Titles by Laurie Cass

Book 'Em, Eddie

A BOOKMOBILE CAT MYSTERY

Laurie Cass

BERKLEY PRIME CRIME
New York

BERKLEY PRIME CRIME
Published by Berkley
An imprint of Penguin Random House LLC
1745 Broadway, New York, NY 10019
penguinrandomhouse.com

ISBN: 9780593818329

First Edition: October 2025

Printed in the United States of America
1

The authorized representative in the EU for product safety and compliance is
Penguin Random House Ireland, Morrison Chambers, 32 Nassau Street,
Dublin D02 YH68, Ireland, https:// eu-contact.penguin.ie.

To Jon.
Always.

Chapter 1

I propped my elbows on our kitchen island's counter. "Different," I said.

My husband looked at me over the bowl of oatmeal he was sliding in my direction, and his expression was easy to interpret: confusion overlaid with a clutch of anxiety that he hadn't actually been paying attention to what I was saying and that our conversation was about to take a hard turn in a negative direction. His mouth opened and shut a couple of times before he managed to say, "Uh, that's, um . . ."

I quelled a shameful urge to take advantage of the situation and waved my free hand—the other being occupied with eating breakfast—and said, "I thought I'd feel different."

"About?"

His cautiously questioning tone, the verbal equivalent of taking sliding steps on a just-frozen lake, made me take pity on the poor man. "Being married," I said. "It's been, what? Just over a month?"

Rafe glanced at the microwave clock, squinted at the ceiling, then came around to sit on the stool next to me. "Four weeks, two days, and fifteen hours."

Math. Before eight a.m. The man was cruel. "Like I said, just over a month. How long is it going to take to sink in?"

"What? That you're stuck with me for the rest of your life?"

He grinned, the slightly crooked version that always made my heart go mushy. Rafe Niswander, tallish but not so tall that his height overwhelmed my efficient five foot zero, with dark hair almost the same shade as my black (but straight against my annoying curls), had an uncanny knack for making me feel better, even when I wasn't feeling all that bad to begin with.

It was just one of the zillions of reasons that I'd married him, and the fact that it had taken me umpteen years to recognize how much I loved him was something I put down to his regrettable predilection to pretend he was far stupider than he actually was. Mostly to get out of doing something he didn't feel like doing, which might have explained the habit when he was seven, but not so much as an adult, let alone principal of our town's middle school.

"Mrr!"

Rafe and I looked at the source of the sound.

Eddie, the black-and-white tabby cat who'd followed me home one fine spring day three and a half years ago and was now my buddy for life, was sitting on top of his carrier and staring hard in my direction.

"He thinks you're late," Rafe said.

The Chilson District Library bookmobile wasn't scheduled at its first stop for almost two hours. There was plenty of time for me to finish eating, do the dishes, catch up on work e-mail, and even start the pointless task of picking cat hair off my clothes before Eddie and I headed up to the library.

I narrowed my gaze at our furry friend. "Just because you're eager to meet your adoring fans doesn't mean I need to skip my breakfast."

He gazed back, won the staring contest because cats always do, then sighed and curled himself into what might have been the most uncomfortable cat ball ever, right on top of the carrier handle.

"Anyway," I said to Rafe, "it's not that I expected to be a different person or anything now that we're married."

"But, Minnie, you are different."

I squinted at my blurred and distant reflection in the refrigerator, blurred partly by distance and partly because it was my self-appointed chore to clean the stainless steel. "Looks the same to me."

Rafe pointed his chin. "Left hand. Finger between the pinky and middle."

Oh. That. Nodding, I admired the wedding band that had recently been soldered to my engagement ring. "One thing. What else?"

"Have you taken a look at your driver's license?"

In truth, I had two driver's licenses. The normal operator one and a commercial driver's version. The State of Michigan didn't actually require that drivers of the thirty-one-foot-long, twenty-three-thousand-pound (when loaded) bookmobile get a CDL, but it was the library's policy, and since I'd written the policy, I'd had one more thin rectangular piece of plastic in my wallet for the last few years. Both now noted yours truly as Minerva Joy Niswander instead of the Minerva Joy Hamilton that had been my name for more than thirty-five years, and the change hadn't quite sunk in yet.

I nodded again. "Keep forgetting. But all those extra letters are a lot, you know."

"You do realize Niswander is only one more letter than Hamilton."

"It's not the count so much as the shapes. That W is exhausting. And don't get me going on having an R at the end of the name. How am I supposed to deal with that?"

"No idea." Rafe used his spoon to give his oatmeal bowl a final scrape. "But I have great confidence that you'll figure it out. You always do."

He flashed a grin, and two minutes later, after depositing his breakfast dishes in the sink, dropping a kiss onto my upturned face, and giving Eddie a light thump on the head, he was out the door and in his truck, headed up to the middle school. My husband—husband!—was the most popular principal the school had had in years. Popular in that the students actually said hello to him, that the teachers had real conversations with him, and that the school board treated him like an actual human being. All in all, he had a good gig going, and unless something shifted dramatically, I couldn't imagine he'd ever leave.

"Then again," I told Eddie as I buckled the now cat-filled carrier into my car's passenger's seat, "the gig I have going is pretty sweet, too."

He ignored my conversational sally, so I felt obliged to continue to talk as we drove to the library.

"Take Chilson." I twiddled my fingers at the passing buildings. "Oh, wait. You can't see, can you, being inside the carrier and all, so you'll have to trust me that this is the quintessential small resort town."

Our permanent population of about three thousand swelled to more than twice that in the summer, and if you added day-trippers, it went to three times the September through May size.

"Maybe October through April," I murmured. Thanks to the many national and even international Top Ten lists that proclaimed northern lower Michigan as a tourist destination, the shoulder seasons were getting busier and busier. Though this was good news for the region's economy, our recent popularity was also resulting in more traffic, more parking problems, more crime, higher housing prices, and a slight but significant shift in culture. We were no longer the out-of-the-way place no one had ever heard of. We were becoming a place to See and Be Seen In, and not all locals were loving it.

I had divided feelings about the changes. For one thing, I was a transplant myself. I had the classic story of youthful summers spent in Chilson, and as an adult realizing that the quieter life of Up North suited me better than the bright lights and activity of downstate.

Soon after getting my master's in library and information science, I'd had the great good fortune to be offered my dream job. Assistant library director? At the Chilson District Library? What could be better than that?

My aunt Frances, the person I'd stayed with during many long teenaged summers, had offered me an off-season room in her boardinghouse. I got creative for my summer housing and scraped up enough money to buy the cutest little houseboat imaginable. For years I'd moored it on Janay Lake, at Uncle Chip's Marina, and only abandoned that seasonal double move when I got engaged.

We now lived in the large Shingle-style home that Rafe had spent eons restoring from its previous life as multiple tiny and not overly functional apartments. Our house, though not on the water, was a mere stone's throw away from Uncle Chip's and Janay Lake, and so not far away from Lake Michigan itself.

"Anyway," I said to Eddie, "Chilson is my favorite downtown ever. I mean, over there on our right is Benton's, a genuine general store. And it's still owned and run by the Benton family, if you can believe that."

"Mrr."

"I know, right? The candy store is about to reopen, thanks to Corey and Isabella Moncada, and their upstairs apartment is super nice. Plus, Gennell Books & Goods is having a great first year, we have a bakery, a brewpub, a deli, a coffee shop, a jewelry store, the ubiquitous T-shirt and gift shops, a wine store, a toy store, a—"

"Mrr!"

"What kind of architecture? So glad you asked. It's a mix of old and new. The toy store is fieldstone and is one of the oldest buildings downtown. Others are brick, some are clapboard, and the brewpub is corrugated metal." I looked around and saw Older Than Dirt, the eclectic store owned by my friend Pam Fazio that was a mix of antiques and new products. "Pam's is mostly glass, and that one is, um, stucco, I guess." I squinted at the insurance company, wondering at the choice, then shrugged. Tomato, tomahto.

By this time we were through downtown, into the residential part of town, and headed up the hill through tree-lined streets to the library. Only a few leaves still hung on to their trees. The fall had been a spectacular one, with maple trees blazing bright red, orange, and yellow, but most all the leaves were now raked into gutters and hauled away by the city.

With leaves gone, the naked trees revealed what had been hidden for months: homes built more than a hundred years ago, primarily for Chicago-based summer people who steamboated up Lake Michigan with massive trunks and live-in staff. That way of life was long gone, but we'd been seeing a shift back in that direction. Many of those large homes had been purchased by out-of-area companies and turned into vacation rentals. Instead of a single family using the home for the entire summer, there were now new residents every week, sometimes twice a week.

Eddie and I rolled past the houses and I consciously pushed away my concern about Chilson's changing nature. There was little I could do about it, and as Aunt Frances often said, worrying didn't change a thing, so why waste the time and energy?

I drove past the library, pulled into the back parking lot, and stopped next to the bookmobile. "Ready, Eddie? We're here."

"Mrr!"

"In a talkative mood today, I see. So I have that to look forward to," I said. "Well, at least you and Julia will have a great time."

The bookmobile, on the road three to four days a week, was staffed by me and two part-timers. Julia Beaton, one of my favorite people in the world, was a sixty-something native of Chilson. She'd bailed on the small town, left the day after graduating from high school, and headed off to the Big Apple to make her fortune as a model.

That hadn't worked out, so she'd turned to her second choice of acting. That had worked and she had a shelf of Tony Awards and a phone contact list that included actors, directors, choreographers, and producers, some of whose names even I recognized.

Julia had retired from the stage a few years ago and had brought her husband back home with her. Five minutes into retirement, she was bored silly. Part-time work on the bookmobile got her out of the house, supplied us with the best storytime teller in the world, and gave Eddie someone else to talk to.

"Daaah-lings!"

I grinned. Julia put on accents like most people put on socks. On any given day, you never knew who she was going to be, and you never knew how long any given persona was going to last since she could switch personalities in the blink of an eye. Sometimes I knew what character she was quoting, other times I had no clue, and sometimes she made things up. Just now, she'd sounded like Zsa Zsa Gabor, but the last time I'd thought that she'd actually been playing Agatha Christie, so this time I was going to keep my guess to myself.

"Morning," I said cheerfully. "Just so you know, Eddie is in a talkative mood today, and—"

"Mrr!"

"What I was saying. Might work out well for Honey Hollow."

Julia flipped her strawberry blond braid over one shoulder and took Eddie's carrier from me. "Muffin," she said to the carrier's resident, "you and the senior citizens are going to get along like a house afire."

I devoutly hoped so. Today was going to be our first-ever stop at Honey Hollow Adult Foster Care. A few weeks ago, Wanda Panovich, owner and manager of the small facility, had contacted me and asked if I could incorporate them into the schedule. "Sure," I'd said, and after dozens of e-mails, multiple phone calls, and two visits—one by car, one with the bookmobile itself—we were finally ready to bring books, storytelling, and Eddie hair to the twelve residents of Honey Hollow.

"It'll be fine," I muttered to myself as I walked around the bookmobile, doing the regular preflight check. Nothing horrible would happen. And even if something did go wrong, we'd be able to deal with it. In the three and a half years I'd been driving the bookmobile we'd dealt with everything from a flat tire to engine trouble and we'd survived it all. Come out more resilient, even.

And, anyway, what could possibly happen? Honey Hollow was in the middle of Tonedagana County, a quiet area marked by rolling farmland, second-growth forests, and few people. The most likely thing that could go wrong was we'd lose our Internet connection, but I could always set up a Wi-Fi hot spot if I had to.

The second most likely thing was Eddie being

more of an Eddie than usual. My workaround for that had started last night, when I'd kept him up way past his bedtime by repeatedly tossing his favorite cat toy under the dining table. I'd hoped to tire him out enough to keep him sleepy throughout the visit. That he was being overly vocal this morning wasn't filling me with confidence that the tactic had worked, so I was thinking about a workaround as I climbed the bookmobile steps and shut the door behind me.

Chapter 2

We need to keep him awake." I dropped into the driver's seat and buckled up. "He needs to be as mellow as possible when we get there."

Julia waggled her feet atop the cat carrier she'd strapped to the floor in front of her. "Any ideas how that might happen?"

"You could sing."

She gave me an arch look. "My dear young lady," she said in a crisp English accent. "There are three kinds of people. Those who can sing, those who can't, and those who shouldn't."

I started the engine. "You never acted in a musical?"

"Only one," she said in a doom-laden voice. "It's a dismal story."

"Will it keep Eddie from falling asleep?"

"It will wake hibernating bears." Julia took a breath and began the tale she titled "Why I Never Starred in Any Musical Ever."

By the time we pulled into Honey Hollow's

parking lot, I was wiping laugh tears off my cheeks. Even better, Eddie's yellow eyes had stayed wide open for the length of the half-hour drive. He might have been taking little kitty notes and was now ready to share the story of how Julia's epically tone-deaf singing voice made front-page news of *Playbill*, or he might have just been kept awake by her efforts to re-create her chorus role in *Fiddler on the Roof*. I didn't care which, I was just glad he'd stayed awake.

We parked just outside the front door. The rambling single-story building had started life as a large family home and had been added onto when Wanda inherited it from her mother. Wanda was an Up North native who'd moved downstate fresh out of school, and she'd stayed there until both her parents had passed away. A registered nurse, she was married to Ken, a paramedic who'd grown up in nearby Petoskey, and they'd made a major life change decision an hour after her mom's funeral.

"It was during the luncheon," Wanda had told me a few weeks ago. "Mom's best friend buttonholed us after the service and told us flat-out that we needed to come home, that the house was waiting for us, and that we didn't need jobs because she knew exactly what we should do."

"And you decided to go ahead? Just like that?" I'd asked, fascinated. My life decisions involved weeks of thought, to-do lists, Internet research, and, depending on the complexity of the decision, multiple spreadsheets.

She'd laughed. "Pretty much. We did our due diligence later on, to make sure the numbers worked, but we loved the concept from the get-go."

And now the bookmobile was visiting Honey

Hollow Adult Foster Care, which after almost two years of operation was thriving. Before agreeing to the stop, I'd done my own due diligence with figuring out the distinctions between adult foster care, nursing homes, assisted living, and independent living. It turned out that all meant a particular level of care, and that in Michigan at least, adult foster care homes were licensed and provided twenty-four-hour care for people who can't live alone but don't need continuous nursing.

Wanda practically bounced out the front door. "You're here! Come in, come in! Everyone is so excited to meet Eddie!"

I'd long ago become resigned to the fact that there were far more people who knew my cat than knew me. If Eddie missed a bookmobile run, I got e-mails, text messages, and phone calls of concern. If I left him home because of a little kitty cold or because he'd eaten one basement mouse too many and was hacking up unmentionable things, he got more get-well notes than I got Christmas cards.

Wanda, though in her late forties, had the energy of a two-year-old. From the top of her ponytailed head to the bottom of her bright pink running shoes, she radiated happiness and good cheer. I'd never seen her in anything but medical scrubs, and today's version was black pants with vertical yellow pinstripes and a sunny yellow shirt dotted with bumblebees.

"How was the drive?" she asked. "See any deer? There are a lot of bow hunters in the woods and they're stirring them up. Do you think Eddie would like a bowl of water?"

The questions and commentary blended into one long sentence with no pauses. Julia, who hadn't met Wanda, sent me a bemused look. I gave a small shrug, and in short order the three of us were transporting multiple book crates—and one cat carrier—inside.

Wanda talked over the top of the crate she was carrying. "Julia, it's so great to meet you. My mom told me all about your career. How exciting! I'm sure you didn't know my mom, but she took a seniors bus trip to New York City about ten years ago, and she saw you acting in . . . oh, sorry I don't remember the play. Anyway, she said it was amazing to see someone from little old Chilson in the big city. And here we are," she said, huffing a bit with exertion. "We're setting you up in the dining room. Everybody wanted to see you and Eddie, and that's the only space big enough. Where do you think we should put the books?" She twisted around, looking.

The room was at the back of the house, with wide windows that brought in a view of a wooded backyard. Four small tables, some set with chairs, some without, were covered with tablecloths in autumnal colors. The walls, painted a warm off-white, were crowded with framed posters of past events. County fairs, art shows, concerts, car shows, Fourth of July picnics—it was history at a glance.

Julia nudged my elbow and I blinked away from reading about a dune buggy race, to be held on Chilson's City Beach in July 1971. "Under the windows," I said. "Is that okay, Wanda?"

It was, and in short order she'd headed out to notify her residents, and Julia and I were emptying the crates, flipping them over, and putting books on top for display. This was a routine we'd developed over the years we'd been visiting the Lake View

Medical Care Facility, up the big hill from the library. It kept the books low enough for the folks in wheelchairs to view, and was high enough for most ambulatory folks to reach without too much effort.

Eddie, from inside his carrier, supervised with a critical eye. He gave an occasional "Mrr" of commentary, which I ignored, and Julia pandered to him by rearranging whatever book she'd been holding at the time.

"Is this a better location, Sir Edward? Yes, you're right. Of course you're right. Thank you so much for voicing your opinion."

"It's a good thing," I said, "that he doesn't actually understand human speech. His head would get even bigger. And it's already pretty big."

His head had always seemed large for a cat his size. I'd asked Dr. Joe, the vet, if that could mean Eddie might have any special abilities, and he'd given me a look so odd that I'd forced a laugh and passed it off as a joke.

Julia smirked. "What makes you think he doesn't understand? Maybe he's just really good at hiding his comprehension level."

"The only thing he's good at hiding is his cat toys," I said. "Last week I found one of his fuzzy purple frogs in the bottom of the clothes hamper." Which had a lid. How he'd managed to get it in there was a complete mystery.

"Hope you're ready!" Wanda came into the room, pushing an elderly woman in a wheelchair. "This is Betty. She's the main reason I called you in the first place. We can't keep up with her demands for new reading material, can we?"

"Not even close," Betty said. She spotted the array

of books and rubbed her hands together. "Now we're talking. That's right, get me up close and personal. My hips don't work for beans, so I can't walk anymore, but that isn't going to keep me from reading as much as I can the rest of my life."

I laughed. "A woman after my own heart." After introducing myself, Julia, and Eddie, and showing her how the books were arranged—history, biographies, travel books, historical fiction, romance, mysteries and thrillers, general fiction—I told her that if there was anything we didn't have, to let us know and we'd bring it next time.

"Lovely," she murmured, opening a copy of Jacquelyn Mitchard's *The Deep End of the Ocean*, and she was gone, having dropped immediately into a fictional world. As so often happened when I got the right book to the right person at the right time, I smiled and gave a huge sigh of happiness. Truly, I had the best job ever.

"Where's that Eddie?" A bald man using a walker shuffled into the room. "Been a long time since I had to pick cat hair off my pants."

"Now, Charlie," Wanda said. "Eddie may not want to share his hair with you."

Charlie snorted. "He's a cat. Of course he does."

"There's plenty to go around," I said. "Trust me."

More and more Honey Hollow residents came in, and Julia and I got busy helping people find books, telling them to go ahead and cuddle a sleepy Eddie, and taking down book requests. Time went by lickety-split and it wasn't until Wanda called out, "All right, everyone. Time to listen up!" that I realized we'd been there two hours.

Julia swirled on her new storytelling garb of a

midnight-blue cape with dazzling rhinestone designs of flying carpets, treasure maps, and books opened to illustrated pages. "It was a dark and stormy night," she whispered in an Eastern European accent, and the audience was hers.

As she told a mash-up tale involving elements from *Dracula*, *The Wizard of Oz*, and what might have been *Hamilton*, I packed what was left of the books back into their crates.

"Need help?"

I turned, a book in each hand. A silver-haired woman, even shorter than my five foot nothing, peered at me through glasses with lime-green frames. She also looked frail enough that a mild west wind would send her and her multicolored cane into Canada.

"Not that I'm going to carry anything heavier than a tall glass of water," she continued in her raspy voice. "Gave up that kind of thing the day I turned ninety. But I can give you all the good gossip."

I glanced at the residents clustered around Julia. Did I want to hear about who was holding hands with who? Absolutely I did not. "Um . . ."

She cackled with laughter. "I don't spread rumors about my friends. But I do have the dirt on what happened a hundred years ago. I saw you looking at those old posters and thought you might be interested in the real story of this place."

That sounded like news I couldn't possibly use. Then again, it would probably be fascinating, and might be something I could tell Rafe. He'd been born and raised in Chilson, so it was a rare occasion when I could tell him something he didn't know about the county. "I'm all ears," I said.

She gave me a sharp nod and introduced herself as Alicia Gwaltny, widowed since before the turn of the millennium, and no children, grandchildren, or great-grandchildren left in Michigan. "If I go live with one, I'll never hear the end of it from the others, and what would I do with myself in North Carolina, Maine, Colorado, or Oregon anyway? This is home." She stamped her cane on the floor. "And there's not much that's gone on here that I don't know about. Do you know why?"

I shook my head, enthralled.

"Because I used to clean houses."

At this point we were in the lobby, out of earshot of the others. I let the book crate slide to the floor, helped Alicia to a handy bench, and sat next to her. "You cleaned houses? In Chilson?"

She snorted. "No, missy. In Gainsborough. Hah. You've never heard of it. I can tell by that blank look on your pretty face."

Laughing, I said, "You're right. Not a clue what it was or where it is."

"Over there." She gestured with the end of her cane. "On Deer Lake. And there's no 'was' about it. Still there, although it's a shadow of what went on, way back when."

A dim light was going on in the back of my brain. "Are you talking about those old summer places on the east side of the lake? I didn't know it had a name."

"Gainsborough," she said again. "Like the painter. And the hat. All those houses were built in the logging years."

My interest, already high, zipped up another notch. The logging heyday, from the 1860s to the early 1900s, was an era filled with stories of hard work, hard living, and hard men. Lumbering was a cold-weather endeavor. Maple, pine, and oak trees were cut down with huge two-man saws, then heaved onto horse-drawn wagons piled freakishly high. The sleds were hauled to railroad tracks or, if no railroad was handy, to the edges of rivers and frozen lakes. Come spring, the logs got heaved into the water and floated down to ships that steamed them downstate or to Chicago. Legend had it that trees from Tonedagana County rebuilt Chicago after the great fire of 1871, and for all I knew that was actually true.

"The people who built those houses were lumber barons?" I asked.

"One way or another," Alicia said. "You know how the people who made the most money in gold out in California were suppliers, not prospectors? Well, there was good money to be made right here"— she stamped her cane again—"in dry goods and foodstuffs. Maybe not as much as the lumber, but money enough, if you weren't greedy. That's how Gainsborough started. With the twins."

"Twins?" I echoed.

"Eliza Creighton and her brother Foster. Walked all the way from Detroit behind a wagon filled with everything from soup ladles to long underwear, sure they were going to make their fortune at the logging camps. All the profit from that first sale went into two wagonloads, then three, then four, then they built a bunch of fancy stores so they could sell to the Chicago summer people."

I blinked. "Are you talking about the E & F stores? That's where the name came from?" E & F were luxury linen stores. The single time I'd walked into one, I'd been so startled at the cost of a single pillow sham that I wasn't sure I'd ever fully recovered.

Alicia nodded. "Eliza and Foster. They built identical houses side by side on Deer Lake."

It sounded sweet. "That doesn't seem very gossipy," I said.

"Just getting started." Alicia smirked. "Eliza and Foster passed the twin houses down to their children, and that's when the trouble hit the fan. The kids got the houses right around the time the Volstead Act was passed."

She paused and let me make the mental leap all by myself.

"Prohibition," I said. "They were using the houses for, what? Rum-running?"

Alicia grinned. "Had you pegged for a smart one. Rum, whiskey, moonshine, champagne, whatever they could get across from Canada. The Creighton and Duvall cousins made a killing."

The Prohibition-era lawlessness of Sault Ste. Marie, aka "The Soo," was legendary. There was a Sault Ste. Marie, Michigan, and a Sault Ste. Marie in Canada, right across the St. Marys River. The Soo on the Canadian side was quadruple the size of the Michigan version—and Canada didn't have a Volstead Act. From 1919 to 1933, alcohol was smuggled across the river on anything that floated. In canoes, on powerboats, tied to rafts, in barrels—it was impossible to enforce that porous border, and there were many legends that told of law enforcement that had turned a blind eye, had helped move crates of bottles, or had even set up entire operations themselves. It had been a wild time, and I was glad it was long ago.

"And it wasn't just Prohibition," Alicia said. "Skip forward a generation or two, and the same thing happened. Only this time it wasn't alcohol. It was marijuana."

My mouth dropped open, and Alicia pealed with laughter.

"You should see the look on your face, young lady. Back in the day, there was a grass air strip next to Gainsborough, built during World War II because the boys in charge at the time thought we needed it." She made a snorting noise. "A handful of local youngsters used it to train before heading off to war, but after that no one used it except for summer people. And boy howdy, did they use it." Alicia winked.

"Marijuana from Canada flew in right here?" I looked around. "It seems . . . so unlikely."

"Ask around," Alicia said, nodding. "It's the dirty little secret of Tonedagana County. People don't like to talk about it, of course. It would tarnish our touristy image, and goodness knows that these days the people at Gainsborough act like butter wouldn't melt in their mouths. But just like the war between Chilson and Dooley for the county seat, those flights were real."

"War?"

Applause for the end of Julia's performance crashed over us, and my attention was diverted. When I turned back, my new friend was up off the bench and away down the carpeted hallway.

When Julia, Eddie, and I were back on the bookmobile, I asked Julia if it was true about the county seat.

"Not sure I'd call it a war," she said as she buckled Eddie's carrier into place. "More a squabble. And there might have been a minor burglary or two, but who was going to prosecute anyone for stealing meeting minutes?"

I made a mental note to talk to the historical society people about the early days of the county. Clearly, there'd been more going on than I'd ever suspected.

Once we were all buckled in, I started the engine and dropped the transmission into gear. We rolled forward and I stopped at the end of the driveway, wheels angled right. But instead of curling out onto the road and going back to Chilson, where an afternoon of library work waited for me, I looked left. "Are you familiar with Gainsborough?"

"Those summer homes out on Deer Lake? Sure. A New York friend of mine was college roommates with someone who used to have a place there. Hubby and I went out there oodles of times for drinks and dinner."

I tapped my fingers on the steering wheel. "What's it like, roadwise? Think we'd fit?"

Julia gave me the one-eyebrow look. "Yes, but why the sudden interest in Gainsborough?"

So I had to tell her about Alicia's story of the twin houses and the years of smuggling. "I've never been back there," I said. "All that history, and I didn't know anything about it. How do you feel about a quick side trip?"

"Beyond that road is an episode," she said in a singsong tone.

"That's a quote, right?"

"Only since 1960."

My right foot eased down on the gas pedal. And we turned left. "If it's something that old, do I need to know what it is?"

"How old are Jane Austen's books?"

"Fair point." But I'd already lost interest in the Name That Show game. It was Julia with ten million points and Minnie with maybe three. "How many houses are in Gainsborough?" I asked.

"Last time I was there, probably twenty. But it's been years. The friend of my friend passed away."

"Wouldn't happen to have been a Creighton? Or a Duvall?"

"No. Why?"

I told her about the twins and their houses, and she was just as entranced as I'd been.

She beamed and clapped her hands. "I never knew. How adorable! Born together, went into business together, lived next to each other. Does anyone do that kind of thing these days?"

"Don't need to," I said. "Cell phones, texting, and social media let us stay together even when we're hundreds of miles apart."

"Not the same." Julia shook her head. "Not even close. I understand that as a millennial you have to support technology, but you're wrong. So very wrong, and I'm pretty sure you know it."

"When did I become the sole representative of my generation?"

Julia tapped her wristwatch. "Since the day I realized you don't wear one of these."

"Why on earth do I need to encircle my wrist with a tight handcuff when I have a perfectly good way of finding out the time in my pocket?"

She heaved a dramatic sigh. And when Julia

heaves one of those, it can be easily heard over the noise of the vehicle's engine, the road noise, and a flyover of the Blue Angels, if they happen to be in the neighborhood. "Don't you ever want to be free of your phone?" she asked. "To be unfettered, unleashed, footloose and fancy free?"

"Not if it means being without a way to look up song lyrics," I said promptly.

Julia laughed. "Point to Minnie Hamil—no, Minnie Niswander."

"My first point as a married woman." The thought made me smile, and I was still smiling as we turned onto Deer Lake Road.

The road sign was green, which meant it was a public road. Blue road signs indicated private roads, and taking the bookmobile down one of those without permission was a big no-no. And not only was Deer Lake Road public, it was also asphalt, which made me happy.

For half a mile we drove through a thick second-growth forest of maple, white birches, and the occasional cedar, winding around small hills and over streams, and finally down from a low ridge into a large open space.

A long row of Victorian cottages, each with a deep front porch, lay in front of us, dotting the shore of Deer Lake. The paint colors of the clapboard siding and gingerbread trim ranged from white to pale pink to midnight blue. "They're like those houses in San Francisco," I said. "What do they call them, Painted Ladies?"

"I remember that house," Julia said, pointing. "That fish scale siding on the peak, each row of scales a different color? It looks the same as it did last time I was out here. Actually"—she looked left and right, taking in the full row—"everything looks the same. I don't see anything that's different."

In an enclave like this, there was almost certainly a homeowners' association of some kind that had all sorts of rules. No construction during the summer, approval required for paint colors, all landscaping to be harmonious and done by a single company. But more than that, it had the feel of a place frozen in time. A place untouched by the passing years.

"No, call me a liar," Julia said. "Those garages weren't here before." She nodded at the far side of a grassy, parklike open area. Five long low field-stone buildings were nestled into the edge of the hill and tucked in underneath towering maple trees. Each building had four garage doors made to look like doors to carriage houses.

It made sense, I supposed. There wasn't room for garages next to the cottages themselves, not if you wanted to retain the atmosphere of the place. And if the drawn shades and lack of porch furniture were any indication, it looked like these were still summer places. No need to worry about traipsing through a foot of snow to get to your car.

"Those must be the twin houses your new friend was talking about," Julia said. "Funny. I never noticed that they're identical."

I followed her gaze. In the middle of the row of lakeside cottages, two stood closer together than any of the others. Not to the point where you could lean out of a window to shake the hand of your opposite number, but not much farther apart than that. "Well, they are painted way different."

Both houses had the same long front porch with

a lattice skirt, tall double-hung windows, two full stories, dormer eyebrow windows, and decorative stone chimneys. The house on the right, though, was a sedate gray with white trim. The house on the left also had white trim, but it was painted what to my eye was the same warm peach my cousin Celeste had painted the boardinghouse she'd bought from Aunt Frances.

I looked around. Not a soul to be seen. "I'm going to take a closer look," I said, unbuckling my seat belt. "You coming?"

"Nope." Julia reached down to adjust her seat to semireclining. "Mr. Ed and I are going to take a nap. Performances exhaust us, you know."

"Eddie was part of the act?"

"Well, duh. Who else was going to play the part of Toto?"

"Mrr" came a sleepy voice.

Of those two, I sometimes wondered who was the bigger ham. "I won't be long," I said.

"Take your time." Julia yawned and squirmed into a more comfortable position. "But leave the door open, will you, please? It's warm enough."

So I swung the bookmobile's door wide and stepped out into the past.

Well, sort of. That was the feeling I'd hoped for, the one I searched for every time I visited anything older than myself. Sometimes I could feel time turn back when visiting Mackinac Island, with its banning of cars and its many bicycles, horses, and carriages, but its popularity meant tourists. Though that was fantastic for the island's economy, it also meant that I found it impossible to put myself back in time. My imagination just didn't stretch to shifting discussions of fudge shops to waterfront discussions of fur trading.

Maybe today, with no one around, I'd feel a bit of what it had felt like to be here a hundred years ago. No, that would have been in the thick of Prohibition. Make it a hundred and thirty years ago, just before the turn of the century.

I half closed my ears and was almost able to hear, instead of road noise from the U.S. highway two miles to the east, the clip-clop of horse hooves and the distant whistle of a train's steam engine.

Then I half closed my eyes and could almost see young girls in shin-length frocks and boys in knickers rolling hoops across the open space's lawn. Nannies in long black skirts with starched white aprons pushing wicker perambulators. Men wearing jackets and bowlers. Women with their hair pinned up and hats pinned on, wearing dresses that swept the ground, petticoats and corsets underneath.

I put my hands in the pockets of my light coat and wandered across the grass toward the twin houses. As I drew closer, I noted how the clever use of fencing and shrubbery hid metal propane tanks that supplied fuel for hot water tanks and furnaces. There were enough cool nights Up North that even summer places needed a way to get heat.

Closer still, I could see sheet-covered furniture through the front windows of the gray house, and pulled shades in the upstairs windows. The more colorful twin house had wood window blinds slanted to open. I caught a glimpse of puffy upholstered furniture, a fieldstone fireplace, and framed artwork that to my uneducated eye looked original.

There was also a light on inside, a faint one, about the intensity of a night-light.

I tried to imagine it as a gas lamp. That didn't work, so I tried to imagine this summer cottage in Tonedagana County as one of the first locations for northwest lower Michigan's rural electrification. That didn't work, either, so I sighed and gave up my attempt to pretend time travel. It was a silly thing to do anyway, and—

"Eddie!"

Whirling, I saw Julia run down the bookmobile steps.

"You get back here!" she shouted, a command that, as anyone who's ever lived with a cat knows full well, had exactly zero chance of being obeyed.

The black-and-white blur that was Eddie in full gallop streaked across the lawn, over a line of boulders that marked the edge of the circular road that ran around the park, and up into the forested hillside.

"Now what?" I muttered as I trotted after him. It had been years since he'd shown any inclination to escape the bookmobile. The inside of the vehicle was his safe and happy place. It was where he got adoration, accolades, and more treats than were good for him. Why on earth had he suddenly decided to run rogue?

I waved off Julia and her loud apologies for opening his carrier door, calling out not to worry, that he wouldn't go far, that I'd get him back in no time.

"At least you'd better not go far," I panted as I entered the woods. "What got into you? Little kitty nose out of joint now that we have a new last name and you weren't consulted? Sorry, and while I understand your point of view, there are some social conventions that are just too hard for me to buck."

I kept up the running babble as I scanned for signs of a passing cat. If he'd panicked for some reason—he'd been known to levitate from a sound sleep at the loud squawk of a seagull—the sound of my voice often calmed him down.

"Yes, I know, having an S right next to a W is tough spelling, but—"

"Mrroooo!"

I stopped short. That wasn't a normal Eddie howl. That was something else altogether, something I hadn't ever heard. It sounded—

"MrrooOO!"

His second howl gave me direction. Ignoring the thick carpet of newly fallen leaves and the tree branches slapping at my face, I ran toward my cat, my little buddy, my furry friend, my pal.

Panting, lungs searing, I ran to the top of the hill, wanting to hear his voice again, but also not wanting to hear it because he'd sounded like something out of one of those nightmares that wake you up at two in the morning, sweating and heart pounding.

Where was he? If something had happened to him, I'd never forgive myself. If—

"MroOOO!!"

I shifted my trajectory slightly. At that decibel level, he had to be close by. "Nearly . . . there," I huffed. "Where . . . are you? Where . . ."

And there he was, staring up at me with his big yellow eyes, mouth starting to open for another howl.

But if he gave one, I didn't hear it, because I was too busy scrambling down the small ravine that had hidden Eddie, who was standing by the feet of a woman lying on the ground. Her hands were pressing against her abdomen, and blood was seeping its raw red way through her fingers, turning her brown jacket a maroon so dark it was almost black.

She groaned and I floundered forward to kneel by her side. Which was when I saw the reason for the blood—an arrow was buried deep into her.

My mouth opened and closed a couple of times before I managed to say, "My name is Minnie. I'm here to help," as I reached for my phone. Mercifully, there was enough cell signal. I dialed 911 and a dispatcher answered after a single ring.

"Central dispatch. Where is your emergency?"

I talked fast, trying not to sound as panicked as I was. When I'd told him everything I could think of, I looked at the ragged rise and fall of the woman's breathing, and whispered, "Please hurry."

"An ambulance is already on the way," he said, over the clicking of a computer keyboard. "Estimated time of arrival is ten minutes. Do not remove the arrow. I know it's hard, but you need to leave it there."

I nodded into the phone. "Should I . . . do something?"

The woman groaned and her fingers twitched.

"If you have padding," the dispatcher said, "use it to lightly press down on the area around the wound."

I pulled off my coat, wadded it up, and did as instructed. The woman's eyes fluttered and I saw that they were a bright blue, the blue of Janay Lake on a brilliant summer morning.

"Minnie?" Julia's voice floated around. "Where are you?"

"Down here!"

Her head appeared over the top of the ravine. "What are— Oh . . ."

"An ambulance is coming," I said, as calmly as I could. "Take Eddie, will you? Get him back in the bookmobile. When the EMTs get here, show them the way."

She nodded, picked up Eddie who was by now wandering around her ankles, and disappeared.

Then I was alone with a woman with a horrific wound. "They're coming," I murmured, trying to transmit a sense of calm and peace, which was the only thing I could think of doing. "On their way. Ten minutes, he said, but that had to be a few minutes ago, so let's say five. Another couple of minutes to get up here, and—"

"Bee . . ."

I glanced up. Her hair was as black as mine, but her skin showed her age as around sixty years. Then again, if she'd stayed out of the sun, she could be ten or twenty years older than that. "Is that your name?" I asked. "Bee?"

She turned her head back and forth. "Bee . . . hind."

A jag of fear sizzled down my spine. Oh so slowly, hardly breathing, I turned my head. But there was nothing there, other than trees and leaves and rocks. "Behind?" I asked.

She nodded, her breathing fast and shallow and sporadic.

"Behind." I looked at my jacket. No blood was showing, but I had no idea if that was good or bad, and when I'd tossed my phone aside to start the pressure, I hadn't thought to put it to speaker, so I couldn't ask the dispatcher. "What's behind?"

Her breaths were frighteningly uneven. "Behind the . . ."

I heard the faint sound of an ambulance siren and the slightly different-sounding siren of a sheriff's vehicle. "They're coming," I said, and then because I didn't know what else to do, I started to babble. "Help is almost here. That was way less than ten minutes, right? Must have had a rig in the area, because I don't think there's a—"

Her hand gripped my wrist with a surprising strength. "Behind the . . ."

I studied her face. "I can tell this is important. I got the first two words. 'Behind' and 'the.' Save your energy and don't repeat those, okay? Behind the what?"

The time between her breaths was long and frightening. I waited and watched, but her mouth didn't try to shape any words, just opened and closed as air went in and out.

Voices and rattling noises came toward us. "They're nearly here," I said. "They'll take care of you. It'll be okay."

Her head went slowly back and forth, and her lips moved.

"Down here!" Julia called. "She's down here!"

EMTs carrying equipment hustled over the crest of the ravine and down toward us. I started to sit back, but the woman grabbed my wrist again. I leaned close, and just as the professionals pushed me aside, I heard her say one more word.

"Books."

Chapter 3

After the ambulance had left and I'd shown the sheriff's deputies where I'd found the woman, I found a trash bin and shoved my jacket inside. "Let's go," I said. At least that was what I meant to say. What came out was more a whimpering croak.

"Oh, honey." Julia reached out and wrapped me into her long arms. "We did everything we could. That woman has a chance because we were here."

"Because of you," I said into her shoulder. "Because you felt sorry for Eddie and opened his carrier door."

Julia nodded. "Guilty as charged. He gave me that look, you know the one. 'Please just let me out, I'll be good, honest, I just need some fresh air.'"

"He hasn't run off in forever." I sniffled and pulled away to wipe my eyes. "There was no way for you to know."

"I don't usually say that things happen for a reason, but maybe this time they did."

We looked up the drive, in the direction the

ambulance had disappeared. Only the faintest hint of a siren could be heard, and then even that was gone.

I looked up at the bare tree branches, at the pale sky with layers of scudding autumn clouds.

Books. Behind the books.

What had she meant? Had it meant anything? She'd been barely conscious from pain and blood loss. She'd been rambling. Maybe hallucinating. I blew out a deep breath, and this time when I said, "Let's go," the words came out.

Once we were back on the road, I told Julia about what the woman had said.

"Hmm." Julia's toes tapped the top of Eddie's carrier. "That's an odd thing to say."

I told her my theory about hallucinations, adding, "It probably didn't mean anything. Maybe she'd been meaning to dust behind her books. Or maybe that's where she kept her grandchildren's birthday presents."

Julia half nodded, half didn't. "With any luck she'll come out of this and we'll hear the rest of the story."

Some version of a story was a certainty. I just hoped it had a happy ending.

After dropping Eddie at the house, I walked up to the library and spent part of the afternoon on the phone with the sheriff's deputies and part of it staring at my computer, seeing nothing. After I'd done a seventh reading of an e-mail request for scheduling the community room, I gave up.

"About time," my boss said after I poked my head into his office and asked if it was okay to take the rest of the day off. "If I recall correctly," Graydon went on, "and I'm pretty sure I do, I told you to go home when you called from Deer Lake to tell me what happened."

"Um." He might have done, but back then my eyes and ears had been so full of ambulances and deputies that I hadn't had much room for anything else. "Okay. Thanks. I'll see you tomorrow."

"Or not," he said. "Take a mental health day. We have those, you know."

We did indeed, thanks to his taking the concept to the library board of directors and being its champion.

"Good idea." I nodded. "I'll think about it. But even if I come in, it's nice to know I could have used the day. You are the best boss ever."

The unflappable Graydon Cain waved me off. "Go home and don't come back."

I smiled and headed out.

Up until that point I'd thought I was okay, that what I'd seen and heard and felt a few hours earlier hadn't really bothered me. After all, more than once in the past few years I'd come across dead people, and that had to be harder. This woman, whoever she was, might not die. She might be fine. But . . . she might not.

Sighing, I climbed the steps of our front porch.

Eddie materialized and did the figure eight thing around my ankles as I took off my coat and put it away. "Mrr?"

"Don't know, buddy." I picked him up and snuggled him as we went upstairs together. "The deputy"—whose name I'd already forgotten—"said he'd call and tell me what happens."

"Mrr." He burrowed his head into the inside of my elbow.

"Yeah. I know." I deposited him on the bed, changed out of what I still called school clothes and into comfy sweatpants and a fleece sweatshirt and curled up with Eddie, letting his purrs wash over me.

It might have been ten minutes later that Rafe got home, or it might have been ten hours. Either way, when he came into the bedroom, he took one look and sat down next to me and my furry security blanket. "What's wrong?" he asked, putting a hand on my leg. "Is it the Honey Hollow stop? What happened?"

Honey Hollow. I'd almost forgotten.

"No." I curled tighter around Eddie. "That went fine. It was after." There was a small squeak. I released my grip on the poor little guy, whispering an apology into the top of his head.

"After?" Rafe kicked off his shoes and lay down on the bed, pulling me, pulling Eddie, close to his heart. "What happened after?"

My eyes, which had been dry, started streaming tears.

And I told my husband what had happened at Gainsborough.

The next morning, Rafe proved once and for all that he was the best husband ever.

After hours of fitful sleep, I'd finally slid into oblivion. I hadn't heard Rafe's alarm go off, hadn't heard his shower, and I hadn't heard the noise that usually woke me up—the sound of Eddie jumping off the bed and onto the floor in anticipation of following Rafe downstairs.

"Morning, my little pumpkin patch."

I blinked open bleary eyes and, in the dim light cast by my bedside lamp, saw a steaming mug of coffee. "For me?"

"Can't think of anyone else in this house who would drink out of a mug that says 'World's Best Bookmobile Librarian.'"

Yawning, I sat up, took the mug, and put my nose into the rising vapor. "Wait. This isn't drip. This is the big stuff." That was the term we used for stove-top percolator coffee. Even though we'd specified no gifts at our wedding, a handful had sneaked in, and one of them was a classic stainless steel coffee-pot, complete with an adorable little glass knob on top that let you peek into coffee secrets. Though it made the best coffee I'd ever had in my life—and I'd had a lot—we only used it on weekends, when we had more time.

"Figured you could use a treat." Rafe kissed the top of my head. "And the treats will keep on coming, because I'm bringing you breakfast in bed."

"You're . . . what?"

"Don't get too excited. It's just oatmeal. Not sure I love you enough to make bacon on a Tuesday morning."

I smiled into my mug. "Married barely a month and we're already drawing lines in the sand about levels of love?"

"Well, they did say it wouldn't last."

Five minutes later, he brought up a small tray of oatmeal, apple juice, a piece of toast with orange marmalade, and more coffee. "Don't get used to this," he said, settling the array on my lap.

"Wouldn't dream of it."

"Mrr!"

Rafe and I looked toward the foot of the bed, where Eddie was glaring at us.

"Cool your jets, pal," Rafe said. "This is for you." He took the tiny bowl of milk that had been hiding behind the juice and put it on the floor.

All through breakfast, I wondered if Rafe had made a dreadful mistake. Had including the tiny bowl set a horrifying precedent that would haunt us the rest of Eddie's life? The probability was high.

I continued to ponder the question as I showered, dressed, and texted my best friend Kristen about the events of the previous night, but it wasn't until I was walking through downtown and up to the library that I came to an obvious conclusion. Yes, Eddie would absolutely expect to get a tiny bowl of milk every morning from here on out. I knew this to be true because he still waited at the bookmobile door to get a treat from Charlotte, the clerk for Wicklow Township, every time the bookmobile stopped at the township hall, even though that had only happened once. Three years ago.

Which made you think that he had the memory of the proverbial elephant, but if so, he had a very selective memory because he couldn't seem to remember that he hadn't actually liked that treat. Had in fact sneered at it as only a cat can sneer.

Smiling at the memory, I used my new fancy electronic key fob to let myself in the library's side door. After a short run of vandalism late last summer, the library board had directed Graydon to invest in enhanced security. The key fobs and security cameras were the sum total of the physical purchases, and our IT guy was working on additional cybersecurity measures. I'd reluctantly accepted the added measures as inevitable, but at least most of the physical changes were unobtrusive.

The back hall was quiet, which was expected as it was still two hours before the library opened. I wanted to check e-mail and finalize the bookmobile's holiday schedule before the doors opened at ten, but first things first.

Halfway down the hall, I took a sharp left turn into the break room and started brewing the first coffeepot of the day. House rules were that whoever made coffee got to make it whatever strength they preferred, but there was one inviolable caveat—you would absolutely be judged for your actions.

I added the correct amount of grounds into the filter and pushed the Start button.

"Morning," Josh Hadden, our IT guy, said. "Uh, Kelsey isn't here, is she?"

"If she is, she missed out on making coffee."

"Cool."

Josh was a couple of years younger than my thirty-five and was classic IT inside and out. Cargo pants, oversized polo shirts, overly long hair, and a razor-sharp mind. The first few years I'd known Josh, he'd been a dedicated drinker of diet soda, but a jump to home ownership—and marriage—had made him reevaluate how he spent his disposable income. Overnight he'd switched his caffeine intake from cold carbonated to hot drip, solely because the library paid for coffee.

I had two solid work friends. Josh was one and Holly Terpening, also about my age, was the other. Maybe it was our similar ages, maybe it was our personalities, maybe it was that we'd all been hired within a few months of each other. Whatever the reason, the three of us often acted more like siblings than coworkers, with Holly and Josh being the siblings who fought the most.

When I'd returned to the library the day before, I'd holed up in my office and hadn't talked to anyone. Today, however, I knew I had to tell the rest of the library staff what had happened at Gainsborough.

But it could wait.

"See you later," I said, earning a grunt from Josh, who was already sitting at the break room's table, tapping at his oversized cell phone.

I took my happy mug, the one emblazoned with the Association of Bookmobile and Outreach Services' logo, and wandered out into the lobby. Careful to stay on the hard tile floor, because spilling onto the carpet would earn me a look of deep disappointment from Gareth Dibona, the library's maintenance supervisor, I took a long look at the place where I worked. After years of being in the building almost daily, its beauty could still take my breath away.

When I was a kid, spending summers with my aunt Frances, the library had been a flat-roofed 1960s-era structure. Back then, the building had served Chilson's needs. But needs shift over time— a big one being the integration of computers into the library's functions—and just before I was hired as assistant director, the good citizens of Chilson approved a short-term construction millage to renovate a two-story elementary school built in the early 1900s into a library.

The result of that vote was in front of me, and I breathed in the peace and calm I always felt whenever I took the time to really look.

What had been the school's gymnasium was now the main stacks. The light that came in through the tall windows was augmented by the amber glass chandeliers, all of which warmed the maple bookshelves and the wide maple trim that was used throughout the building.

Carpet softened the noise in this room, the children's space, the young adult space, and the community rooms. The heavily trafficked areas had large earth-toned quarry tiles, colorful metallic tiles decorated the drinking fountain surrounds, and all signage was in an Arts and Crafts style that deeply satisfied my font-loving soul, but my hands-down favorite spot in the building was the reading room. Just past the checkout desk, the large and popular space had wood-paneled walls, upholstered chairs, a deep window seat, and a working gas fireplace.

"Not so bad, is it?"

My boss was suddenly at my elbow, also with a mug in hand. We often ran into each other first thing in the morning, both of us doing the same thing; loving our jobs.

I shrugged. "Could be worse, I suppose."

"That's right." Graydon took a sip of coffee. "We could be working in any other library in the world."

"Oh, I don't know. I hear the Library of Congress is okay. And I've always thought working in the New York Public Library might be nice. Or the Long Room in Dublin."

"Working in any of those means living in a major metropolitan area."

I made a scrunchy face. "Never mind. Still, they'd be fun to visit."

"So would Alexandria," Graydon said.

We sighed simultaneously. The ancient loss of that fabled Egyptian library tugged at the heart of every librarian I'd ever met.

"What's on your agenda today?" he asked.

I shook away the image of dusty parchment scrolls piled high on shelf after shelf. "Finalizing schedules, restocking the bookmobile, and staffing the reference desk this afternoon."

"Would you have time for a meeting with the new Friends president at eleven this morning?"

For years, the Friends of the Library had been bulldozed into submission by their former president, Denise Slade. That all ended two weeks ago when Denise put up her house for sale, announced she was moving downstate, and resigned from the Friends. Three days later, the Friends unanimously voted Duffy Ulrich as their new president.

The library staff was crossing fingers and toes that Duffy, who'd recently retired after selling her commercial sign design and fabrication business, would be a breath of very fresh air to the group. Though I hadn't yet crossed paths with her, I had been meaning to reach out.

Graydon was watching my face. "We can reschedule if you're not up to it. You know, after yesterday."

"What? No, eleven is fine." I'd been reliving one of my many run-ins with Denise. Whatever Duffy was like, she had to be easier to work with than her predecessor.

At least I hoped so.

We met in Graydon's office. His second-floor space was roomy and quiet, and it was also the only office up there. The rest of the floor was taken up with the boardroom, a conference room, the computer lab, and the Friends book sale room.

Though the silent calm was probably conducive to deep thoughts, for me it didn't hold much appeal. Part of the fun of working was the synergy of being with other people. An office distant from coworker camaraderie would make it harder to have those silly conversations that led nowhere but to laughter, harder to form friendships, and harder to feel part of . . . well, everything.

For instance, just half an hour ago, Josh, Holly, and Donna, our part-time seventy-something clerk who worked only to fund her travel budget for running marathons all over the world, listened to me tell the tale of what had happened yesterday at Gainsborough. Sure, their muted shock made my eyes sting all over again, but their concern was obvious and comforting, even if Josh's reaction was more raised eyebrows than the sympathetic hugs I got from Holly and Donna.

If I had an office on the second floor, would I have that kind of relationship with my coworkers? I thought not.

Graydon said he didn't mind being up there, and maybe some distance was appropriate for the library's fearless leader. Then again, not that I watched his movements that closely, but it sure seemed to me that he was spending more time downstairs than he had when he first arrived.

When I popped upstairs five minutes before the meeting time, someone was already sitting with Graydon at his small conference table.

"So you're the bookmobile lady." The new Friends of the Library president looked me up and down.

If I'd been asked what I'd expected her to look like, I'm not sure what I would have said, but there's no possible way I would have come close to the reality that was Duffy Ulrich.

Bright blue block-heeled boots that rose up to her knees, sleek black pants in a thick shiny space-age fabric, a wide belt of navy blue yarn, a loose black-and-white buffalo plaid shirt over a shockingly pink tank. That clothing ensemble was on a figure slender enough and short enough to be mistaken for a ten-year-old, and topped with fiery red hair curlier than my own unmanageable mess, something I hadn't thought possible.

I was smiling as I held out my hand, and her grip fit her looks exactly: firm and confident, with nothing to prove to anyone. I'd found another role model, which made my day.

"Frances is your aunt," Duffy said. "Can't believe we've never met."

"How do you know her?" Most people in Chilson knew Aunt Frances. She'd married a Chilson native and had lived here far longer than I'd been alive. Her husband had passed away decades ago, and she'd recently remarried, but leaving Chilson had never occurred to her. To make a living after becoming a widow, she'd turned the house her first husband had left her into a summer boardinghouse and taught woodworking classes at the local community college. Now retired from teaching, and with the boardinghouse sold, she'd set up a small business as a wedding planner.

Duffy's expression was closer to a smirk than a smile. "Ask her."

I laughed and made a mental note to do that exact thing.

Graydon leaned back in his chair. "Madame President has an idea for you."

"Last thing I want," Duffy said, "is to step on toes. Seems to me there's been a lot of that going around the last few years with the Friends. If I'm wrong, about that or anything, tell me up front."

"Yes, ma'am," I said. "I mean yes, I'll tell you when you're wrong, but it hasn't happened yet."

"Well, we've only known each other five minutes. Give it time."

I nodded, putting on a fake frown. "Noted." And just like that, my mild anxiety about the new president of the Friends vanished, as if it had never been. Duffy was going to be fun to work with. Right off the bat, we understood each other. That was important, because it was part of my job to liaison with the Friends, to make sure their efforts integrated smoothly with official library efforts. That Duffy had a sense of humor compatible with mine was going to make this infinitely easier than the previous president. This was going to work out just fine.

"What do you think about a bookmobile scavenger hunt?" she asked.

I spent a short period of time imitating a large-mouth bass—jaw dropped, eyes wide—then asked, "A what?"

"A scavenger hunt. With the bookmobile."

I squinted at her. Hearing what she'd said repeated, this time with a couple more words, didn't help communicate the concept. My imagination flared with images. Driving the bookmobile all over Tonedagana County, trying to find clues hidden by the Friends, none of whom had ever driven anything close to bookmobile size, squeezing it down private roads that ended in tiny driveways, having its poor sides scraped by overgrown tree branches and shrubs. "A scavenger hunt," I said.

"Sure, with prizes for finding it the most times."

"For . . . finding?"

"Not all on the same day," she said. "Over a couple of months, maybe. The Friends could make up passports of some sort, and you stamp people's passport for each location."

At long last, I clued into what she was talking about. Not the bookmobile going on a scavenger hunt, but people hunting down the bookmobile all over Chilson. Duffy didn't seem to notice the light bulb going on inside my head, but the half smile on Graydon's face indicated that he absolutely had.

"Get each page of the passport stamped," she said, holding out her hands, palms up, "and you win a free book from the Friends book sale room!"

It was an interesting idea, but I wasn't sure what its focus was all about. "This is for getting more interest in the bookmobile? Or the Friends? Or for the locations where it's parked?"

"All of the above!" She laughed. "Triple whammy!

We can talk to the city, the county, the chamber of commerce. I bet all of them have places they'd like to bring more attention to. I mean, what business wouldn't like the bookmobile parked out in front of it for a couple of hours? Think of the new customers that could bring in. And I bet the city has parks they think should get more attention. And maybe the sheriff would like to do some outreach."

I was pretty sure the sheriff would, but the problem was hours in the day. This would be a huge project to manage, with zillions of things to wrangle into place, and it wasn't as if I was sitting around twiddling my thumbs, waiting for work to find its way to me.

"Well," I said. "That's an interesting idea, and—"

My phone went off with the ringtone from *Hawaii Five-O*. "Sorry." I pulled my phone from my pocket. I looked at Graydon. "It'll be about yesterday. Is it okay if . . ." I gestured at the phone.

He nodded. I made a quick apology to Duffy and hurried into the hallway to hit the Answer button. "Hey, Ash. Do you have news?"

Sheriff's deputy Ash Wolverson was inches away from becoming a full-fledged detective. Ash and Rafe had been friends for years, but before Rafe and I got together, Ash and I had dated for a very short period. We'd quickly realized there were zero sparks between us, Ash was now engaged to Chelsea Stille, office manager extraordinaire for the sheriff, and the four of us were all good friends.

I'd known Ash for so long that I tended to forget how drop-dead handsome he was and tended to focus on his increasing and regrettable tendency to take after Detective Hal Inwood, who was training and mentoring him. Hal was a solid human being, but he did not play well with others. Or at least he didn't with me.

Ash cleared his throat. "Where are you?"

"At the library."

"You're not at your desk."

I frowned at the floor, in the direct direction of my office. "No, I'm upstairs."

"Can you come down here?"

The clipped tone to his voice meant he was in Serious Officer Mode, so I skipped over my normal tendency for light banter and headed for the stairs. "On my way."

When I got there, Ash, in his brown deputy uniform, was standing, waiting for me. I paused in the doorway and eyed him. His shoulders were stiff and his square jaw was set, and there wasn't a hint of a smile on his face.

"Hey," I said quietly.

Ash gave me a long look, and I knew what was coming. "Minnie, I'm sorry to tell you this."

I held up my hands, trying to ward off the words, but he went inexorably on. "Yesterday, after Paige Ferrer was transported to the hospital, she had a five-hour surgery. However, the damage was too great, and—"

"No," I whispered.

"—and at 9:24 this morning, Paige Ferrer died."

I sat heavily in my chair. "She was murdered."

Ash nodded.

I studied my tightly clasped hands and breathed, in and out, in and out. Then I glared at Ash. "You're going to find who killed her."

"Yes, ma'am," he said.

"Well, then." I drew in and released one more breath. "Go do that."

He touched my shoulder lightly. "Yes, ma'am."

When he'd gone, I stared at the place he'd been. Paige Ferrer. At least now I knew her name.

Behind the books.

Chapter 4

When I returned to Graydon's office, Duffy was gone and my boss was in a virtual meeting with what looked like a screenful of librarians from all over the state.

"Talk later?" I asked quietly, and he nodded.

Back downstairs, I stood at my window and looked at the world. The library's lawn. The city street and sidewalks. The houses across the street. The hill rising to the north. The maple and birch trees, bare-branched and swaying gently in a light wind. It was a view I'd seen almost every day for years and enjoyed every time, but today wasn't going to count because I wasn't really seeing it at all. What I was seeing was the look on a woman's face, a look of frustration, of entreaty, of despair.

"Behind the books," I said softly.

The words rang inside my brain, bouncing around and around and not losing any momentum. Gaining speed, if anything.

I shook my head, trying to bring my internal

mind loop to a full stop. After all, Ash and Hal Inwood would figure out who killed Paige Ferrer. Her family would get answers, and justice would be served.

I'd passed on Paige's words to the deputy yesterday, and I'd seen him write them down in a notepad. Ash and Hal would figure out if they meant anything. There was no need for me to call Ash and make sure he'd seen the deputy's notes. Absolutely no need at all.

It was close to noon and not raining, so I pulled on my coat and went outside. I walked along the waterfront, strong-mindedly staying away from the direction of the sheriff's office.

The walk, and the phone call I made to Rafe, helped get the whispers out of my head. It also helped me think about what I was going to do with the knowledge that the woman I'd tried to save had died. Mourning someone I'd never known seemed odd, but our lives had intersected in a very powerful way, and I couldn't ignore that.

When I got back to the library, with my unruly hair in even more disarray than usual because the wind had picked up something fierce, I made a quick stop in the break room to heat up my lunch.

Holly was there, eating her regular ham and cheese on a hamburger bun. That she managed to put together a lunch at all with two grade-school children in the house and a husband who was out of the state for months at a time never ceased to amaze me. She swallowed and asked, "How did it go with Duffy?"

My mind was so full of other things that a meeting I'd had an hour before had been completely pushed out. "Duff . . . oh. Right." I gathered up my memory. "She knows my aunt Frances."

"No surprise." Holly shrugged. "Between the two of them, I bet they know ninety-five percent of Chilson. Probably the whole county. What did Duffy want? Is she going to shake up the Friends?"

I thought about the staid and comfortable Friends group, who'd been doing the same things the same way for decades. "Probably."

"Cool," Holly said around a bite of sandwich. "But you don't look too happy about it."

I shut the microwave door on my tub of leftovers. "Different reason," I said, sighing, and told her what Ash had told me.

Holly jumped up and gave me a hard hug. "You poor thing. Are you okay?" she asked, releasing me and looking into my face.

I smiled. Sort of. "Not really. But I will be."

The microwave beeped and I took leftover spaghetti with marinara sauce to my office and sat down in front of my computer. The first thing I did was type her name into a search engine. "Paige Ferrer," I said out loud, and the first thing I found out was the many ways that both Paige and Ferrer could be spelled.

Adding "Michigan" to the search string helped narrow the focus; adding "Chilson" helped even more, something I should have done in the first place.

The very first thing I found out was that Paige was actually Dr. Paige Ferrer, an orthopedic surgeon. And that she was part of Maple Street Orthopedics, a practice just north of Petoskey.

I recognized the name, and when I opened their

website and looked at the photos, I recognized the brick building, too, as one I'd driven past dozens of times. Remembered it being built, even. Through luck and grace, I'd never needed an orthopedic surgeon, but I knew plenty of people who had—my best friend and top-notch restaurateur Kristen Jurek, for one—and everything I'd heard had always been positive.

My cursor hovered above the *Meet Our Doctors* link. Did I want to go there? Yes . . . no . . . yes . . . no . . .

"Yes," I murmured, and clicked.

I had to scroll a bit through doctors with A through E last names, but suddenly there she was. Shoulder-length black hair loose and full. A smiling face. A happy face.

"I'm so sorry," I told the image quietly. "I wish I could have done more to save you. I did my best, but it wasn't good enough."

Paige kept smiling at me, and I had to look away.

How could she be on that website, as if nothing had changed? It felt cruel that her picture should still be up there, having her look like she might have yesterday morning. Before someone had aimed an arrow at her and left her for dead in the woods.

"I'm so sorry," I repeated, and once again I could hear the wheezing of her breath and the desperation in her voice as she struggled to speak what might have been her final words.

Behind the books.

I looked directly into her smiling eyes. "I don't know what you meant," I told her. "But I will find out. And that's a promise."

* * *

After my library day was over, I made a quick trip downtown, then walked up to the middle school. It was Rafe's school board night, and he'd taken to staying at the school to prepare for the meeting rather than come home and get something to eat. Rafe had told me multiple times that he was fine missing a meal now and then, and that he didn't get cranky hungry like I did, so I could quit worrying, but he was wrong about all of it. He wasn't fine, he did get cranky, and I was never going to stop worrying about him.

I walked into his office and plopped a Shomin's Deli bag on his desk. "Eat," I commanded.

He did the one-eyebrow thing. "Now?"

"Yes. I'm stopping at Sophia's after this. I want to see what she's done to my old room. And then . . ." I busied myself with opening the bag and distributing the sandwiches. "Then I need to tell Aunt Frances and Otto about . . . everything."

"Huh." He took a huge bite of corned beef, sauerkraut, dressing, and rye bread. "Kind of surprised Frances isn't already on you about getting involved in another murder."

I was, too. My aunt had an uncanny knack for hearing insider news before it became news. It simply wasn't possible that she hadn't heard about what had happened yesterday at Gainsborough. She'd also almost certainly heard that the poor woman had died, so the missing bit to the puzzle was that her niece had been on the scene.

Telling her wasn't something I was looking forward to, as she felt free to play loco parentis whenever she felt the occasion arose. The many times

I'd talked her out of contacting my parents had sharpened my negotiation skills, but doing so was exhausting. Though now that I was married, maybe she wouldn't be so inclined to pass judgment on my extracurricular activities. But she'd known Rafe his entire life, so I wasn't going to count on it.

My husband took a huge bite, finishing his sandwich. "Gotta go, my little acorn. Meeting with the prez ahead of time."

I ignored the acorn comment. For more than a year Rafe had been trying, and epically failing, to stick me with a nickname. "Have a good meeting. I'll lock the door behind me." After he left, I ate the last few bites of my Swiss cheese and olive with Thousand Island dressing on sourdough, then headed out.

A thick cloud cover had rolled in, so it was hard to tell if the sun was still up or if it had set. Either way, it was dark. Streetlights gave me some indication of where the sidewalk lived, but I had to rely on the city laying straight and flat concrete most of my way through the residential streets.

Now that it was late October, and a Tuesday, most of the homes that had been converted to short-term rentals were empty and as dark as the sky. Of course, many of those houses had been owned by summer people and would have been empty this time of year anyway. Still, having so many houses in Chilson now being rented to people from all over was giving the town a different feel.

What had once been summer cottages visited by generations of the same family were now filled with wedding parties, golf weekenders, and general tourists. It was a good thing for many area businesses, but not long ago you'd have been able to depend on your summer neighbors keeping an eye out for, say, a runaway cat. And you'd keep an eye on their house all winter long. Now, with companies from out of state owning so many houses . . .

I shook my head as I climbed the stairs of the former boardinghouse, walked across the wide front porch, and did something that felt super strange: knocked on the front door.

The door was opened almost immediately by Sophia Aguilar, whose Mexican heritage did not reveal itself to the naked eye. The maternal side of her family had given her wavy blond hair and pale skin, but her dark brown eyes must have come straight from her father's side.

"Well, if it isn't Mrs. Niswander." Sophia grinned. "Come on in. I'm all alone tonight, my housemate is at the school board meeting. Have you eaten? I wasn't thinking and picked up a full sub from Fat Boys, instead of a half, so there's plenty."

"Save it for your lunch tomorrow," I said when she paused for breath. "Rafe and I had Shomin's."

By this time we'd passed through the living room with its stone fireplace, pine paneling, and deep sofas, through the dining room with its long table and bank of windows that, when the drapes were pulled, revealed a thickly wooded backyard, and had entered the kitchen. Sophia's dinner was sitting on the pedestal table that was still in the same kitchen corner it had always been in.

I tried not to look around with a critical eye, but it was hard. I'd spent my childhood summers in this house. I'd also spent a number of adult winters here, all cozy with my own upstairs bedroom, and not remarking on the changes was taxing my abilities.

Sophia, besides being the person to unite Rafe and me in holy matrimony, was also the county's district court attorney magistrate. She was hardworking and smart and had an offbeat sense of humor that meshed so well with mine that I wished she could have been a part-time bookmobile librarian. She was also observant and noticed my sliding glances around the kitchen.

"It's weird for you, isn't it?" she asked.

I ripped my attention away from the towel rack— a blue flower-print towel? Seriously? That was clearly a spot for a red-and-white check!—and to her amused face. "Sorry," I said. "But, yeah, it is."

Sophia laughed. "It would be weird if it wasn't." She wadded up her sandwich wrappings and got up to toss them into the kitchen garbage can, which looked no different than it had for decades. This made me feel better. Childish, but better.

"Come on," Sophia said. "Let's go rip the bandage off."

And we headed upstairs so I could see what had happened to the last of my childhood.

Half an hour later, I was in the house across the street, sitting in the kitchen nook and watching my aunt Frances and her husband Otto Bingham work on a new recipe, this time for shredded beef enchiladas, complete with homemade tortillas.

Aunt Frances had the tall, rangy grace looks of Katharine Hepburn, and you could mistake Otto for a younger brother of Paul Newman. Though they hadn't been married long, I'd rarely seen a couple so in tune with each other. Not only did they have complete conversations with a couple of mouth twitches and come to agreements about complicated plans with a nod, but they also made cooking look like a choreographed ballet dance for two. For which there was a term, but I couldn't think what it was, so I pulled out my phone and did a quick search.

Pas de deux. That was it.

"So what did you think?" Aunt Frances asked. "I haven't been inside since Celeste left."

When our thirdish cousin had purchased the boardinghouse from my aunt, Celeste had made it clear that she was going to be a fair-weather occupant, traveling with her cute little camper October through April, visiting friends, relatives, and national parks around the country.

Last summer, Celeste had come to understand the depth of the housing crisis in Chilson and decided that, instead of renting rooms to summer visitors, she'd convert the house to apartments. After getting cost estimates that were prohibitively high, she'd thought about it and decided the boardinghouse could stay the same and she'd just rent rooms on a long-term basis instead of short-term.

She kept a suite of rooms for herself and was renting out the remaining bedrooms one at a time, as she came across reliable people who were interested in a different type of housing.

"Well," I said, "right now Sophia and one of Rafe's new teachers are the only renters, but Sophia said there are two new people coming in right after the holidays."

My aunt gave me a look over the top of their

scary-looking countertop mixer. "Not what I meant and you know it," she said, and turned the mixer to the Drown Out Anything Minnie Says level.

After my eardrums recovered, I took a sip of wine from the glass Otto had poured for me. "It'll be okay," I said eventually. And it would be. Aunt Frances, though she'd lived in the boardinghouse longer than I'd been alive, was having an easier adjustment time than I was. One more reason to be like her when I grew up.

I watched my aunt add a single drop of hot sauce straight into the mixer bowl, something that I would have been terrified to do for risk of adding ten drops instead of one, and said, "Sophia is in my old room. She painted it a pale yellow and brought in her own furniture, but it works."

Yes, seeing the scarred pine dresser and matching double bed I'd used for years replaced by snappy white spool-style furniture had been jarring, but after that first shocking glance, I'd been able to nod appreciatively.

"So glad you're able to accept change," my aunt said, "when it's being thrust upon you."

I eyed her, then looked at Otto. "Was that snark? Pretty sure that was snark."

Otto gave me his gentle smile. "She's just tired of waiting for you to tell her about what happened at Gainsborough."

"So you heard about that."

My aunt did an eye roll so dramatic she must have learned it from Julia. "I'm old and mostly retired, but I'm not dead. I still get out of the house. And I hear from people even if I don't get out of my pajamas. There's this thing called social media, maybe you've heard of it? And gosh, isn't that a telephone? In. Your. Hand?"

Instinctively, I slid my cell phone away from me. "Yeah. Well. But telling you is one of the reasons I wanted to stop by tonight. Does that count?"

Aunt Frances abandoned the cooking dance and came over to sit across from me. She reached for my hands and covered them with her own large ones, lightly scarred in various places from her years of woodworking and teaching woodworking. "Of course it counts. I was starting the conversation, that's all. You do have a history of giving me news of this sort on a very reluctant basis."

True enough, and it was yet another character flaw that I should think about working on. Someday soon. Just not today. However, there was a reason behind not wanting to tell her, one that had nothing to do with dealing with her reaction, and everything to do with me.

I didn't want to relive it.

But I needed to be a grown-up—or at least represent a facsimile thereof—so I took a deep breath and started the sad tale, ending with how Ash had stopped by to tell me that Paige Ferrer had died that morning.

"That poor woman," Aunt Frances said. "I'm so glad you found her. Not easy for you, but at least she wasn't out there all alone."

I hadn't thought about that. "I suppose so."

Otto, who'd come over and sat next to my aunt, gave me a kind look. "You did your best, and that provided a chance. If it hadn't been for you, she wouldn't have had any chance at all."

Sighing, I said, "Part of me knows that to be

true. The rest of me feels like I didn't do anything at all. If I'd had more medical training, maybe I could have saved her."

"You've taken more first-aid courses than anyone I've ever met," my aunt said. "Any more training and you'd be a doctor and would never have been at Gainsborough to begin with."

Though I was pretty sure you couldn't accidentally become a medical professional, as a bookmobile driver in a rural county I was very conscious of how far we could be from assistance. I'd enrolled in every in-person emergency first-aid class I could find, and a slew of online ones.

Aunt Frances and Otto were right, I didn't need to take on any responsibility for Paige's death. That belonged to the person who'd shot her. But I did want to learn more about her. Who she was, what she cared about, who she'd left behind.

I looked at my aunt. "I don't suppose you knew Paige."

"Not this time," she said. "Sorry."

"Um."

My gaze swung over to Otto. "Um? Did you say 'um'?" I glanced at Aunt Frances. "He said 'um.' You heard it, didn't you?"

"I did indeed." She gave her husband a speculative look. "Very uncharacteristic of him. Wonder what he meant by that?"

"You do realize that I'm right here," he said.

"But are you?" I asked. "You said 'um.' Clearly your body has been taken over by aliens. Ones who don't know your inability to speak other than in precise sentences that diagram cleanly."

Aunt Frances squinted. "Or maybe this isn't

Otto at all. Maybe it's a simulation. An android." She reached out and pinched his skin. "Hmm. Feels real."

"If you two are done," Otto said patiently, "I have information about Dr. Ferrer that I can share."

My eyes opened wide, matching my aunt's. "Really?" I asked. "Were you a patient of hers?" I couldn't remember either one of them needing an orthopedic surgeon.

"No, it was the other way around." He smiled at our puzzled expressions. "Dear Minnie. You do remember that you convinced me to volunteer my time at the library as a financial counselor? Yes, of course you do."

Otto had been a very successful accountant, and in his retirement he'd discovered a latent talent for nurturing young business owners.

"You were giving free financial advice to a surgeon?" Aunt Frances gave her husband a hard "are you serious?" look.

He smiled. "Not exactly. One of her employees was interested in a business start-up, medical bookkeeping, and Dr. Ferrer had seen a notice in the library's e-newsletter about my services. She contacted me, set up an appointment, and came in with her employee for emotional support, it seemed."

The knowledge that Paige had been a library patron, and that I'd never met her, made my heart twist.

"Sounds a little overbearing," my aunt said.

Otto made a noncommittal gesture. "On the surface, perhaps. But the young woman had a solid business plan and the capital to start a small home-based business. All Sharrow appeared to need was confidence, and Dr. Ferrer was doing her best to supply that."

He gave me a steady look. "She did share some personal information about herself, if you'd like to hear it. Yes, I thought you would. Dr. Ferrer grew up downstate, in the Lansing area. She did her undergrad work at MSU, and was in medical school at Michigan. After that, she worked at a practice in Grand Rapids for a number of years, and moved north about ten years ago to become a partner at Maple Street Orthopedics."

"Why did she move Up North?" Aunt Frances asked.

"She didn't say, and I didn't ask. This was a meeting about her employee. I only asked about Dr. Ferrer's background to start the conversation."

Which made sense, if the employee was nervous.

"The only other point of interest," Otto said, "was she mentioned that she'd purchased the house in Gainsborough, the Duvall house, as an investment. She spent some time there, but its primary use was a short-term rental."

Just like so many others. I looked at Otto. "It sounds as if you liked her."

"I did," he said, nodding. "We met only the once, but she was articulate, smart, and savvy. Plus, she cared enough about her employee to make an appointment with me, and to make the time to come along."

Everything Otto said spoke of a woman I wish I'd known. A woman I wish I could have saved. A woman whose last words to me were still echoing in my ears.

Behind the books.

* * *

Bright and early the next morning—not that the sky was actually bright, because we wouldn't see much of that for months, but it was early—I walked through the front door of the sheriff's office.

A smiling Chelsea Stille came toward the security window. "Well, if it isn't the friendly neighborhood bookmobile librarian," she said, tucking her brown hair, cut into wavy layers that always did what she told them to do, behind her ears. "What's up, Minnie?"

Chelsea and Ash's wedding was coming up in a few months, so I asked how things were going. She gave me a look. "Seems to me you've had enough wedding talk. Are you asking because you want to know, or because you feel obligated to?"

I laughed. "How about both?"

"Executive summary, then." She put her elbows on the counter and leaned close to the round metal speaker. "Wedding at Ash's church, conducted by his childhood minister. Catering by Angelique's, flowers by that place in Harbor Springs, photos by a talented high school friend of mine. Dress is ordered, and I almost have Ash convinced to do the tux thing." She winked.

Since Ash, with his classic good looks and broad shoulders, had the body type that tuxes were designed to highlight, I applauded her efforts. "And the reception venue?"

Chelsea laughed, a contagious peal. "You are not going to believe this," she said, still laughing. "You know that boat place just south of town? The one that sells massive boats that cost more than most houses? Ash knows the manager. He stopped in after doing a car accident report nearby, just to say hello. Turns out they've started building a fancy-schmancy showroom and they're happy to rent out the space for events. Plus," she said, grinning, "since we're first, and kind of like guinea pigs for the whole thing, it turns out that they're only going to charge us cleaning costs."

"That's . . . great!" Timing my wedding reception with the end date of a construction project would have been way too much stress for me, but maybe people who worked in law enforcement had a higher tolerance for things like that.

The door to the inner sanctum clicked open. "It's going to take some time," Detective Hal Inwood said, looking down from his—to my mind—excessive height, "to grow accustomed to saying Ms. Niswander."

I sketched a wave at Chelsea and went in. "You could call me Minnie," I pointed out, and got a mild grunt in reply. Part of his ill humor might have been because I'd e-mailed him and texted Ash an hour ago, asking to meet with one or both of them as soon as possible, but I also knew that gruff and distanced was his default personality. How this man could have been married to the irrepressibly cheerful Tabitha for decades was a total and complete mystery.

The detective led me to a small room that held nothing but a scarred rectangular table, four battered chairs, and Deputy Ash Wolverson. I sat across from Ash.

"Question about the reception," I said. "Do we get to dance on the boats? Because I see some serious photo opportunities."

Ash glanced at Hal, then shook his head. "They'll move all the boats ahead of time."

Well, that was disappointing. Understandable, but disappointing.

Detective Inwood sat next to Ash, folded his hands, and gave me a long look. "To what do we owe the pleasure, Ms. Niswander?"

"It's about Paige. Dr. Ferrer. I was hoping you'd have some news about what happened, is all. It's early in the investigation, I know," I added hurriedly, seeing the glance exchanged by the two men. "But I was . . . well, I was there, and I'd like to know whatever you can tell me."

Hal tipped his head at Ash. "Deputy."

"Dr. Ferrer," Ash said, pulling a small notebook out of his shirt pocket and flipping through pages, "grew up in Lansing, maiden name Millar. She was valedictorian at Lansing's Sexton High School, graduated from Michigan State magna cum laude, and was near the top of her class at University of Michigan's medical school."

He paused. "This is all public information, which is why I can tell you."

"Understood," I said. Otto had already told me most of that anyway. "What else?"

Ash went back to his notes. "She married Rob Ferrer, an attorney, when she was a resident. They moved to Grand Rapids, where she worked with a large group of orthopedic surgeons. They had two sons, Alec and Logan. She and her husband divorced about ten years ago, after which she moved north and joined Maple Street Orthopedics, specializing in sports injuries. She'd been living just outside Petoskey and moved to Chilson about a year ago, around the same time she purchased the house in Gainsborough."

A page flipped. "It seems the Gainsborough house was primarily an investment purchase, that she was using it as a short-term rental."

I felt a pang for Paige's sons. They were probably about my age, maybe a little younger. Sure, in a vague way you expect to lose your parents at some point, but this was far too soon.

"She had a renter leave the morning that . . . that morning," Ash said. "We're using the working theory that she was out there to check on the place. The cleaning company she used said that was standard procedure for her."

They'd found out a lot in a short period of time. I was impressed, and was about to say so, when Ash went on.

"We have another working theory." He paused. Cleared his throat. Continued. "The morning of the incident, there was heavy cloud cover and a light mist in many parts of the county. Dr. Ferrer was wearing a light brown jacket. It is currently bow hunting season, and—"

"No," I said quietly.

Ash plowed on. "And our working theory is this was a tragic accident, and—"

"No," I said, slightly louder.

Hal sighed. "Ms. Ham . . . Niswander—"

"No," I said again. "Let me tell you what is *not* going to happen. You are *not* going to write this off as a hunting accident, then not look very hard to figure out who killed her because, gee, why should some poor guy's life be ruined because of one mistake?"

By this time I was standing and glaring at the men, neither of whom was looking me in the eye. "A woman has been killed," I said, my voice increasing in volume with every word, "and someone needs to be held accountable!"

The last few words were at full shout. I gave them a final glare and walked out, brushing past a surprised Chelsea on the way.

"Don't worry," I muttered to Paige, as I pushed out into the stark October morning. "I'll make them do a real investigation. And if they don't find out who killed you, I will."

Chapter 5

My walking speed up to the library was stoked by fury. Arms pumped, legs flashed, and lungs heaved. Halfway there, I took a deep breath and slowed to a more normal pace.

"Don't worry," I said again to Paige, just in case she was listening. "Now that Hal and Ash know how invested I am in finding who killed you, they'll make sure to dot all their *i*'s and cross all their *t*'s." My words were coming out in short puffy breaths, so I dropped my speed one more notch.

"Not that they wouldn't even if I had nothing to do with the investigation," I murmured, because of course they would have. Their slightly guilty—or if not guilty then abashed—expressions had only revealed what they'd been secretly thinking, not that they wouldn't look at every possibility.

"They'll pursue every avenue of investigation," I said, quoting Detective Inwood. I was pretty sure it was his favorite expression. That they were leaping to a hunting accident assumption mostly meant that he was trying to prepare me for a possible result of death by persons unknown, or whatever the non-television equivalent might be.

Probably.

Though I spent the rest of my library day doing normal library things, I also ended up spending a significant portion of it staying out of earshot of anyone speculating about what had happened at Gainsborough. I wasn't ready to talk to anyone else about Paige, so I kept to my office, stayed focused on what was in front of me, and ended up getting a tremendous amount of work done.

"My entire to-do list was almost finished," I said to Rafe over our dinner of calzones and steamed broccoli, the last because I was making a real effort to eat healthy. Or at least healthier. The volume of broccoli was a teensy fraction of the calzones, but you had to start somewhere.

"Does this mean you're going to stay in your office every day from now on?" Rafe stabbed a piece of broccoli with his fork, studied it, then put it back on his plate and cut it in half.

"Mrr," Eddie said.

"You want this?" Rafe held his broccoli-laden fork in Eddie's direction.

"He does not," I said, "and stop feeding him from the dining table. We have standards, you know."

"We do?" Rafe looked around the room, which was lined with bookshelves packed with my books, his books, and a growing collection of books that we'd bought together, a fact that warmed my heart. "Since when?"

"Didn't say they were very high." I sliced into my calzone, letting the lava-hot steam escape. "Might begin and end with not feeding Eddie from the dining table."

"So feeding him from the kitchen island is okay, you're saying."

I looked down at our furry friend, who was sitting upright in Egyptian cat statue mode and staring at me with unblinking yellow eyes. "What do you think?"

"Mrr!"

Rafe nodded. "Pretty sure he said he prefers a linen tablecloth."

"On it. Just let me get the iron."

My husband frowned. "We have an iron?"

"And an ironing board. We're like real adults here. I thought you knew."

"All day, every day?"

I snorted. "As if."

"Well, okay then." He blew out a fake sigh of relief. "Being a grown-up all the time would be exhausting. Not sure I have it in me."

I reached over and patted his hand. "No one would expect you to. Trust me."

"Glad I can meet expectations."

An odd *thump* came from the corner of the room. I craned around and saw Eddie's back feet squirming themselves behind a row of my childhood books. It was one of my Nancy Drews that had landed on the floor. *The Hidden Staircase*, if I was remembering the covers correctly.

"You are so weird," I told the disappearing tail, and returned to my dinner. "Speaking of travel," I said, "one of these days we should talk about our honeymoon."

We'd chosen our late September wedding date

partly by virtue of detaching the honeymoon from the wedding. Now that we were actually married, it was probably time to figure out the travel part.

"Question." Rafe half closed his eyes. "When does it stop being a honeymoon and when does it start being a vacation?"

This was something I'd thought about more than I'd like to admit. "Our first anniversary."

He nodded. "Makes sense. So we need to go somewhere before next mid-September. Almost a whole year."

"Gives us basically every season to consider." Then I thought about that. "Well, this fall would be hard. There's not even two months left, and traveling during Thanksgiving would be brutal."

"Going down to your parents' house is bad enough, and we're going in the easy directions."

One fun fact of Up North life was that the heavy traffic was almost always in the other lanes. Driving south on a summer Friday meant watching a steady stream of bike-laden and boat-towing cars, trucks, SUVs, and RVs head north, with the reverse happening on Sunday. Smugness was not an attractive thing, but it was hard not to smirk at the long line of slow-moving vehicles.

"Unless we want to go north, Thanksgiving is out," I said.

"Not sure that late November is when we want to tour the Upper Peninsula. Or Canada."

"Narrowing things down quickly. Excellent." I heard, and ignored, a muffled "Mrr!" Forking up a big bite of calzone, I said, "Any other time of year we can eliminate? And is there any location we can remove from our itinerary?"

"Time of year." Rafe waved his second bit of broccoli about. "We have to go between December first to mid-September."

"Agreed."

"To narrow things down, let's stick to the Northern Hemisphere. We can always take a Southern Hemisphere trip some other time."

I felt a pang of regret. I'd been wanting to visit Australia ever since I'd read the Phryne Fisher books, Botswana ever since I'd read the No. 1 Ladies' Detective Agency books, India ever since I'd read the Perveen Mistry books, and Laos ever since I'd read the Dr. Siri Paiboun books. But all that could wait. "Also agreed."

"Then we're almost there." Rafe grinned, the slightly lopsided one that he saved just for me.

And my heart went mushy.

The next day was Thursday, which had turned into a bookmobile day for me and Eddie. When I'd made the staff schedule, I'd put Hunter down for Thursdays, but he'd had to cancel this week.

Hunter Morales had hired on as a part-time driver because he liked books and driving and because he and his wife Abigail were taking every job they could find and investing every penny they could into their welding business, and the business was booming. This was fantastic for that particular pair of twenty-somethings, but it was also resulting in Hunter having less and less time to come out and play on the bookmobile.

I knew I needed to start working on finding someone else willing to work infrequent hours for not much pay, but I was also hoping to delay having to do so as long as possible. It hadn't been easy to find a driver as qualified as Hunter in the first place, and it wouldn't be any easier this time around.

"Besides, we like him," I said out loud.

Julia turned. "Eh?" she asked in a voice that crackled with age. "What was that, dearie?"

I had no idea if Julia was playing a real part or a made-up part, or if her voice had suddenly changed, so I ignored the new persona. "Hunter. We like him."

"Mrr!"

Julia nodded, toe-tapping the cat carrier, and said, still in her aged-wise-woman voice, "That young man and his wife are salt-of-the-earth types. Their parents should be proud."

My guess was that Abigail's parents would really be proud the day she and Hunter were able to move out of their basement, as that was where the couple was living for now to save money. "One of these days Hunter is going to leave us. Might even be soon."

"And what, pray tell, are you doing about that?" She arched an eyebrow. "Eh?"

"Putting my head in the sand," I said promptly. "How about you?"

"Hah." Normal Julia was back. "I am not the assistant library director. I am a part-time clerk with no responsibilities."

"Do you want some?" I flicked the turn signal and pulled off the county highway and into a church parking lot.

"Responsibilities?" She scoffed. "Been there, done that. It's your turn."

After I braked us to a slow stop, we unbuckled our seat belts and started the short list of opening tasks. Julia and I had done this so many times that we hadn't looked at the checklist taped to the inside of a storage cabinet in years.

I unlatched the driver's seat and rotated it all the way around to face the back, then unlocked the flip-down countertop that served as a desk and pulled out one of the two laptops. Meanwhile, Julia had gone to the back, where she unhooked the bungee cord that held her rolling office chair in place. We fired up our computers, Julia double-checked the shelf of book holds set aside for this stop, and I opened the cat carrier door, checked on Eddie, and went to unlock the side door.

Already waiting for us, his hands full of returning books, was Lawrence Zonne, a widower in his mideighties. Not that anyone would have guessed he was that old. Sure, he had white hair and the associated wrinkles, but he moved more easily than many twenty-year-olds, he had vision sharper than mine had ever been, and his memory was the envy of pretty much everyone.

If we had favorite patrons—which we didn't, because that would be sort of like having a favorite child and would be wrong—the facts that Mr. Zonne had a witty intelligence and he talked to Eddie just like we did would have put him in the top ten.

"And what," he asked, "is this I hear about you two being out at Gainsborough the other day? Don't tell me you were the ones who found Dr. Ferrer."

Julia and I looked at Eddie, who was sitting in his new favorite spot in the exact middle of the floor.

"Ah," Mr. Zonne said, climbing up the stairs. "Mr. Edward. I should have known. Because of you, Dr. Ferrer did not die alone. Thank you." He crouched down and gave Eddie a long pet.

I cleared my throat, which had gone tight. "You knew Paige? I mean, Dr. Ferrer?"

Mr. Zonne stood. "She replaced numerous parts of both me and my lovely late wife."

"Knees?" I asked.

He smiled at me. "Child. If only 'twere so. Knees and hips for me and my bride, with the addition of shoulders for me, thanks to my football-playing youth."

The idea of a young Mr. Zonne in uniform and running down a grassy field distracted me momentarily, but I was brought back to the here and now by Eddie rolling over and whacking my ankles with his tail. "Did you know much about her?" I asked.

"Other than that she was much too young to die?" He gazed out the front windshield and suddenly looked his age. He shook his head and turned back to us, sighing. "Very little, I'm sorry to say. Divorced. Two sons. Alec and Logan, I believe, alphabetical by birth order, which I always appreciate."

"Do the sons or the ex-husband live around here?" I asked.

"She never talked about her ex-husband, but it was my understanding that Logan and his wife live in Oregon. Alec, the oldest, lives downstate, in Kalamazoo." He frowned. "She didn't share overmuch about her personal life, so that, I'm afraid, is all I know. Apologies."

"None needed," I assured him, and Julia murmured the same. The three of us spent a few minutes in quiet conversation, grieving over a woman's life cut short in such a tragic way, and then we took a collective breath and moved on to the business of the bookmobile.

But after Mr. Zonne departed, a load of new books under his arm, I realized that he'd left one thought behind.

Paige was a successful surgeon, and at her age, she had likely accumulated a significant net worth. Was it possible that one of Paige's sons had killed her in order to speed up his inheritance?

And if possible, was it probable?

I had no idea. But what I did have were my first suspects.

Chapter 6

Another obvious suspect," I said to Eddie on our way home, post-bookmobile, "is Paige's ex-husband. What was his name again?"

"Mrr."

"That's right; Rob. Thanks for the nudge. The divorce was, what, ten years back, but some people are excellent at holding grudges. Maybe this Rob was biding his time, waiting until no one would realistically think he'd still have strong feelings. And he's an attorney," I said, warming to the idea, "so he'd know all about the advantages of playing a long game. Makes sense, right?"

There was no answer from the cat in the car. I glanced over and saw that my fuzzy friend had rotated, turning around so that his back end faced me.

"Okay," I said, relenting. "Maybe it doesn't make that much sense. Besides, the ex-husband is an obvious choice for Ash and Hal to investigate. Even if they think it was a hunting accident, they'll do their due diligence and check on the former spouse." I'd make certain of it. Yes, I'd give them a few days, but there was no reason for me not to hound them a bit, just to guarantee there was some momentum to the investigation.

Momentum. The Big Mo, as Rafe called it. I was pretty sure that was a sports reference, but I was also sure I'd never ask him, because then he'd tell me the origins of the phrase, I'd have to pretend to listen, and worse, I'd have to try to remember what he said. Far better to save us both the irritation and frustration and never ask the question in the first place.

"What I need to do next," I said as I parked the car in the garage and hauled Eddie inside, "is to learn more about Gainsborough. Who should I talk to?"

Eddie exploded out of the carrier, across the kitchen, and toward the dining room, giving me a dirty look over his shoulder as he went.

"You're right," I called after him. "Amelia Singer is the obvious choice. Thanks so much for your help!"

Amelia was another local who'd moved away, then returned after retiring. Downstate, she'd been a teacher, a school principal, and a school superintendent, and retirement had hung heavy on her hands until she'd taken over directorship of the Chilson Historical Museum.

She'd had a busy first couple of years, and she was now making serious inroads on her goal to turn a slightly musty and ill-lit warehouse of castoffs into a showpiece. Talking to her was always an interesting experience, as her busy brain was constantly whirring at top speeds.

After anticipating the conversation, I decided against calling, or even stopping by. "I am millennial, hear me text," I said, misquoting a Helen Reddy song lyric my mom had often used.

Minnie: *Hey, there. It's Minnie. I have a local history question for you.*

Amelia (after a short pause): *Hey, Ms. Niswander! Whatsup?*

Minnie: *Do you know anything about Gainsborough? A late 1800s settlement out on Deer Lake?*

Amelia: *Heard of it. Don't have any solid information.*

Minnie (sighing): *OK. Thanks anyway.*

Amelia: *Try Camille. She might have something for you.*

Minnie: *Great idea. Thanks!*

Camille Pomeranz was the benevolent ruler of the *Chilson Gazette*, our local weekly newspaper. She was a dark-skinned woman in her late forties and was a downstate transplant, having moved Up North after the large newspaper she'd worked for since college had cut their staff to the bare bones.

It had all worked out for Camille and for the *Gazette*, because the paper had gradually shifted from a staid publication that had been little more than a glorified gossip sheet to a news-gathering powerhouse that was winning national awards.

I knew Camille from publishing advertising for library events ranging from author talks to computer classes, and we'd formed a solid work friendship that was on the cusp of becoming a real forever friendship. I sent her a quick text, asking if she knew anything about Gainsborough.

Camille: *Not a thing. But Pam Fazio has made some buying runs out there.*

I thanked her and started a text to my friend Pam, owner of Older Than Dirt, an eclectic store that sold antiques, vintage clothes and jewelry, a smattering of artwork, and a generous number of new items. Pam always said she bought whatever caught her eye, and her eye must be quality, because her store was one of the busiest downtown.

My text to her was the same as the others, with the added sentence "Are you coming back to the Friends of the Library, now that Denise is gone?"

My phone instantly started showing the rippling three dots of an incoming text and then:

Pam: *Wait, what?!? How did I not know about Denise? What happened? Did she vanish in a puff of smoke? Was it spontaneous combustion? Or did she get summoned by her masters to that fiery place?*

Minnie (after laughing out loud): *She moved downstate last week. Duffy Ulrich was voted president.*

Pam: *Best news I've had in months. I'll be at the next meeting, with bells on.*

Minnie: *I'm sure they'll welcome you with open arms. But what I wanted to ask you about is Gainsborough. Camille said you've been out there. Do you know anything about the place?*

Pam: *Not much, really. But you know someone who does.*

Minnie: *Who?*

Pam: *About the last person you'd expect.*

Minnie: *The last? You don't mean . . .*
Pam: *Yup. Mitchell.*

Laughing and crying vied for top billing in Minnie reactions. Of course it was Mitchell Koyne. I thanked Pam, gave Eddie a bobbing pat on the head, and, since I hadn't taken off my coat, headed back outside.

Mitchell Koyne had, for years, been at the tippity-top of the library's list for late fines owed. For most of his adult life he'd cobbled together a living by doing seasonal work: construction and landscaping in the summer, snow plowing and ski lift attendant in the winter. He'd also spent a serious amount of time using the library computers and, after a former library director had cut him off from borrowing until he paid his late fines, cozied up next to the reading room fireplace.

All that had changed, however, after he'd started dating and then married Bianca Sims, one of the area's top real estate agents. Somewhere along the way, Mitchell had been hired as manager of Chilson's toy store and had turned it from a marginal business into a wildly successful one. The cleaned-up Mitchell was undoubtedly an improvement, but part of me missed slacker Mitchell in his untucked flannel shirt, worn jeans, and ancient pickup truck with its mismatched hood, doors, and tailgate.

Bells jingled as I opened the door to the toy store.

"Hey, Minnie." Mitchell was at the DO NOT CLIMB ABOVE part of a stepladder, hanging a new addition to his fleet. The ceiling accessories had started with a couple of model airplanes he'd made as a kid but had expanded into papier-mâché birds, balloons, flying dinosaurs, and now, apparently, weather formations.

"What do you think?" He grinned.

"Very cool." I had no idea how he'd managed to make such a realistic-looking cloud. "It looks as if it could float away any second."

"Yeah?" He peered at it, shrugged, and clambered down. "What's up?"

A Mitchell on ground level was almost as hard for me to talk to as a Mitchell on a ladder. He was far more than a foot taller than my efficient five feet, and he had a tendency to stand close enough that I got a stiff neck from looking up at him.

Surreptitiously, I backed up a few inches. "I hear you have insider information about Gainsborough, out on Deer Lake."

He shrugged. "Yeah, I guess. Did work for a bunch of those families. Lawn mowing. Cottage openings and closings. Kept an eye on them in the winter. Stuff like that."

"What was it like out there?" I got a blank look in return, so I started babbling. "Did the families get along, or did they have long-running rivalries? Feuds?"

Mitchell cocked his head. "Those are weird questions."

He was right. They were. I took a deep breath. "You heard a doctor was killed out there the other day? Dr. Ferrer. I'm the one who found her."

His eyes went wide. "Geez, Minnie, that was you? Wow. I had no idea. So you're, what, looking into this? Investigating?"

I was sharply and suddenly reminded that Mitchell had once upon a time hung out a shingle as a private investigator. Those efforts had lasted about as long as his other former money-making enterprises, but apparently a spark for the trade still burned.

"Not really," I said. The last thing I wanted was for Mitchell's size-thirteen shoes to stomp around in what I was doing. "Just getting . . . closure, if you know what I mean."

"Sure." He nodded. "Okay, then. Let me think," he said, scratching his chin. "Last I worked out there, and it's been a couple of years, there are two cottages with year-round people. Callaways, one door down from the north end, and Gauthiers, three places up from the south end."

"And they all get along?" I asked.

"Callaways and Gauthiers?"

"Yes, but I was wondering more about the place as a group."

"Well, I know none of them liked it when a family sold to an outsider. What did they say?" He used air quotes and put on a fake English accent. "Letting in the riffraff, none of whom have any sense of history."

He shrugged and went back to normal Mitchell voice. "Can't say I mind not working out there. They didn't want anything to change, ever, and that included trees. Ever try to keep a white pine from growing?" He mimicked shoving down an imaginary tree with his bare hands.

I laughed, thanked him, and wandered home, thinking.

It wasn't a huge surprise that the Gainsborough people were opposed to change. Few people loved it, and summer people had a reputation for resisting it more than anyone.

But the interesting fact was that two families lived out there full time. And Paige had brought short-term rentals to their lives.

"Huh," I said to myself.

Definitely huh.

My night was punctuated with snores (Rafe), tossing and turning (me), and heavy sighs (Eddie). The tossing and turning was a direct result of my conversation with Mitchell, and Eddie's sighs were a direct result of my inability to drop down into dreamland. What Rafe's snores were the result of, I didn't know, but wished I did so I could imitate him.

At some point sleep claimed me, so hard and deep that I slept through my phone's alarm and woke to the love of my life poking me in the shoulder.

"You sick?" he asked.

I blinked out of a dream involving hoop skirts and crossbows. "What time is it?"

"Just past seven. Weren't you meeting Trent at seven thirty?"

And just like that, I was wide awake, because yes, I had arranged to meet up with Trent Ross, president of the library board, for breakfast. "Why didn't you wake me up earlier?" I shrieked, flinging back the covers as I leapt out of bed. "You're my husband! That's one of your jobs!"

"Don't remember that being in our vows," he said idly, backing away to avoid my trajectory to the bathroom.

"Inherent, pal," I snarled.

"Mrr!"

Rafe muttered something to Eddie that sounded like "Thanks for sticking up for me," but that was a conversation I'd follow up on later, as I had twenty-seven minutes to shower, dress, and get to the Round Table. Twenty minutes would be more accurate, as Trent had an almost annoying habit of arriving early to everything, and arriving after he did would be a bad look.

Halfway through my speed shower, I decided to drive the quarter mile instead of walk, so I was able to slide my knees under my favorite booth at the same moment Trent walked into the diner.

"Morning," he said, sitting across from me. "How are you?"

I was almost sure my hair was still dripping, but this was one time my curly hair worked in my favor, because its wetness wasn't detectable by anyone other than me. "Just fine," I said, glad my breathing had already steadied. Trent was a good guy and wouldn't have cared if I was a few minutes late, but it was never a good idea to be late to an appointment with the boss of your boss. "I hear the sun might actually come out today."

"Hmm. I'll believe it when I see it." He glanced out the front window, but since sunrise wasn't for another half hour, and because even if the sun had been up it wouldn't have made much difference, all he could see was a black reflection of the restaurant's interior.

Which, to be honest, wasn't all that interesting. Carpet so worn it didn't have any trace of its original color, ceiling tiles that hinted of an era when smoking had been allowed in restaurants, wide pine paneling, vinyl booths down both sides, tables in the middle with the eponymous big round one in the back where elderly males gathered every morning for coffee and set the world to rights. It hadn't changed in years, and we liked it that way. Changing the interior of the Round Table might create a spark that could flare up into a world-destroying conflagration, and who wanted that?

Sabrina, the Round Table's forever waitress, came over and poured coffee into the two mugs we'd already turned right side up. She pulled a pencil out of her bun of silver hair and slid a pad out of her apron pocket. "Cinnamon apple pancakes and sausage links for her; fried eggs, hash browns, and bacon for him. Anything else?" Though it was technically a question, she walked away before either of us responded, so it ended up as more of a directive.

I watched as she made a detour to top off the coffee of the not quite sixtyish man in the back corner, a man she'd married about three years ago. Bill D'Arcy was, as always, hunched over a laptop computer, doing whatever mysterious financial things he did that made him buckets of money. He rarely made eye contact, spoke mostly in grunts, and was typically completely unaware of his surroundings, but after Sabrina filled his mug, he patted her hand without looking up from his screen. While this didn't make Sabrina smile, she did exude a mild glow.

Why Bill had chosen Chilson as a preferred work location when he could have been anywhere in the world was something I'd never been able to find out from him or from Sabrina. And though he'd had a frightening diagnosis of macular degeneration a while back, he was getting treatments in Traverse City that had stabilized his vision.

"So," Trent said. "What's this about a bookmobile scavenger hunt?"

I focused on the man in front of me. Trent was a retired downstate attorney and looked like it. Sure, he was wearing jeans and a pullover fleece, but I was pretty sure the price tag of each one had been more than I spent on cat food for a year.

"Well," I said. "Here's the idea." I described the project in as much detail as I could, which wasn't much because the e-mail conversations that Duffy and I had been having tended to spin off into discussions of other projects she wanted the Friends to explore. Still, the concept was simple enough.

Trent nodded. "I think it's a great idea."

"You do?" I blinked. And here I'd been hoping he'd give the whole thing a huge thumbs-down. Not that I was afraid of additional work; it was more that I wasn't convinced the efforts would be worth it. Then again, this was the man who'd gifted the library with a handmade book bike, so clearly he was okay with trying new ventures.

"Sure. But I'd like you to present this to the full board at the next meeting. Getting their ideas will make this an even better event."

I buried my dismay in caffeine. In my experience, the larger the group of people involved in putting together an event, the larger, more sprawling, and less focused the event became. The term "herding cats" came to mind. On the plus side, I had a lot of experience in cat herding. On the minus side, the success rate of those experiences was not what you'd call stellar.

"Sounds like we have a plan," I murmured, wishing the board had meetings every other month instead of once a month.

Quarterly would be even better.

*   *   *

After breakfast, the sky had indeed started to clear, so I drove the embarrassingly short distance home so I could walk up to the library. I popped my head inside the house. "Hey, bud!" I called. "Do you need anything?"

Silence.

"Eddie?"

More silence.

Huh. There was always a chance that he'd slipped outside, so I wandered around the house, calling his name and checking every traditional Eddie hideout.

Still nothing.

I was starting to get a little worried, so I pulled out the big gun—went to the kitchen, got the treat can out of the cupboard, and gave it a vigorous shake.

"Mrr."

I whirled around. There was Eddie, sitting upright, not five feet away from me. "Where have you been?"

He stood, walked four and a half feet in my direction, sat, and looked up at me. "Mrr," he said.

"Fine. Don't tell me." I took the lid off the can and shook a few treats out onto the floor. "I'd recommend saving some of those for later . . . okay, never mind. Hope you enjoyed them!" I called, because he was already walking away, tail in the air, leaving behind a few wafting cat hairs.

Curious, I trailed behind, wondering if he'd return to wherever it had been that I couldn't find him. An odd raspy noise alerted me, and I peered around the dining table just in time to see his tail disappear behind a shelf of local history books.

"Is this going to be a regular thing?" I asked. "Are you going to be behind a different shelf every day?"

"Mrr!"

"Fine. Just keep the books on the shelves, please. You know what happened on the bookmobile that day." I'd had to drive through a massive pothole and all of the three thousand books on the vehicle had bounced to the floor. Every. Single. One.

My furry friend declined to answer, which I decided to take as a sign of acquiescence, and on my walk up to the library, I once again heard Paige's whispered words. "What was behind the books?" I asked the sky. "What was so important? And why?"

The sky was just as responsive as Eddie, so I stopped in the middle of the sidewalk and sent Ash a text, reminding him of Paige's last words, and asking if they'd checked bookshelves at both of Paige's houses and at her workplace.

He didn't reply until I was in my office, mug of coffee in hand and e-mail half dealt with. The response was terse and very Detective Inwood–like: *Thank you for the suggestion. Investigation is proceeding.*

I made a face at the words and flipped my phone over to make it a teensy bit harder to send a rude text in return. The satisfaction of sending it would only last a fraction of a second, but the regret for being mean to a friend who was just doing his job would last far longer.

"Not worth it," I said, sighing, and wondered if

being an adult meant a lifetime of balancing base reactions against the greater good. Probably, but I didn't want to think about that, so I woke my computer from its nap and was about to go back to work when I decided to see if Paige's obituary was anywhere to be found.

And there it was, right at the top of the Scovill Funeral Home website. "Paige Holton Ferrer," it said, right there with the smiling photo from her practice's website. I scanned the text and learned nothing I didn't already know, except the fact that she played viola in the Petoskey Symphony Orchestra.

The obit confirmed the names of her sons, Alec and Logan, and their locations of Kalamazoo and Salem, Oregon, respectively, and that Logan was married but Alec was not.

I scrolled down and started reading the public notes of condolence. "Dr. Ferrer was a wonderful surgeon and an even better human being." "Thoughts and prayers with the family." "She will be greatly missed by many." Some people had left their names, others hadn't, but one name caught my attention. Blaine Callaway.

Callaway was one of the families that Mitchell had mentioned lived at Gainsborough year-round.

Huh.

I pulled out my phone so I wasn't using a library computer to do a short stint of cybersleuthing, and quickly found that there weren't many Blaine Callaways on social media. Happily for me there was one in Michigan, and his Facebook page was not only active but wide open to the public.

He didn't have a profile picture online, but he

did post regularly. Some were reposts of memes; others were links to comic video clips; others were photos of what I assumed was Deer Lake, but others were his own words. Mild complaints about the weather, congratulations to someone for getting married, asking about recommendations for restaurants in Marquette.

I'd scrolled down through almost months of posts and hadn't seen anything noteworthy, until I saw an all-caps rant during the Fourth of July weekend.

SHE'S AT IT AGAIN!!! What kind of person rents their house out to strangers and doesn't talk to her neighbors about it?!? These people aren't following any of our rules, parking every which way they want, playing awful music at all hours, and not understanding that voices carry across water. For crying out loud, I don't WANT to know about some guy's argument with his boss!! THIS HAS GOT TO STOP!!!

I read it once, then a second time, more thoughtfully.

If Blaine Callaway was this angry in July about Paige's short-term rental, how much angrier would he have been by October?

I didn't know, but I was going to do my absolute best to find out.

Chapter 7

That night, Rafe and I had dinner with his parents at Three Seasons, the restaurant owned, managed, and ruled by my best friend, Kristen Jurek.

I'd met Kristen on Chilson's city beach when we were both knobby-kneed preteens. Our differences were many. In height (she was tall, I was not), in hair (hers was Scandinavian blond and beautifully straight, mine was neither of those things), in temperament (she was larger than life, I was a classic introvert), and in ambition.

Kristen was ready, willing, and able to make the world acknowledge that quality cooking was the path to universal peace and prosperity, and I was content with bringing the bookmobile to a few more people every month. Her marriage to Scruffy Gronkowski and the recent arrival of twins Eloise and Lloyd did, however, hold a huge potential to shift her priorities.

Most of the summer I'd wondered if her dedication to Three Seasons might wane, now that she was a mother, but the twins were six months old and sleeping through the night and I was seeing a resurgence of the old Kristen.

Lois, who looked far too young to be Rafe's mother, scanned what was visible of the interior of Three Seasons. "I remember when this was Betty and Gerald Darden's cottage."

The restaurant had once been an old stately summer home. To purchase and renovate the building, Kristen had gone heavily into debt since she wasn't willing to cut corners. The kitchen, complete with top-quality cooktops, ovens, refrigerators, freezers, and ventilation, was an addition. Plumbing, electrical, roof, and windows had all been replaced, and every room had been refurbished as intimate dining rooms.

It was a wonderfully comfortable place, and the food was so good that it had now reached destination status. The fact that Three Seasons had been featured a few years ago on Trock Farrand's nationally syndicated *Trock's Troubles* hadn't hurt, of course. The fact that Scruffy (not his real name) was Trock's son and producer also didn't hurt.

What might hurt me was that Kristen and family were spending more and more time in New York, home base for the TV show. I was used to my coldaverse best friend disappearing to Key West at the end of October and returning north in April, but summer New York trips were getting longer. She'd made a recent decision to hire a full-time manager for Three Seasons, and though I was very glad of that—she'd been working far too hard for far too long—I had the uneasy feeling she'd be spending less and less time in Chilson.

Rafe's dad, Rick, who looked like what his son would look like in thirty years if he took care of himself, gave his wife a glance over the top of his reading glasses. He'd been studying the menu since we sat down, although I wasn't sure why, because Kristen would serve us what she wanted. "You remember that?"

"I used to babysit their kids when they went golfing," she said. "I was, oh, fourteen. Maybe fifteen. Before I could drive anyway. I rode over on my bike."

Rafe started humming the Miss Gulch melody from *The Wizard of Oz* and I elbowed him. "Stop that. Your mother must have been adorable at that age."

"She was cute as a shiny button," Rick said, though his attention was back on the menu. "Had a smile a mile wide."

Lois eyed him. "Interesting use of past tense."

"Was, is, will be." He shrugged and turned a page. "The past Lois, the current Lois, and the future Lois. All button cute. All wide smiled."

Though it wasn't what you might call swoonworthy, it was the most romantic thing I'd ever heard my father-in-law say. And if the faint shade of red on my mother-in-law's face was any indication, it wasn't anything he said on a regular basis.

"So," Rick said, putting his menu on the white tablecloth. "You two make any honeymoon decisions? When, where, why, how? Anything?"

I hesitated. I'd wanted to talk to them about Paige, asking if they'd known her or anything about Gainsborough. But maybe tonight wasn't the time or the place. It was Final Friday, after all.

"When you go will make a difference in where you go," Lois said.

"That's what we were just talking about," Rafe said. "First thing is to decide the when."

"And?" his mother asked.

"Spring break," Rafe said at the same time I said, "In June, after school lets out."

Lois laughed and Rick nodded, saying, "Five bucks says you do it in June. Happy wife, happy life."

For years, Rafe and I had been making five-dollar bets on everything from who could list the most words starting with the letters AB to guessing the date when the snow pile next to the city garage would finally melt. It had been a fairly even contest, so we typically traded the same now-tattered five-dollar bill back and forth. I wondered if Rafe and his dad had a similarly dedicated five-dollar bill and decided I was okay not knowing.

"There you are." Kristen, all six feet of her resplendent in checked chef pants, chef apron, and towering chef hat, beamed down at us. "Welcome to Three Seasons' Final Friday dinner, there will be no more Friday dinners here until May, and for which I will accept no money from any of you, because I still owe Minnie here a deep debt."

A few months ago I'd helped her out with something, but as far as I was concerned, she'd never owed me anything. Friends helped friends, no questions asked, no favors owed. I sighed. "You can't keep doing that."

"Can and will," she said, flicking off my objection as if it were an annoying fly. "Now. Let me describe the culinary journey upon which you are about to embark."

Rafe leaned over and whispered, "Save us time. Bow to the inevitable."

He was right.

So I did.

I woke up Saturday morning feeling as if I'd been rolled through a laundry wringer. "Sick," I croaked, trying to sit up without disturbing the lightly snoring Eddie, who'd laid himself out lengthwise along my outside leg.

"What is?" Rafe asked. He was already out of bed and pulling on working weekend gear of jeans, T-shirt, and loose flannel shirt, all of which were laden with paints of many colors. I couldn't remember if he was working on our house or if he was helping a friend, but at that moment I didn't particularly care.

"Not sick as in the trendy adjective," I said, over the scratchy gravel stuck in my throat. "Sick as in a descriptor of physical status." I couldn't remember the last time I'd felt this sick. Every winter I tended to get a mild cold, but this was not that. This was the Real Thing.

Rafe took a long look at me. "Huh," he said, and headed downstairs.

I stared after him. What happened to the "in sickness" part of our wedding vows? I flopped back and pulled the covers up past my chin. My husband of barely one month had abandoned me at the first sign of trouble. How nice. And here I'd thought we'd make it forever. We'd done many things together before getting married, all of which were tryouts for marriage. Vacations, home improvement projects, cooking. We'd even gone camping, something my mom said was a surefire test for life-long compatibility.

But neither of us had ever been sick, and now he was bailing on me at the slightest hint of illness. I sniffled, felt sorry for myself, and at some point must have fallen asleep, because next thing I knew, there was a gentle poke at my side.

"Hey," Rafe said softly. "Can you sit up?"

Blearily, I slid to a position of extremely poor posture. "I thought you'd left me."

"Not a chance, my little fresh biscuit."

I fumbled for my glasses—no way was I going to put in my contacts today—and peered at what he was holding. A tray I recognized as part of a floral set Rafe had inherited from a long-gone great-aunt was laden with a cup of oatmeal, cut-up bits of melon, a small plate of scrambled eggs, a half piece of buttered toast, a biscuit, a mug of steaming coffee, and another mug of what smelled like hot chocolate.

He noted my wide eyes. "I don't know what you like to eat when you're sick, so I made your favorites. Just tell me what you want and I'll take the rest downstairs."

"This is . . . You're . . . But . . ." I scrubbed my face with the palms of my hands. Yep. There was moisture. I wasn't absolutely sure where it had come from, my teary eyes or my dripping nose, so I pulled the napkin Rafe had put on the tray and wiped my whole face. "Why are you being so nice to me?"

"Duh." He rotated the coffee mug so the handle was closest to me. "I love you. Remember? Now, what don't you want? Because that'll be my breakfast and I'm supposed to be at my buddy Bob's house to help drywall their bathroom."

Bob. Right. I remembered. Not that I had any real idea who Bob was. Rafe's legion of friends was wide and deep and I'd long ago realized I'd never keep them all straight.

I gestured that he could take away the eggs and the toast. "Thank you," I croaked out. "This was really nice. Just what I needed."

"Doesn't seem like you're running a fever," he said, kissing my forehead. "Should I get the thermometer? Do you want aspirin? Anything?"

I shook my head at all his offerings. This felt like a bad cold. All I needed to do was lay low for a day or two and it should be gone.

Rafe stood over me, hesitating. "I can stay, if you want. Bob will understand."

A concerned husband bringing me breakfast in bed was wonderful. A concerned husband hovering over me all day would drive me batty. "Thanks, but I just need to sleep," I said.

He eventually left, and after I ate, I snuggled up with Eddie and slept away the morning and a good chunk of the afternoon. When I woke up, I felt almost fine. Still a slightly raspy throat, but my head was clear and my sniffles were gone.

"It was the biscuit," I told Eddie as I slid out of bed. "Rafe made magic biscuits."

My cat, who was curled up in the middle of the comforter and clearly had no intentions of moving any time soon, did not respond. I patted him on the head and changed out of pajamas and into the most comfortable sweatpants and fleece pullover that I owned.

I'd planned on a Saturday of cleaning bathrooms, cutting down the outside plants for the winter, and paying bills, but I didn't have the energy and/or brains to do any of that, so I sat on the couch, turned the television to a nature show of deep blue oceans, and pulled out my laptop.

One quick mini crossword puzzle proved to me that my head could conjure up rational thoughts, so I pulled out my cell phone and started a text to Bianca Koyne, formerly Bianca Sims. Though she was the only real estate agent I knew, she was also one of the most successful in the area, so she was my go-to contact for insider info on property sales.

Minnie: *Are you working today?*

(A very short time later) Bianca: *I'm a Realtor. I'm always working, and happy to so do! What's up?*

Minnie (after a short pause while she thought about the best course of action): *Do you have a few minutes for a phone call? I have some questions.*

Five seconds later, my cell rang.

"Hey, Minnie," Bianca said breezily. "Let me guess. You and Rafe are expecting quadruplets and need a bigger house."

My insides clutched. Having children someday soonish? Sure. Four at a time, less than a year after getting married? Absolutely not. "Not unless you know something about my reproductive parts that I don't know."

She laughed. "I know all sorts of things, but not that."

"What I'm hoping you know something about is Gainsborough, out on Deer Lake."

"Mitch said you'd been asking about Gainsborough. That you're the one who found that poor woman."

It took me a moment to realize that the Mitch

she was referring to was Mitchell. So weird. "Yes, the whole thing is hard to wrap my head around. I don't suppose you sold that house to Paige?"

"No, I believe that was a private sale. Most are, out there. Family-to-family kind of thing."

"Oh." My insides deflated. I'd really hoped I'd get some inside scoop from her. "Well, thanks anyway."

"Hang on," Bianca said. "I've never listed or sold that house, but just yesterday I had a call."

"A call?"

"From one of that poor woman's sons. Alex. No, call me a liar. Alec, that's it. He's looking for a potential sale price for both the Duvall house and Dr. Ferrer's house in Chilson. It'll take time for the probate details to get figured out, but like I told him, everything is negotiable. Keep checking my storefront," she said. "If they list it, you'll see it there first."

"Even before it goes online?"

"Got to give people some reason to come to my office." She laughed.

"So her sons are looking to sell," I said slowly.

"Probably. Alec lives downstate, his brother lives out west. Montana? Something like that. Anyway, it sounded more like they didn't want to deal with the hassle of owning multiple houses."

Possibly.

But wasn't it also possible that contacting a real estate agent less than a week after your mom's death meant a desperate need for money?

And for murder?

The call with Bianca left me at loose ends.

"What do you think?" I asked my cat, who now

was sleeping full length on the parts of my legs that weren't covered up by my computer. Not that I could look him in the eyes, because that wasn't the part of him facing me.

Instead, his tail kept curling around the edges of my computer screen, and every time I started to reach out to move it away, he flicked it out of my reach. Whether all cats had this ability or whether this was an Eddie thing, I did not know, but I was also pretty sure I was never going to ask around to find out.

"Do I put the sons on the suspect list?" Eddie didn't reply, so I continued without his assistance. "Why yes, I do. But how do I find out more about them? And more about Paige?"

Eddie turned his head and gave me a classic cat look of disdain.

"Well, sure," I said. "Obviously, I'll see what information is available online. Goes without saying." Not that I'd done so yet, but I would have come to that conclusion without Eddie's help.

A quick look at the popular social media sites provided essentially no information. Either Alec and Logan didn't partake or they had their privacy settings set to keep people like me at a distance. Paige also had no social media presence, but that could have been because the family had already requested that her accounts be removed.

Using the general search engine turned up too many results for me to want to deal with on a Saturday afternoon when I was still feeling under the weather, so for lack of anything better to do, I went back to the Maple Street Orthopedics web page.

This time, Paige's photo was front and center on the home page, along with a short note. *With deep sorrow, we regret to inform you that our great friend and esteemed colleague, Dr. Paige Ferrer, has passed away suddenly. Dr. Ferrer's patients are being contacted regarding their wishes for referrals. Our thoughts and prayers are with all who feel her loss.*

I clicked around and saw that the About Us page no longer included Paige's photo, and I suddenly wondered what the library would do if something happened to me. Not that anything would, because I'd promised Rafe to live just as long as he did, and longevity was a thing in his family, but still. What if? Would the library post a picture of me on their website? And who would let my Association of Bookmobile and Outreach Services friends know?

There were so many things I wondered about, and most of them I would never admit to wondering about to anyone other than Rafe. "And you, too," I murmured, jostling my legs just enough to garner a Look That Could Kill from my furry friend.

Idly, I scrolled past the doctor photos and down into the staff pictures. I didn't know any of them, which wasn't a huge surprise since I hadn't yet had need for an orthopedic surgeon, and since the practice wasn't even in Tonedagana County. Then a name caught my attention. Sharrow Joss.

Sharrow . . .

I patted around on the couch until I found my phone and started texting Otto.

Minnie: *Was Sharrow Joss the employee of Paige Ferrer's that you talked to about a medical bookkeeping business?*

Otto (after a couple of minutes): *Yes. Any particular reason why?*

Minnie: *I'd like to talk to her about Paige. Do*

you think she would meet with me tomorrow morning for coffee? My treat?

Otto: *Are you investigating?*

Minnie: *Yes. Any chance you won't tell your wife?*

Otto: *None.*

Minnie (sighing): *Understood.*

After some back and forthing with introductions and assurances that Minnie Niswander was an upright and honest human being, Sharrow and I arranged to meet the next morning at North Perk Coffee in Petoskey.

Sharrow: *Can you be there right when they open?*

Minnie: *Absolutely!*

Sharrow: *I know it's early, but I'm playing piano for my church's early service, and I need to do warm-ups.*

Minnie: *Not a problem. I appreciate you taking the time.*

It wasn't until I tossed my phone back onto the couch that I looked up North Perk's Sunday opening time. "Six thirty?" I shrieked. "Who opens that early on a Sunday morning?"

Apparently North Perk did, so the next morning I dragged myself out of bed when the outside was still extremely dark, gave the snoring love of my life a kiss on the forehead, patted my cat, and headed out.

I'd just sat down with a tall cup of coffee and a muffin, with a second muffin in a box for my beloved, when Sharrow walked in, looking exactly like Maple Street Ortho's photo. Short, full sandy-brown hair cut to curl under, square face, stocky frame, and, when she spotted me, the same wide smile I'd seen on the website.

"Minnie?" The pitch of her voice was high and bright, like a chirpy chickadee. "I'm Sharrow. You look just like Otto said."

I laughed and got up to shake hands. "Short, with curly hair that's totally unmanageable?"

"And a face full of curiosity and kindness."

That had the ring of a direct quote, and I was touched. "It's the curiosity part that gets me in trouble," I said ruefully. "What can I get you?"

Soon enough, we were settled at the table, crumbling our breakfast into bits small enough to eat and sipping the nectar of the morning gods. "I'm not sure what I can tell you," Sharrow said after swallowing a mouthful of bagel. "Dr. Ferrer, Paige, was a wonderful person. I'm sorry you were the one to find her, but I'm glad someone did, that she wasn't left out there alone. You know what I really want?" Her blue-eyed gaze held me fast. "Is whoever killed her to pay the price."

The harsh sentiment conflicted with the sunny persona she projected, and I thought a moment before responding. "Has the sheriff's office talked to you?"

She shook her head. "They've just talked to the partners. It sounded like they'll interview the rest of us this week."

Hmm. "I'm sure this is all hard for you," I said. "And the last thing I want to do is make it harder."

"It's okay." Sharrow wrapped her hands around her coffee cup. "I get it. I mean, I think closure is a bunch of hooey, but talking to people about traumatic events is a kind of therapy, I figure, so I'm happy to help."

It was a point of view that hadn't occurred to me. Was self-care why I inserted myself into murder investigations? "Thanks," I said, trying to smile. "I was just hoping to learn more about anyone who might have had a grudge against Paige. The sheriff's office"—I caught back what I'd started to say about the working theory that her death was a hunting accident—"will be asking all sorts of questions, I'm sure, but they can be intimidating, and maybe talking to me first will help you think things through."

"A grudge." Sharrow's eyebrows drew together. "Well, her oldest son was a piece of work, but he wasn't violent or anything. Just a jerk. Takes after her ex-husband, Paige always . . ." She sniffled and looked at her hands. "Always said," she finished softly, changing the verb tense.

Oldest son. Hmm. "That's Alec?"

"He lives in Kalamazoo," she said, tipping her head in a southerly direction. "In the ten years I've worked at the clinic, I've only seen him once—maybe two, three years ago."

I made a mental note to put Alec high on the suspect list. "Does anything else come to mind? How about disgruntled patients?"

"Paige's patients loved her." Sharrow smiled into the distance. "She was that kind of person, if you know what I mean. And it wasn't an act, she was just nice. You know what they say, that if people like their doctors, they don't sue them. It's doctors who are jerks that get sued for malprac—" She stopped abruptly, leaving her mouth half open.

I leaned forward. "You remembered something."

"Yes," she said vaguely. "Just the other day. I forgot."

"About what?" I asked.

Her eyes focused on me. "Norris Wilcox. He was suing Paige for malpractice. He said she'd ruined his life."

Chapter 8

When I replayed the conversation with Rafe an hour later, I had to rewind a number of times before I was sure he completely understood.

"Okay." He popped the last bit of muffin into his mouth, chewed, and swallowed. At least I hoped he did, because if he was talking and eating at the same time we would have to start having etiquette lessons, and that did not bode well for our young marriage. "To recap," he said. "Norris Wilcox, who to no one's surprise goes by Will, not Norris, is one of two people in a malpractice suit against Dr. Paige. The other person is his wife, Rila. It's her knee surgery that Will Wilcox is claiming was botched, causing his wife permanent pain and suffering, which in turn causes him permanent pain and suffering, for having to watch his wife suffer."

I patted him on the arm. "There you go. I knew you'd get it eventually." I wasn't sure I did, but then I couldn't imagine suing anyone over anything. It just wasn't the way my brain worked. Maybe it was a genetic thing. I couldn't think of anyone in my family who'd ever talked to an attorney for anything other than drawing up a will.

"Is it a real lawsuit?" Rafe asked. "Did they hire an attorney, file papers, all that? Or are they threatening a lawsuit in hopes of getting a settlement check without the pain of going to court?"

I shrugged. "Sharrow wasn't sure. The only reason she knew anything about it at all was because she'd made the initial contact with the practice's liability insurance. It wasn't something she typically deals with, but the person who normally does was out on vacation."

"Huh." Rafe rubbed his chin, and since he hadn't shaved yet that morning, the action was also making a sandpapery sound that I was making a determined effort to find endearing instead of irritating. "You know who might know."

But I was already pulling out my phone, and a few text exchanges with Sophia Aguilar later, we'd arranged for the three of us to meet for a late lunch at Hoppe's Brewing.

Sophia was already there when Rafe and I walked in. She spotted us and waved. "No, you're not late. I'm early, is all. Sundays, you know?" She pushed two menus across the table—a single page for food, two pages for beverages—and Rafe got down to the serious business of choosing beer.

I ignored both menus. Beer wasn't my thing, Rafe always ordered the day's lunch special, no matter what it was, and I always dithered between a lovely, gooey grilled cheese sandwich and a romaine salad replete with black beans, corn, and tomato bits.

After our orders were taken by a fresh-faced waiter who didn't look old enough to walk to school by herself, let alone take adult beverage orders, Sophia cocked her head at us. "So what's up?"

Rafe pointed at me. "This is her thing. I'm arm candy today."

"Today and every day," I said, patting his hand.

Sophia snorted a laugh into her pale ale. "You two make me laugh. You're going to invite me to your silver wedding anniversary party, right?"

"And the golden." Rafe held up the oatmeal stout the waiter had just slid over, I held up my locally made root beer, and the three of us clinked glasses.

"What I wanted to ask you about," I said, "was insider information on how courts work."

Sophia gave us a long look. "You know what? I'm going to tell you the court system's dirty little secret." She leaned forward. "No one knows how it works," she said in a stage whisper, then sat back and laughed. "You should see your faces! Priceless."

I shifted around in my chair, suddenly uncomfortable with the universe and everything in it. "Um, you're joking, right?"

"Mostly." She took a long sip of her drink. "But not completely. There are a lot of very smart people working in the courts, from the Supremes all the way down to the smallest county trial court. The judges are, for the most part, very good at what they do. Staff is hardworking and dedicated."

"And yet?" Rafe asked.

She nodded. "And yet no one is taking a look at the big picture, not from top to bottom. There are efforts to streamline and improve this and that on a statewide basis, but as far as making sure the systems are an integrated part of the community, making sure the courts are working with the social services, making sure the metrics parse out . . ." She stopped talking. "And now I'll get off my hobby-horse. If your eyes glaze over any more you won't be able to see across the room."

Smiling, I said, "I'm glad you're passionate about improving the courts. It's people like you who will make a difference."

"Yeah, yeah." She waved off the sentiment. "On good days, I almost believe that. So what's your question? I'm guessing you don't really want a workshop on Michigan's courts."

"I'd love to learn more. I really haven't a clue how it all works. But today I'm mostly wondering how to get information about a lawsuit. Or even if something is an actual lawsuit."

"Sounds specific," Sophia said. "What details do you have? I'm assuming this is a civil suit. Named parties, attorneys involved, date filed?"

"Um." I shifted again. "I'm not sure I know any of that."

She gave me a look. "Without something, it'll be a needle-in-a-haystack-massive-time-suck kind of search."

Rafe elbowed me. "Don't let the court jargon mess with your head. You know the named parties, or at least one of them."

"Right." I gave myself an eye roll. "Norris and Rila Wilcox. I've heard they were suing Dr. Ferrer, the woman who was killed at Gainsborough, for malpractice. Is there any way to tell if that was actually happening?"

"Depends." Sophia squinted. "If nothing has been filed into the court's software system, then it's virtually impossible to find out. If something has been filed, then it might be hanging out there, waiting to be assigned, it might be a pending case, or it might be an active case, and I can see those eyes going glassy."

"Sorry."

"Apology not necessary. This isn't your world, and mine is a complicated one with lots of rules and acronyms and insider language."

Sophia was a truly nice person. "You said court software," I said. "Is this something the general public can access? Can I just log in and look up some of this?"

"You can, but it's not the friendliest thing to use." She tugged on her lip. "Tell you what. I'll take a look for you."

"What?" I sat up straight. "No, I can't ask you to do that. You're busy, and—"

She waved me off. "Don't worry about it. I don't have any plans for the rest of the day. And going on a lawsuit hunt can be fun."

The woman clearly had a different concept of fun than I did, but then again, I thought it was fun to work on the library's strategic plan. If she was willing, who was I to object?

At some point in the next morning's early hours, I woke up remembering that Mitchell had given me the names of two families that lived at Gainsborough year-round. Callaway was one, and I'd learned that Blaine Callaway had been anti-Paige because of the short-term-rental thing, but who was the other family? The name had started with an F, hadn't it? And had more than one syllable.

I tumbled around last names in my head. Fuller. Fountain. Fortune. Fazio. Faber . . .

Then it occurred to my mostly asleep brain that the F last name in my memory was probably Paige's, and that the name of the other family started out with a different letter altogether. Twenty-five other letters in the alphabet, but probably not X, or Z, so down to twenty-three, so gee, I was almost there and . . . hang on. G! That was it. Now for the name itself and I could go back to sleep. Almost there . . . almost . . .

"Gauthier," I said out loud.

"Umm?" Rafe asked.

Snuggling up to my husband, I whispered, "Nothing. Go back to sleep."

"Mmm," he said.

A few hours later, when we were sitting down to breakfast, he squinted at me. "Did you wake up in the middle of the night and try to talk to me?"

I squinted back. "I don't think so."

"You sure? I could have sworn you said something about being gaudy."

"Why would I be talking about being gaudy in the middle of the night?"

"You tell me, my pretty little pumpkin."

"Stop that," I said mildly. "Either you were dreaming, or I was, because I don't . . ." My voice trailed off as I remembered. "I take it all back. You were right. I was wrong. I'm sorry."

"Ah, my favorite eight words. And it's not even seven thirty. On a Monday morning, no less." He patted me on the head, something I didn't tolerate from anyone else on the planet. "Excellent start to the week."

I explained about remembering the second name. "I'd assumed I'd remember when I woke up this morning."

"Brains are funny things. Any ideas on how you're going to stalk the Gauthiers?"

"Not stalking. Investigating. Completely different."

"Tell that to the judge." He grinned. "And now I have to go. See you tonight, honeybunch."

I rolled my eyes and tipped my face to accept his good-bye kiss. "I live in fear that one of these days you'll come up with a nickname that sticks and I'll be called that the rest of my life."

"That's the plan," he said, pulling on his coat. "Be good."

When the door shut, I looked down at Eddie, who was sprawled on the floor in front of the heat register. "He was talking to you, not me," I said. At least I assumed he was. "So. How do you think I should find out more about the Gauthier family?"

My cat opened one eye, closed it, then heaved an audible and very visible sigh.

"You're right. Stupid question. Sorry to disturb you, buddy." I got up, put our dishes in the dishwasher, poured myself another cup of coffee, and took it into the dining room, which was where I'd left my laptop.

I browsed the comments on the funeral home's website, hoping to strike gold a second time, but if a Gauthier had posted a note, they hadn't used their name. Next stop was the property information web page on the county's website. It took a few minutes of poking and prodding, but I eventually learned that the Gauthier Family Trust owned the cottage half a dozen doors down from the Duvall place that Paige had purchased. At least I had the correct spelling of the last name.

With little else to go on, I typed "Gauthier" and "Michigan" and "Tonedagana County" into the search bar, paused, then added "Carlow Township," because nothing ventured, nothing gained.

I hit the return key, picked up my coffee mug, and slowly put it down.

At best, I'd hoped for a couple of quality returns, but I was looking at a full screen of them, all bringing up entries mentioning a Verity Gauthier. "Interesting," I murmured, and clicked on the top entry.

It took all of two paragraphs for me to figure out why the search returns had been so healthy: Verity Gauthier was chair of the Carlow Township Planning Commission, and for over a year they'd been discussing an ordinance that restricted short-term rentals. The meeting minutes weren't anything close to verbatim, but I'd read enough sets of minutes over the years to get the gist.

"'Chair Gauthier stated that short-term rentals were a commercial use, and so did not belong in residential zoning districts,'" I read out loud. "'Vice-Chair Nelson noted there was pending state legislation regarding short-term rentals. Commissioner Braddock said the Planning Commission needed to consider private property rights. Commissioner Heubel noted that any ordinance regarding short-term rentals would almost certainly result in legal action against the township. Commissioner Minshew said a fear of litigation shouldn't keep the Planning Commission from doing what was right. Discussion ensued.'"

I skipped to the end of the minutes and looked for the time of adjournment. The meeting had run more than three hours.

And it sounded as if it had been a very long three hours.

I closed the laptop and went to get dressed for work, thinking about what I'd just learned. Of the two year-round Gainsborough families, precisely one hundred percent of them were vehemently against short-term rentals.

Huh.

How very, very huh.

I arrived at the library just ahead of nine o'clock; long before our ten a.m. opening, but later than I typically showed up on non-bookmobile days, and when I walked into the break room, I saw the price I was going to pay. Kelsey was already there, whistling what might have been "Yellow Submarine" as she dumped scoop after scoop of coffee grounds into the filter.

"You snooze, you lose," she said, seeing my disappointed face. "And besides—"

"I can always water it down," I chanted along with her.

Kelsey laughed. "I know it's not the same, but you usually get here so early I hardly ever get to make a pot. Give me this small win, okay?"

"Employee engagement is key to any successful organization," Graydon said, walking in the door. "If making coffee strong enough to hoist a horse is what it takes to keep you happy, Kelsey, I'll make sure that's what we have every morning."

"Hang on," I said. "What about my happiness? If I drink Kelsey coffee every morning, I'll end up with heart palpitations."

"Water it down?" he suggested, and smiled at my disgusted look. "Sacrifice, Minnie. Servant leadership has sacrifice at its very core."

I gave him a look. "Have you been reading management articles again? You really shouldn't."

"Disagree," Kelsey said, grinning at me over the mug she was filling with freshly brewed mud.

A thought occurred to me. I turned and started moving the loose miscellaneous items on the counter. Mugs, boxes of tea bags, canisters of sugar and powdered cream . . .

"What are you looking for?" Graydon asked.

"That." I shoved aside a chipped mug full of stirrers and pointed. "It's another outlet. Is there any reason we can't get a second coffeepot? One for Kelsey's ooze, one for the rest of us."

"I'll have you know," Kelsey said loftily, "that Mr. Goodwin is a big fan of my coffee."

Mr. Goodwin, a dapper cane-carrying man in his late seventies, was everyone's favorite bricks-and-mortar library patron, not that we had such things. The original intent of the break room had been for employee use, not public, but that line had blurred years ago.

I nodded in acknowledgment. "Kelsey and Mr. Goodwin's ooze."

"A second pot." Graydon laughed out loud. "Sheer genius."

"Really?" I asked. "Here I was thinking how stupid I was for not thinking of this before."

"The difference between stupidity and genius can be a fine line." Graydon gave me a nod and headed out. "Take it out of the office supplies budget," he called over his shoulder.

I filled my mug to the two-thirds level, topped it off with water, popped it in the microwave, carried the substandard brew back to my office, and an hour later, I was at the front door of Benton's, waiting for the forty-something Rianne Howe to unlock the door of the general store her family had run since its birth.

"Hey, Minnie," she said, smiling and pushing the hundred-year-old door open wide. "What brings you here this time of morning?"

"Coffee."

She closed one eye at me. "You do know that we don't have any, right?"

"Coffeepot, to be more exact." I explained the dilemma and the extremely obvious solution, and a laughing Rianne led me over the slightly squeaky wood floor to the kitchen wares. Though there were only two options, one looked almost exactly like the one on the library's counter. I happily pointed to that one, and Rianne took it to the register and rang it up.

I walked back up to the library with a smile on my face, feeling childishly proud of myself for the entire episode. A problem solver, that's what I was. See a problem, find a solution. That was what I did. Sure, this particular problem had taken me years to solve, but better late than never, and—

The ringing of my cell phone halted my personal admiration party. I pulled it out. "Morning, Sophia. How are you this fine Monday?"

There was a slight pause. "You're a morning person," she said, making it sound like an accusation.

I laughed. "I'm a blue-sky-and-sunshine person. Can't help but be perky when the clouds have blown off."

"Yeah, well, what I'm about to tell you might take a shine off that."

My steps slowed. "Oh? What's up?" I spotted a bench and went over to sit down. It wasn't really warm enough to sit outside while dressed in school clothes, but I also didn't want to walk and listen to Sophia at the same time. Any tiny sidewalk inconsistency had the potential to trip me at the best of times, let alone when I wasn't paying any attention to what my feet were doing.

"First thing is that I haven't found anything in the court dockets about a lawsuit by Norris and Rila Wilcox, or any combination of those names."

"Oh." I deflated. I'd thought one of the two would be an excellent suspect. "Well, thanks anyway. I appreciate your time and—"

"Not done yet," Sophia said. "What I did find out was that Rila Wilcox is much better known by her maiden name. Does 'Rila Shutleff' ring any bells for you?"

Frowning, I said, "Don't think so. Is she from around here?"

Sophia sighed. "You are so not a sports person. It was the first name that tipped me off. How many Rilas can there be? Rila Shutleff was a high school and college soccer phenom. Saline High School, then college at Notre Dame. One of their best forwards ever. She played pre-professional for a couple of years, and then a few months after she signed a contract for a big-league team, she injured her knee. That was two years and multiple operations ago. No one in the soccer world has seen her since."

"Paige did the surgery?" I asked.

"Easy to assume that, given what you heard about a lawsuit, but you know what they say about assumptions. And you now know everything I do about this, and I have court in ten minutes. Talk to you later."

She was gone before I could thank her, so I texted her a quick thank-you meme that included a cartoon cat who looked a lot like Eddie, and got a thumbs-up emoji in return. I stood and continued my way back to the library.

How was I going to investigate a world-class athlete and her husband when I'd never met them, didn't know anything about them, didn't know anyone who knew them, and had no idea where they worked, lived, played, or even what they looked like?

"Solve this problem," I murmured to myself. But I would find out a way. I'd promised Paige.

And I kept my promises.

Chapter 9

That afternoon, Graydon and I were sequestered in the conference room with the library board's finance committee, working through the planning stages for the next budget year.

I was beyond pleased to see that the special capital fund for replacing the bookmobile was hale and hearty, and even ticking upward thanks to donations and the magic of compound interest. Vehicles only lasted for so long, and bookmobiles were expensive. Keeping the program sustainable meant money. Sure, the vehicle wasn't even four years old, but its purchase had been thanks to a donation, and I'd made a replacement fund a high priority.

The fund's healthiness was due in large part to the generosity of Barb and Russell McCade. Russell, known widely as Cade, was one of those artists that critics hated and people loved. He and his wife Barb had donated one of his paintings to the library for the express purpose of its sale price going to the bookmobile, and the replacement fund had been growing ever since.

"Looks solid," Bruce Medlar said, tidying up his stack of budget paperwork. Bruce was also on Chilson's city council, and if anyone could recognize a solid budget, it was him.

"Agreed." Carolyn Mathews smiled across the table at Graydon and me. Carolyn, a high-powered hospital administrator, was new to the library board and was becoming a mentor of sorts to me. "Nice job, Graydon."

Linda Kopecky tapped her stack of papers. "What about cybersecurity? I see some increases in Josh's IT budget, but is that enough?"

Graydon and I exchanged glances. It had been Josh's plainspoken assertion that you could never spend too much on cybersecurity. "If you're interested in additional measures," Graydon said, "we can have Josh draw up options."

"In time for our next meeting?" Linda asked. "It would be nice to have him come talk to us."

"Not a problem." Graydon glanced at me, and I nodded, accepting the responsibility of getting Josh to the next board meeting. It wouldn't be easy, because Josh hated public speaking as much as I hated the smell of burned toast, but I'd find a way.

"Excellent." Carolyn slid her draft budget into her briefcase. "Now, Minnie. What's this I hear from Trent about a bookmobile scavenger hunt?"

Bruce, who had been starting to stand, sat back down. "A what? You're hunting with the bookmobile?"

I should have known that Trent would talk to his fellow board members about the project. Staff talked to staff; board members talked to board members. It was the way of the world.

"More the other way around," I said, trying to resummon the temporary enthusiasm that had found me while breakfasting with Trent. I gave a quick explanation of the project and, as I talked, saw the light bulb go on in Bruce's head.

"Love it," he said, nodding. "Sounds like a Duffy idea, top to bottom. She doesn't do dumb. And I'll talk to the city manager. We'll definitely want to be part of this."

"Have you talked to the chamber of commerce?" Linda asked. "That new director will have lots of ideas. And they're finally at full staff. Play your cards right and they just might do the lion's share of the work." She gave me a sly wink.

Carolyn looked around the table. "Ladies and gentlemen, this might be the start of a very fruitful collaboration. Just think of the expansion possibilities. We could wrap in service vehicles from across the county. Across the region. The bookmobile. The bloodmobile. EMTs, fire trucks."

"The secretary of state," Linda said thoughtfully, "has a mobile unit that does vehicle renewals and driver's license renewals."

Graydon nodded. "And don't forget the book bike."

"I would never," I said, putting my hand on my heart. Much as I wanted to forget that behemoth of a bicycle, it simply wasn't possible.

Carolyn rolled her index fingers. "Coming back to reality here. I think the scavenger hunt is a wonderful idea. Excellent exposure for our outreach program, and for Chilson in general."

Linda and Bruce agreed, and I suddenly got that special frisson of excitement, the kind that had the potential to energize and inspire me for months to come. Duffy had been right. A bookmobile hunt was an excellent idea, and I was going to do everything I could to make sure it was a success.

I left the conference room, ideas spinning around in my head. My friend Pam, who'd said she would come back to the Friends now that Denise was gone, had been a big-shot corporate graphics designer in her previous life, down in Ohio. We could tap her to design the passport booklet. And I could talk to my friend Cathy at the city. And I'd talk to the chamber. And the—

"Earth to Minnie."

I stopped short. Josh was standing three feet in front of me, pushing a cart piled high with monitors, keyboards, and miscellaneous cables.

"Do you ever watch where you're going? I was about to deke around you."

"Deke?" I echoed. "Sports term, right? No, wait. Don't tell me. Hockey. Or is it soccer?"

"Both." He shrugged. "Mostly hockey, I guess."

"Just so you know, the finance committee is thinking about adding more into next year's budget for cybersecurity. Can you put together some options? Varying costs." I hesitated, then took the plunge. No time like the present. "And, um, talk to them at their next meeting?"

"You mean, be in the room with them?" At my nod, he leaned back on his heels and crossed his arms. "Who's on Finance? Bruce and Linda, right?"

"And Carolyn."

He twisted his mouth so far I hoped it wouldn't

freeze that way, then shrugged. "They're not so bad. Shouldn't be a problem."

I let out an inaudible sigh of relief. "Thanks," I said, moving out of the path of the cart. Then I quickly moved back. "Say, do you follow soccer? More specifically, women's soccer?"

He squinted at me. "Sort of. But everything I know comes from Mia. She's a huge fan. Stuff oozes in, if you know what I mean."

I did indeed. Essentially all my sports, beer, and public school funding knowledge came from Rafe. That Josh was learning things from his wife made me wonder what my husband might be learning from me. I let that particular thought float off and asked, "Do you know anything about Rila Shutleff?"

"Well, sure. Everybody does. She was huge."

His definition of "everybody" was different than mine. "I hear she and her husband live around here." At least I assumed they did. Otherwise, why would Paige have been her surgeon?

"Yeah, up the hill, over on Curfman." He gestured with his chin. "Mia said she bought that house with the turret a couple of years ago, right after she went full pro. Don't remember her married name, though."

"Wilcox."

"That's it. Sucks about her knee."

"Do you know what either one of them does for a living?"

He did not. But knowing where they lived gave me a solid next step.

That evening, Rafe and I met up with Ash and Chelsea for a quick dinner at Shomin's Deli. Because of complicated work and life schedules, this was the first time since our wedding that the four of us had been able to sit down together, and there were a lot of things to catch up on.

Rafe, of course, had pushed for Hoppe's Brewing even though we'd been there yesterday, but in our group text, Ash had said he needed to spend some time at the shooting range after we ate, and going to Hoppe's when he couldn't drink would be cruel.

We all arrived about the same time, placed our orders at the counter, and sat at our usual booth: in the far corner near the back door, with Ash sitting closest to the door and facing the room.

I'd learned, in the few months that I'd dated Ash, that this was typical for law enforcement. Every time they entered a room, they assessed it for threats and exits, and whenever they took a seat, they made sure to sit where they could continue to monitor what was going on. Ash had been with the sheriff's office for so long that he could do a room assessment with a single glance, and probably barely registered that he even was doing it.

Though it was a good thing that he was so aware of his surroundings, I wondered about the long-term personal price. Would that hypervigilance wear him down? Age him before his time? If he and Chelsea had children, how would they interpret his situational awareness? Would they grow up thinking they were surrounded by threats and live a cautious, fear-filled life? Would they grow up angry at the world for being such a scary place?

I took my time removing the wrapper from my straw as I thought about these things, which I would never ever tell anyone as long as I lived, not even Rafe. Sometimes thoughts needed to stay where they belonged: permanently inside my head.

"You in there?" Rafe rapped his knuckles on the wood tabletop in front of me. "What's going on in that busy brain of yours?"

"What the first song at Chelsea and Ash's wedding should be," I said promptly. "I have a prepared list of suggestions." In actual fact, I did not, but I also knew Chelsea would head off that discussion.

"No wedding talk," she said, making a time-out gesture. "If you care for me at all. Please."

"Not even a continuation of the tux-versus-suit argument?" Ash asked. "I think this could be a good time to make the final decision."

His beloved gave him a look. "Exactly how stupid do you think I am?"

Ash looked straight back. "If you're stupid enough to want to marry me, you could easily be stupid enough to have the tux-versus-suit argument in front of the guy who convinced his now-wife that suits would work just fine."

Rafe and I exchanged a glance. I tipped my head in his direction, indicating that it was his turn to mediate. "Not my pig, not my farm," he said. "Wedding opinions are not available on this side of the table."

"How about if I pay you?" Chelsea asked.

"Especially not then."

"And moving on to other topics," I said smoothly, "have I told you about the bookmobile scavenger hunt? It was Duffy Ulrich's idea, and it's really starting to take on a life of its own."

I'd just come to the end of the finance meeting

when our order was called up. Rafe and Chelsea were sitting on the outside ends of the booth, so they went to hunt and gather our food.

Now that an opportunity had presented itself, I leaned forward. "Do you know who Rila Shutleff is?"

"The soccer player who totaled her knee?" Ash asked. "Yeah, who doesn't?"

Ignoring his question, I talked fast. "Did you know she married a guy named Norris Wilcox, and that they're living in Chilson?"

"I—" He stopped. "Well, no. I didn't. Why would I?"

"Don't go getting all defensive. I'm trying to help. What I heard from an employee of Maple Street Orthopedics is that the Wilcoxes were suing Paige for malpractice, for a knee surgery gone wrong."

"The partners said there was a malpractice," he said slowly, looking off into the distance, "but they didn't have details. I've been meaning to follow up but haven't had the time." His gaze refocused on me, lasering in, and I tried not to squirm. "Who gave you that information?" he asked.

"Sharrow Joss." I opted out of mentioning her connection to Otto. Sharrow's entrepreneurial efforts to start her own business were no business of the sheriff's department. "She's worked at Maple Street for years. I wanted to make sure you knew about this before you talked to the staff. This week, right?"

He nodded.

I glanced at the pickup counter, where luckily

Rafe and Chelsea were chatting with the youngster who was running the cash register and giving every appearance of continuing to do that for some time. What was that kid's name . . . Scrooge? No, that couldn't be it. Bob? Tim? Marlow. That was it. I turned back to Ash. "Sharrow said that Norris Wilcox, who goes by Will, said that Paige had ruined his life."

"Ruined *his* life?" Ash's eyebrows went up.

I shrugged. "What she said. Maybe she didn't recall the dialogue exactly, but no matter the case, a malpractice suit about a surgery on a professional athlete who now can't compete could be a motive."

"Huh." Ash drummed the tabletop. "That is interesting. Thanks for letting me know."

I sat back, glowing a bit from what I interpreted as praise. "You're welcome."

"And," he went on, "Hal said I can let you know what we learned about the arrow that killed Paige, and I can practically see your ears pricking up. Nice poker face, Minnie."

Rafe and Chelsea were almost to the table. "Just tell me."

"There was nothing," he said. "Nothing out of the ordinary, I mean. About as standard an arrow as you can get. No fingerprints, no nothing. We'll send it downstate for a deeper forensic analysis, but we're not expecting anything."

I sighed. "Well, that's disappointing."

"Yup."

We shared a glance of frustration. Our spouses returned, food in hand, and we went on to talk of other things.

But though the conversation went on, my mind wandered back to Gainsborough.

Behind the books.

Rafe and I had talked about going for a wandering walk through Chilson's darkened streets after dinner, but when we walked out of Shomin's we quickly reevaluated that plan.

"Holy camoley," Rafe said, zipping his jacket all the way up. "Who flipped the winter switch to full-on mode?"

As I often did, I thanked my past self for having the wisdom to put gloves in the pockets of every coat I owned, because it hadn't occurred to my present self that I might need them tonight to avoid frostbite. "Well, it is almost Halloween. And it's northern lower Michigan. Cold is a thing here."

"Sure, but not like this."

He had a point. The wind had shifted from its earlier mild southwesterly to a hard north-by-northwest blast straight from Canada's northern reaches. I yanked up my own coat zipper and pulled up the hood, but despite all that, tail ends of gusts were finding their way down my neck and into my bones. In seconds, I was shivering and I couldn't talk without my teeth chattering. "L-let's s-start a f-fire when we get home," I managed to eke out.

The love of my life grunted agreement, and neither one of us said another word as we hurried the half mile home, barreled up the front steps, and hurled ourselves inside.

Eddie, sitting halfway up the stairs, looked us over critically as Rafe shut the front door, pushing hard against a final gust of wind and throwing the deadbolt as he used his foot to hold the door in place.

"Mrr," our cat said.

"What was that?" Rafe asked. Though he was getting pretty good at Eddie interpretation, there were times that he needed me to translate.

I put my coat in the entry closet and held out my hand for Rafe's jacket. "He said he didn't expect us home so early, that we're disturbing his sleep, and that he's going to wake us up at three in the morning as punishment."

"Really?" Rafe squinted at Eddie.

"Or he could have been saying that his dry food isn't mounded properly and I should go fix it as soon as possible, otherwise he's going to starve to death."

"Sounds more like him."

"Then again," I added, stepping into my slippers, "he could have been saying that he's figured out the answer to life, the universe, and everything, and that if we play our cards right, he might just pass that along to humans."

"Be careful with the knowledge, pal." Rafe, in his stockinged feet, went up the stairs, patting Eddie on the head as he went. "Don't want it to fall into the wrong hands."

Our feline friend swiveled his head, watching Rafe go past, then turned back to face me with unblinking yellow eyes. We stared at each other, and I lost the staring contest for the ten-thousandth time in a row. "If you have something to say, go ahead and say it."

"Mrr." He bounded down the stairs, brushed past my legs, and stalked into the living room.

Since he'd seemed as if he had a plan, I trailed after him and quickly discovered that his plan entailed curling up on the super fuzzy lap blanket that someone had left wadded up on the coffee table instead of folding it and laying it along the back of the couch.

"Nope." I picked Eddie up, earning another stare, and sat down, blanket first, cat second. Though he squirmed throughout the process, he settled down when I put my feet up. Sadly, I'd planned poorly and the TV remote was out of reach. I didn't dare disturb Eddie again for fear of having my hair chewed off in the middle of the night, so I started talking.

"Did you hear? No, of course you didn't. You weren't there. Ash said there was nothing unusual about the arrow. Standard, whatever that means, and no fingerprints. They're sending it downstate for more analysis, but hope is slim."

Eddie sighed and suddenly weighed an additional five pounds.

"Yeah, I know. But they're working on the investigation, so at least there's that. What I need to think about is my next steps. Should I start an actual suspect list?"

"Mrr," Eddie said.

I looked over and saw that I'd left my laptop on the side table. Judging from the noises upstairs, Rafe was changing out of restaurant clothes and into make-a-fire-and-watch-TV clothes, so since my restaurant attire of leggings and an oversized sweatshirt doubled as TV attire—efficient Minnie!—I had a tiny window of opportunity.

Carefully, in a manner meant to not disturb the cat who'd been sleeping most of the day, I maneuvered my computer onto my lap and opened it. "Let's see what we can find out," I said.

Normally I tidied the screen of open files and apps before closing it, but when I opened it this time, the browser was up and running. Since I was too lazy to go to all the trouble of opening a spreadsheet or word processor, my fingers hovered over the keyboard as I thought about search engine parameters and what I might be able to find out in the next two, maybe three minutes.

Eddie rolled over and gave me an upside-down look, his mouth opening and closing in a silent "Mrr."

"Got it," I said, nodding. "Take a look at the sons." What had Mr. Zonne said their names were? Alec and . . . Logan. And the younger one lived in Oregon.

They were probably a few years younger than me, so the odds of them having an online presence were reasonably high. And the younger they were, the higher the odds, so I typed the name "Logan Ferrer" and "Oregon" into the search engine and hit Return.

"Huh," I said. There were all sorts of entries, so I started clicking, and soon I said "Huh" a second time. Logan Ferrer was, apparently, the instigator of a brand-new film festival in southwest Oregon, which had started the Tuesday before Paige was killed and wrapped up the very day I found her. Assuming all the news articles and photos weren't the result of some deepfake Internet efforts—an assumption I was willing to make—Paige's youngest son was thousands of miles away when she died.

Logan was off the suspect list.

Chapter 10

The next day was a bookmobile day, something that typically made my heart sing and my soul sparkle. But the raw weather of the night before was continuing unabated, and I wasn't sure anything about it had the ability to make anyone sparkle. This was proven when I took the Eddie-laden carrier out of my car and a massive wind gust nearly tore it out of my hand.

"MRR!"

"Hang on, buddy!" I wrestled the carrier into submission and hurried it into the bookmobile, out of the wind and cold and what I was pretty sure was white rain, because it couldn't possibly be snow. Well, it *could* be snow, but my ice scraper was still in my car's trunk, and I certainly wasn't wearing the right shoes, so I sincerely hoped it wasn't. Tomorrow I could deal with snow, because I'd make sure that tonight I'd move the ice scraper into the back seat, haul my boots out of the back of the front closet, and make triple sure about gloves in all my coat pockets.

The bookmobile door thumped shut behind me, and I breathed in the sudden quiet calm.

"Mrr."

"Completely agree," I said, not sure what I was agreeing to, but going along with whatever Eddie said would save us both time in the long run. I strapped the cat carrier into its allocated space, took a deep breath for courage, and went back outside to do the fastest exterior preflight check ever.

Julia arrived just after I started the engine, whooshing in wearing tall black boots, a long black coat, and an extremely long bright pink scarf that was woven with numerous strands of silver metallic threads.

I looked over at her as she settled in and buckled up. "You're sparkling."

"You're making it sound like an accusation, my dear."

Her accent dripped with elegant disdain. So it was going to be one of those days. I dropped the transmission into drive and grinned. Maybe my soul was going to be able to sing a little today, after all.

"Speaking of accusations," she said, continuing with the snobby mien, "I believe it is only common courtesy to inform me of your investigative efforts regarding the death of our dear Dr. Paige."

"It is?" I asked.

"My dear." Her chin went up. "Are you questioning me?"

"Yes."

She waved her hand languidly. "The very definition of common courtesy requires—no, demands—that you share information."

"And what is that definition? That I tell you everything you want to know?"

"You are finally grasping the situation." She bestowed a condescending smile upon my undeserving self. "There is hope for you yet."

"I'll pass that on to Rafe. He'll be pleased." Then I told her what I'd learned about Paige, her ex-husband, and her two sons, and that the youngest had very publicly been in Oregon when his mom had been killed. I told her what Sharrow had said about a pending lawsuit, and that the people suing were Rila and Norris Wilcox, and that Rila had been the soccer-playing Rila Shutleff before her knee injury.

Finally, I told her that I'd learned Paige had used the Duvall house as a short-term rental, thus displeasing neighbors galore, especially the two year-round residents, the Callaways and the Gauthiers. "Blaine," I said, "was using social media to make his thoughts on the matter very public. And Verity Gauthier was doing the same thing at the planning commission."

Julia tapped her fingers on the console. "That short-term rental thing is a hot-button topic." Her country club accent was gone. "Lots of opinions on both sides. Private property rights versus community stability. Hard to find a compromise on that."

"Which makes me put Blaine and Verity on the top of the suspect list. If they're passionate enough about it in public, how big a jump is it to being passionate enough to kill?"

"Hmm." Julia tapped her fingers some more.

"What was that Blaine's last name again? Callaway . . . Callaway . . . let me think . . ."

I glanced over. Her expressive face was so blank that I wished I could take a picture, show it to her later, and see her reaction.

One round of finger taps later, she woke from her trance and hooted. "Hah! Got it. I went to high school with a Susan Arnhold, who married a Callaway. From Dooley, not Gainsborough, but odds are good they're related."

"Are you still in touch with Susan?"

"Haven't seen her since high school," she said. "But she was one of those organizing types, back in the day, so I bet if I call and ask if there are plans for a"—she squinted and counted on her fingers—"forty-fifth class reunion, she'd have an answer for me."

"Call?" I slid her a glance. "You think she still has a landline you can look up?"

"No idea. But," she said, pulling out her cell and thumbing a text message at the speed of a middle schooler, "I know people who know people and I bet I can get her number by the time we get to . . . to here." She waved the phone triumphantly. "Ta-da!"

"You are genius."

"Thank you, thank you." Julia beamed as she went back to working the phone. "Now, let's see if she picks up." She stabbed the Call button and held the phone to her ear. "Ringing . . . ringing . . . ringing . . . ringing . . . Susan! This is a blast from your past, Julia Beaton!"

Julia quickly worked in a question about a reunion as the ostensible reason for the call, the answer to which seemed to be no, and for the next ten minutes, I heard a one-sided conversation about people and events I'd never heard of.

When that seemed to be tailing off, she asked, "Did you hear about that doctor dying out at Gainsborough? Hope you don't mind if I put you on speaker, I need my hands a minute. Anyway, don't you have some Callaway relatives who live there? What are they saying about it all? Terrifying, I'd think." She laid the phone on the console.

"Yes, Blaine, my nephew by marriage lives out there," Susan's tinny voice said. "Blaine's one son is in college, the other is an electrician. Such nice boys. But Bob and I only see them all at holidays and such. We just . . . well, we just don't see eye to eye on things."

I glanced at the phone. Susan hadn't answered the question about Paige's death. Hadn't even come close to trying.

Julia tried again. "It's unfortunate when family doesn't get along," she said. "Was Blaine friends with that Dr. Ferrer?"

Susan's sigh blew into the phone. "No. Not at all. Blaine simply *hated* that Dr. Ferrer was renting her place as a short-term rental, which I understand, but at our annual family Labor Day picnic Blaine wouldn't stop talking about it. My Bob got so tired of hearing Blaine's complaining that he said well, if you're so angry, call your attorney."

By this time my head and Julia's were so close to the phone our hair was almost touching. This made driving a mild challenge, but the bookmobile was going straight and the road was going straight, so all was well.

"And did he?" Julia asked. "Call his attorney, I mean?"

"Well, not then and there. It was a holiday, remember?" Susan chided. "But it certainly sounded like he was going to. Say, did you hear that Jim Gertz ended up becoming an attorney? Who would have guessed?"

The conversation went back to high school, Julia flipped the phone off speaker, and I returned to a vertical position, thinking.

So Blaine was also considering a lawsuit against Paige.

Interesting.

The information about Blaine popped him to the top of my suspect list. I reviewed the names out loud to Eddie at the end of the day as we drove home. "Blaine Callaway at the top, of course, for obvious reasons, followed by Verity Gauthier, for very similar reasons. Say," I said slowly, as an idea oozed into my head. "Do you think Blaine and Verity could have done it together?"

I considered how it might have gone. Two neighbors, bonded by their obsessive hatred of the constant circuit of strangers coming into their private neighborhood, casual chats on the way back and forth to the garage becoming more pointed talks, culminating in a devious plan for one of them to invite Paige for a friendly walk in the woods, leading her step by step to a place where the other was lurking behind a tree, bow in hand.

"Mrr."

"You're right." I nodded. "Possible, but not all that probable. One of them on their own is more likely. Moving on, the next suspect is Norris Wilcox and his wife Rila now Wilcox formerly Shutleff." Another pairing. Hmm. But a married couple seemed far more probable as a killing duo than neighbors. Definitely something to keep in mind.

"And," I said, "down at the bottom are the family members, Paige's sons Alec and Logan, although I've already eliminated Logan, so it's just Alec, the oldest. One suspect down, five to go."

A rumbling noise emanated from the cat carrier. Not the adorable purring kind of noise, but the less adorable snoring kind of noise, something few people realized a thirteen-pound cat was capable of creating.

The snoring was probably less a commentary on my investigative update than a reaction to the bookmobile day, which had been full of home-schooled children dressed in their Halloween costumes and Julia's spooky and sound-effect-filled storytelling, but it was hard not to take it at least a little personally, so I started talking louder.

"Five suspects isn't so bad, right? I've had lists that were longer. Although . . . hmm . . ."

We pulled into the garage and I started the car and house door opening and closing sequence that ended up with Eddie and me in the kitchen, me still thinking about the suspect list and Eddie still in his carrier curled up on his fuzzy pink blanket, even though the carrier door was wide open. Cats are so weird.

I put my coat in the front closet, started to close the door, then remembered my morning vow about winter boots and whatnot. Huh. What mattered more, the fatigue of my current self or the irritation of my future self when I had to walk through two inches of snowy slush without proper footwear?

"If you put it that way," I muttered, and got down on my hands and knees to sort through the contents of the closet floor. Five minutes later and the minor task was done. I felt unreasonably proud of myself and went upstairs to change. When my head emerged out of my fleece sweatshirt, I saw that Eddie had transferred to the bed, flopping himself against my pillow.

"Anyway," I said, continuing the conversation that he'd mostly slept through, "even though I never put Paige's ex-husband on the suspect list, and even though I'm sure Ash and Hal are looking into him, I feel compelled to take a quick look myself. Just to see."

Eddie paid no attention to any of that, so I patted him on the head and went downstairs. Thanks to the lack of privacy in the modern world, it didn't take long to find that Rob Ferrer, an attorney out of Grand Rapids, specialized in mediations. More specifically, he worked on union mediations, and he'd been in New Jersey to help settle a nationally publicized strike. "That's . . . interesting," I murmured. Mediating unions was undoubtedly an important job, and I was glad there were people who were willing to do it, but it sounded like immense amounts of stress and a total of zero fun.

"So he's out," I said, shutting the laptop and sliding off the kitchen stool to start dinner. Rafe would be home in less than half an hour and it was my turn to cook.

I filled a pot with water and put it on the cooktop to boil. My specialty was spaghetti with marinara sauce from Aunt Frances that I'd put in the freezer, along with salads if we happened to have enough stuff to make them.

As I ripped up the last of the lettuce, I wondered what my next investigative steps should be. What I really wanted was to figure out the meaning behind Paige's last words, but I hadn't yet figured out a way to do that.

If I was going to take the obvious route, the next best thing was to continue looking into suspects. In what way, though? Try looking into alibis? Dive into researching each suspect, one by one? Learn about—

An odd *whoosh*ing noise crossed the room, left to right.

I stood on tiptoe to look over the kitchen island and saw nothing out of the ordinary.

"Eddie?" I asked. "What are you doing?"

This time, the *whoosh* came from the dining room.

I abandoned dinner preparations and went in search of my cat. "If you're messing with Rafe's ear-buds again, he's not going to be happy. And if you're messing with my . . . Eddie, what are you doing?"

My fuzzy feline friend was under the dining table, his hind end high and waggling, his front end crouched low, gaze focused tight. He was in hunting mode, only what was he hunting? And what had made the whooshing noise?

I leaned over. "Are you looking for your imaginary friend? Because I'm pretty sure he's . . . Eddie Hamilton Niswander, you let go of that!"

Eddie bounded away, and I was left to get down on my hands and knees to gather up the remnants of what had been a small feather duster. "Thanks a lot!" I called. "Every six months or so, I actually use this."

"Mrr!"

"If that was a commentary on my housekeeping skills, you should know that ninety-five percent of what I clean up is cat hair."

No response.

"Whatever," I muttered, crawling backward with feather bits in hand. "Now I have to add 'Buy feather duster' to my list and—"

I stopped, midcrawl. Feathers. Arrows had feathers. An arrow killed Paige. The next investigative step I needed to take was, in retrospect, a very obvious one.

Find out which of the suspects knew how to use a bow and arrow.

I scrunched my face into a knot. "Easier said than done," I said, mostly to myself.

"What's that?" Rafe glanced up from the brown sugar he was spooning into his morning oatmeal. "Hang on, let me get my phone out. I want to take a picture of that expression and send it to your mother to show her that your face finally did freeze that way."

Since I wanted to be a good wife and a good sport, I remained immobilized until the photo was snapped. When he opened his messaging app, I unfroze myself. "Don't tell me you're really going to send that to my mom."

"No," he said, tapping away, "but I am going to send it to Kristen, Ash, and your aunt Frances."

"Separately, or as a group text?"

"Group. More fun that way."

"As long as you include me." I reached for my phone and waited. Sure enough, up popped a remarkably unattractive picture of me, along with a message. "'Look what five weeks of marriage has done to this poor woman,'" I read out loud, then looked up at him and nodded. "Glad you're taking some responsibility."

Messages pinged in quickly.

Kristen: *I was betting it would take at least 6 months—nicely done*

Ash: *Hope you got some decent "before" photos*

Aunt Frances: *Or is her true self finally being revealed?*

Rafe texted *Will let you know when I know* and slid his phone back into his pocket. "What were you saying about easier done than said?"

I rolled my eyes at his misquote of the saying. "I was thinking about my next investigative steps. How do I find out which one of the suspects is a bow hunter? If it had been a gun, I could have gone to shooting ranges and talked to people. Or talked to people at local gun and ammunition stores. But you can practice shooting a bow almost anywhere, and I have no idea where people buy arrows." I frowned. "Do people make their own arrows?"

"No clue." Rafe took a bite of oatmeal. "Want me to ask around? I know a guy."

Rafe's network of connections was deep, wide, and strong. If his first guy didn't have the answer, that guy would know another guy, and if the second guy didn't know, the third guy would almost certainly be the region's foremost arrow expert. "Maybe," I said. "Let me think about it. I'll text you."

"Okey-dokey, hokey-pokey." He stood, giving me a smacking kiss.

My face returned to its earlier scrunchiness. "Please promise me you'll never say that again."

"You want me to eliminate words from my vocabulary? What kind of librarian are you?"

"One that wants to stay married for a long time."

He grinned, his teeth flashing white. "If I detach the okey-dokey part from the hokey-pokey part, can they both stay?"

Debating personal lexicons with my husband was not how I'd planned to start my day. "Let me think about it," I said again, but we both knew I wouldn't, because the whole conversation was ridiculous. Rafe would say whatever he wanted whenever he wanted, and I wouldn't want it any other way.

After he left, I tidied the kitchen, then went upstairs to change out of my bathrobe and into library clothes, thinking about doing a couple of minor chores before heading up to the library, then deciding a better use of my time would be going into the library early.

When I walked into the break room, Josh was already there, brewing coffee in the new pot. "The new one is better than the old one?" I asked.

"This one is eighteen inches closer to the faucet."

"Really? Doesn't look like that much."

He gave me a look of complete and utter disbelief. "How can you not know what eighteen inches is?"

"How can you not know under what Dewey decimal numbers you'd find self-help books?"

"Easy. I don't care."

"Well, there you go."

Josh shook his head but kept his mouth shut. This made me think that being married to the adorable Mia was doing him a world of good, because not long ago he would have said out loud the things he was surely thinking. Speaking of Mia . . .

"When I was asking about Rila Shutleff Wilcox the other day," I said, "you told me that Mia knew where Rila and her husband are living."

"Yeah. That turret house. Why, you want to stalk her or something?"

"I'm just curious as to how someone like her ended up in Chilson." Among other things.

He made a rude noise in the back of his throat. "We're on too freaking many Top Ten lists, that's how. Glad I bought my house when I did. Even with Mia's income we probably couldn't afford it now. Did I tell you she got another promotion? She's making way more than I am now."

Mia was also in IT, but she worked in the private sector. "So talk to Graydon about a raise," I said.

"Yeah, I should do that," Josh said, but half-heartedly. He had a good thing going at the library and he knew it. Maybe the pay wasn't what it could be, but he had as much autonomy as he wanted, and Graydon listened to him when he said he needed new equipment.

He started to leave, then stopped. "About that Rila. I mentioned to Mia that you didn't know anything about her, and Mia said she's working part time as the girls' high school soccer and cross-country coach."

That made no sense. "How can she coach two teams at the same time?"

"You really don't know anything about sports,

do you? Girls play soccer in the spring. Cross-country is in the fall, girls and boys. Don't you ever read the sports pages?"

"Of course I don't. Why would I?"

He rolled his eyes and headed off to do IT things. I filled my coffee mug and wandered to my office to do librarian things, which that morning included a quick check of the high school's website for coach names and information about practice locations and times.

I got an e-mail nod from Graydon to leave a couple of hours early, and late that afternoon I drove out to the hiking trail system where the boys' and girls' cross-country teams were scheduled to practice.

Never in my life had I ever had any reason to attend a cross-country practice, and I'd never much thought about what it might look like. What I found in the parking lot was a handful of vehicles, most of which sported "Chilson X-C" bumper stickers, and a small group of high school kids in running tights and nylon jackets hopping up and down in a vain effort to stay warm in the face of a thirty-five-degree windy late afternoon that was spitting a sleety rain.

The kids were clustered around a young woman in a bright red parka, her head topped by a thick multicolored fleece hat with a long curly brown ponytail trailing out. They hopped, she talked, and when she blew a whistle, they hared off, feet flying.

As I walked up to her, I saw that she was peering at a stopwatch.

"Rila Wilcox?" I asked.

Her head came up and hazel eyes gave me a quick top-to-bottom assessment. "That's me," she said, communicating neither friendliness nor fear.

I smiled and introduced myself.

"Eddie's mom!" She grinned. "I've heard all about you and the bookmobile cat. What a great story."

Well, this was going to be easier than I'd anticipated. "That's me," I said cheerfully.

"It's great to meet you." Rila gestured to an SUV that had seen better days. "I'd say we could sit in my car and talk, but I need to time the kids."

I nodded. "Understood. I won't take up much of your time. In addition to driving the bookmobile, I'm also the library's assistant director. We're always looking for interesting people who don't mind talking in front of a group."

Her face closed up. "Thanks for thinking that I'm interesting, but I don't know if I'm in a position to do that."

"Not a problem," I said easily. "And no pressure. Public speaking isn't for everyone, and I imagine your story could be hard to tell."

"Oh. It's not . . . Well, I guess it is that. More or less." She glanced at her stopwatch and said in a soft sigh, "Sometimes I think everyone has a complicated story."

It seemed an odd thing to say, and I wondered what had spurred it. Then I remembered that she and her husband were both murder suspects. To keep the conversation rolling, I asked, "How long have you been coaching?"

"Here? Just a few months. But I was helping coach kids younger than me when I was still in high school. And I'm finishing my education degree so I can hire in full time as a teacher."

"And your husband?" I asked. "What does he do?"

The wind gusted hard and Rila zipped her coat to the top. "Will is a sales rep for Saville Beverages. He drives all over this part of the state."

"Sounds fun," I said, though I wasn't sure I meant it. "And how did you meet? How-we-met stories are my favorite."

She gave a wry smile. "We first crossed paths years ago, when we were both training up for the Olympics. We got married the year after I graduated college."

"Will plays soccer, too?" That I hadn't heard.

But she was shaking her head. "He's okay at soccer, but he's not even close to international level. No, he's an archer. You know, with a bow and arrow?" She mimicked the action, then noticed my face. "Are you okay? You look a little funny."

My mouth opened and shut a few times before I could eke out, "Fine, thanks. Just fine."

I wasn't. Because I was busy mentally rearranging the suspect list, and moving her husband, presumably the love of her life, to the tippy-top.

Chapter 11

The next day was a bookmobile day, and Hallow-een Eve to boot. We had a packed schedule of driving to elementary schools all over the county, doing spooky storytelling here, there, and every-where, and part of the plan had been that Julia would be doing approximately ten thousand cos-tume changes.

When she climbed aboard the bookmobile I gave her a squinting stare. "What, pray tell, is this?" I gestured at her plain garb of a navy peacoat, black leggings, light blue button-up shirt over a black tank top, and loafers. "I didn't know you owned clothes this normal."

She sniffed. "I can be normal if I want."

"Really?" I shot her a look of complete disbelief. "And when was the last time you wanted to be normal?"

"Hmm." She tapped her upper lip. "I believe it was March of 1973. Or was it 1972?"

Now *that* I believed. And when she went back

out to her car, returning with two massive totes overflowing with costumes for her to quick-change into and out of, I finally understood what was going on.

"You," I said, buckling my seat belt and starting the engine, "have been preparing for this day this for weeks."

"Minnie. Please. I've been planning since November first of last year."

For the quadzillionth time in my life, I wished I could do the one-eyebrow thing. "You? Planning ahead? I thought that violated your personal freedoms."

"Pish." She waved away a statement she'd made dozens of times. "Planning is a sign that you have the freedom to choose the life you want."

I blinked. Julia didn't usually wax so philosophical. "Is that a quote or did you make it up?"

"Quote," she said. "My paternal grandpappy. Haven't I ever told you about him?"

She had not, but by the time we reached the first stop, I'd learned where Julia's penchant for the dramatic might have originated. "Seriously?" I asked, as we slowed to a stop at Chancellor Elementary School. "Your grandfather worked at Willow Run during World War II, making airplanes?"

"Yep." She tapped the top of Eddie's carrier with her toes. "The family lived in Ann Arbor. He drove over to Ypsilanti every day with three buddies, and that same group of guys turned into a barbershop quartet that won awards all over the Midwest."

"I don't think anyone in my family has ever done anything that cool."

Julia hooted. "Don't you have a brother who's an Imagineer at Disney World?"

"Well, yeah, but . . . he's still an engineer." I was about to tell my favorite engineer joke, but we got busy hauling cat, costumes, and books into the school and the moment was lost.

When we were four feet from the door, it swung out and a cheerful voice called, "Good morning, bookmobile ladies!"

I blinked. Duffy Ulrich, president of the Friends of the Library, was holding the door open for us. At least I assumed it was Duffy. The voice had been hers, the minimalist height was hers, and the red hair was certainly hers, but hand-on-heart identification would be difficult. Head to toe, she was outfitted in a classic court jester costume: multipointed and multicolored hat with jingling bells, jacket paneled with many colors and decorated with additional bells, breeches of bright green, and felt shoes whose long toes curled up and ended with yet more bells.

"Nice, yeah?" She did a quick spin that set all her bells to jingling. "Chancellor is my grandkid's school and I couldn't wait to volunteer today. I made this for a community theater show a while back and borrowed it for today. Ain't like it's going to fit anyone else," she said, winking.

By this time, my mouth had closed. Julia, however, was circling Duffy with a critical eye. "Not bad," she said, "but I'd add more bells if you want to be heard in Traverse City."

It was at that point that I did some quick mental math—always a risk, but needs must—and figured that they were maybe a year apart. In a high school the size of Chilson's, that meant they had absolutely known each other, and judging from the scene going on in front of me, they'd been friends.

"Now that the Queen of Theater has approved," Duffy said, poking Julia's arm with a puppet-headed scepter as I revised my estimate of their friendship status from Level Two up to Level Three, "I can tell Minnie the good news. I just got an e-mail from Graydon that the library board has put their official stamp of approval on the bookmobile scavenger hunt."

I felt my own spirits rising, buoyed up by her infectious grin, and a wide smile spread across my face. "This is going to be fun," I declared, and wondered why I'd ever resisted the idea in the first place.

"Great green goblins." Julia sighed. "You've been Duffied. Sucked into a wild venture of her making, half convinced that it was your idea in the first place."

Duffy poked Julia with the scepter again. "Just because you got caught sneaking back into your parents' house that night doesn't mean it wasn't fun."

I looked from Duffy to Julia, sensing an excellent story. "What night?"

"Little pitchers," Julia said darkly, her gaze glancing at the empty hallway. "Big ears. Ms. Ulrich, lead the way."

After leaving Duffy and the school behind, we went on to a similar event at the Peebles Elementary School, and after that we stopped in the small town of Peebles itself to grab lunch. I parked us in a large lot behind the single long block of downtown stores and walked around to pick up the on-line order Julia had sent to the local diner.

On the way back, I noticed a small store that had never before registered in my tiny little brain. A single-story concrete block structure, it was tacked onto the back of a two-story building. Its one small window was almost filled with a lit orange neon OPEN sign. Above the metal door, which was flaked with peeling gray paint, was an aging wooden sign that read BUD'S GUNS & AMMO.

Huh.

I climbed the bookmobile steps and, as we ate our lunch of grilled ham and cheese sandwiches on sourdough, I said, "We're what, five miles from Gainsborough?"

Julia squinted in that direction. "About that. Why?"

"Anyone from Gainsborough who's into shoot-ing probably stops there at least once in a while," I said, nodding in the direction of Bud's.

"Do bow-and-arrow people go to gun stores? I mean, bows and arrows aren't, you know, guns."

"But they are"—I searched for the right word—"weaponry." I'd taken self-defense courses and had a working relationship with handguns, but I didn't own one. "Doesn't hurt to ask, right?"

I told Julia and a snoring Eddie that I'd be back in a few minutes, and walked across the parking lot to expand my world and join the ranks of those who'd ventured into a gun store.

Inside, the store was not at all what I'd imagined. Armed with the experience of watching numerous TV shows and movies, I'd expected a darkened and slightly grimy interior filled with shelving stocked high with dusty boxes of various sizes with unfamiliar labels, a long glass counter that held a wide array of black handguns, a wall behind the counter crowded with long guns of increasingly scary sizes, and a fiftyish unshaven man in a sleeveless T-shirt, sitting on a stool, chewing on a toothpick, reading a newspaper.

This was not that.

Though there was, in fact, an aisle of shelves filled with unfamiliar-looking boxes and a glass cabinet of handguns, the store's interior was clean and brightly lit. There was even a faint scent of something familiar.

I sniffed. Lemon. That was it. All-purpose lemon cleaning fluid, just like what was under my kitchen sink and didn't use nearly often enough.

"Hi!" A brown-haired woman about my own age, dressed in jeans and a fleece pullover, hurried in from a back room. "Sorry to keep you waiting. What can I do for you? My name's Aurora, by the way."

"Not Bud?" I asked, smiling.

"That's my grandpop. I took over the store a couple of years ago when he was finally ready to retire." She rested her forearms on the counter and her long ponytail fell forward over one shoulder. "No one else in the family wanted anything to do with it, so here I am."

After introducing myself and gesturing at the bookmobile, I said, "I was hoping to ask you a few questions, if that's okay. You heard about Paige Ferrer's murder the other day, over at Gainsborough?"

"Sure. It's all anyone is talking about."

I took a deep breath for courage. "I'm the one who found her."

Aurora's face, which had taken on a resigned look when I'd intimated that I wasn't going to buy anything, went soft. "Oh, wow. That's tough. I can't imagine what that must have been like."

I didn't want to imagine it, either, but my choice in the matter had been made that day in the woods. I nodded and was formulating a question about weaponry when Aurora asked, "Is it true that she was shot with an arrow?"

"Yes. That's what I was wondering," I said, looking around and seeing nothing but guns and gun-related paraphernalia. "Do you sell arrows? Or bows?"

"Not on a regular basis. Sometimes I special-order bows for customers, but it's been months."

"Oh." I deflated. "Well, thanks anyway. I appreciate your time and—"

Aurora tapped the countertop. "But here's a question for you. Do you know if a guy named Alec Ferrer is related to Paige? About our age, I'd say. Lives downstate. Kalamazoo? Jackson? Something like that."

I went still. "Her oldest son."

"Okay. Well, Alec came in here last summer," she said. "Ordered a bow."

"He . . . did?"

"A nice one. Said he was going to practice all summer and for hunting with it this fall."

Huh.

I thanked her and walked back to the bookmobile, wondering if the object of Alec Ferrer's hunting had been of the deer variety, or if it had been human.

                                    * * *

The next day, Friday, was Halloween, and Rafe and
I spent the busy trick-or-treating hours handing out
horrifically unhealthy snacks to the next generation
of future dental patients. After that, we collapsed
in front of the television and watched seasonally
appropriate movies. Horror movies often had the
unfortunate tendency to give me nightmares, but
this time around they must not have held a candle
to the horror I'd witnessed at Gainsborough, because I slept like a rock.

Saturday morning dawned bright and cheery.

"Good morning, my buttermilk pancake." Rafe
waved a spatula in my direction as I pulled a tall chair
up to the kitchen island. "Showered and dressed already? It's not even eight."

Without me even asking, he grabbed a mug, added
a titch of creamer, poured it full of the staff of life,
and pushed it across the countertop into my waiting
hands. Truly, he was the best of husbands.

"Have you ever been to a high school cross-
county meet?" I asked.

"Dual or invitational?"

Which essentially answered my question. Anyone who knew the difference between must have a
working familiarity with both of them. "Invitational. Six teams are running Chilson's course this
morning."

He ladled dollops of pancake batter onto the
griddle. "Are you saying you want to go?"

What I wanted to do was curl up on the couch
with a vat of coffee, a cozy blankie, a nice thick
book, and Eddie. "Yes."

"Then this must be part of your investigation

about Paige Ferrer." When I nodded, he gave me a long, squinting look, then shrugged. "Okay. I'm in. What's the goal?"

I aimed an air-kiss in his direction. Though I hadn't actually asked him if he wanted to go with me, there he was, volunteering. Of course, last night he'd said he wanted to clean out the basement today, and going to a cross-country meet was nothing but avoidance behavior, but who was I to question the man who was making me breakfast?

"The goal," I said, "is to learn more about Rila Wilcox. Watching her coach the team might . . ." My voice tailed off. I had no idea how seeing a coach in action could contribute to any body of knowledge. "It might help. And," I said, wrapping my hands around the warm mug, "it didn't look like she had an assistant coach, so it's possible that her husband might be there to help her."

Rafe flipped a row of pancakes, one after the other. "The guy training for Olympic archery events? Yeah, I can see why you might want to talk to him about a murder with a bow and arrow."

"He's at the top of the suspect list for a reason."

"You, my little caramel apple," he said, pointing the flipping tool at me, "are among the brightest light bulbs in the house."

I leaned over my coffee, taking in its steamy aroma. "When are you going to get tired of coming up with new nicknames for me?"

"2073?" He squinted at the ceiling, then shrugged. "Maybe 2072."

He sounded like Julia, only in reverse. "Can't wait," I muttered, but it was a mutter with a smile, because what really mattered was the coffee, the pancakes, and the fact that my husband was willing to help with my unofficial investigation, even if his motives were not pure of heart.

Less than an hour later, the two of us were standing on a flat grassy area next to a three-quarters-empty parking lot at the high school's football stadium. Chilson's cross-country course, it turned out, started just outside the stadium and ended at the finish line of the track that encircled the football field.

Boys and girls in various school colors were milling around, bouncing up and down and taking short jogs in an effort to stay warm and limber. A whistle blew, and the boys suddenly started shedding sweatshirts and pants, revealing running tights, T-shirts, and running singlets that had race numbers attached to front and back.

I felt an odd sense of anticipation, and edged closer to the white stripe painted on the grass that was the starting line.

"Line up!" a man shouted, and a gaggle of gangly boys trotted forward. The parents, who had been chatting in small groups, spread left and right around the line of boys and went silent.

"On your mark!" the man called into the quiet. He raised his arm and pointed a starting pistol at the sky. "Get set!"

Bang!

The runners took off en masse, a kaleidoscope of colors and motion and energy. It was an exhilarating sight, one that almost made me want to get back into running.

Almost.

Some parents jogged off toward a city park that

I assumed the runners would be winding through. Other parents started walking toward the stadium. In the middle of that group was Rila Wilcox.

"That's her," I said to Rafe. "The one talking to that guy in the bright green hat."

"Spartan green," my Michigan State University alumnus husband said.

I kept my eye roll to myself and continued watching. "From that body language, I'd say he's a parent, not her husband. And I haven't seen anyone who looks like he might be. Her husband, I mean."

"Nope. But I can find out for sure, if you want."

I did want, and Rafe ambled forward, entangling himself with the parental group. I hung back, letting him chat up a set of parents. He might have known them from the days when their offspring had been in middle school, or he might have known them from his own school days, or he might have known them from church, or he might have known them because he ran into them once at a restaurant. With Rafe all those options were equally likely.

As the main group entered the small stadium, Rafe let them go ahead and came back to me. "Wilcox has never," he said, "been to a cross-country meet since Rila started coaching."

I thought about that, and decided it was not a commentary on their marriage. She'd said Will was a sales rep. Maybe he worked Saturdays. Or maybe she preferred that her husband not attend and distract her from her job.

"Do you want to stay?" Rafe asked.

"Yes," I said, surprising myself. Though organized sports were not my thing, this view into a different world was interesting. We moseyed to the stadium and climbed up a few rows of bleachers. Not very long after, we heard cheers and encouraging shouts, and three runners tore onto the track, arms pumping and feet flying, in an all-out race to be first.

We were on our feet and shouting, caught up in the excitement, not even knowing who we were cheering on.

"Go! Go! Go!"

A few breathless seconds later, one boy edged ahead and crossed the finish line. Other boys came into the stadium, some in groups, some running alone. Parents gave hugs, patted backs, and handed over sweatpants, and half an hour later, we did the same routine all over again for the girls' race.

The scoreboard was dark, as it was for football and didn't lend itself well to however cross-country meets were scored, so we had no idea who'd won until the loudspeaker system crackled and the announcement was made.

Chilson's girls finished second, the boys third. I'd been watching Rila, and she'd shown signs of being pleased with the results, bumping knuckles and giving thumbs-up to her kids.

Not that I knew anything about coaching, but it sure looked like she had a solid rapport with both kids and parents, which had to bode well for team spirit, even if they hadn't won the meet. That didn't, of course, have any direct correlation to her likelihood as a murder suspect, but I could see all sorts of indirect correlation, because it sure seemed to me that a good coach had to be a good person, and good people didn't commit murder. Which would mean nothing to Detective Hal Inwood or to Ash, so I just tucked the knowledge away to think about later.

Rafe and I made our way down to the ground and Rila's gaze swung in our direction. She frowned, then came forward. "Minnie, right? With the bookmobile. What brings you to a cross-county invitational?"

I smiled. "Never been. And since I'd met you the other day, I figured it was past time. Have you ever met my husband?"

They shook hands. "You're the middle school principal, yeah?" Rila asked. "I've heard lots of good things about you."

Rafe shoved his hands in his coat pockets and sighed. "Please don't believe everything you hear."

She laughed. "I get it. High standards can be tough to live down.

"Minnie!" Bob Craw, a library patron, jogged over. "Do you have a minute? Got a question for you."

If I had favorite patrons—which, again, I didn't, because that would be wrong—Bob wouldn't be anywhere on the list. "Morning," I said. "I didn't know your kids ran cross-country."

"Oh, they don't." Bob chuckled. "I just like to keep in touch with what's going on. But I wanted to know if it's true what I've been hearing? That you're the one who found Dr. Ferrer, out at Gainsborough?"

Rila, who'd started to ease away, stopped short.

"How awful that must have been." Bob shook his head. "If it had been my wife, she would have been a mess. How are you holding up? Are you okay?"

I murmured that I was doing fine.

"Good, good. The whole thing was so awful and

weird. One of those things that you remember where you were when you heard about it, you know? I was at Shomin's, getting lunch. Rafe, I bet you were at school. Rila, how about you?"

"Um." She backed away, her gloved hands rising, palms up. "I guess . . . Sorry, I don't . . . I don't remember."

And she was gone.

After Rila's quick exit, Rafe and Bob carried on a desultory conversation, but I stared after her, wondering exactly what had caused her to suddenly switch from normal human being to frightened rabbit. There was only one conclusion that made any sense.

Reluctantly, sadly, and with a sigh, I moved her up one slot on the suspect list.

Chapter 12

Rafe, of course, hadn't noticed a thing.

"Let me make sure I have this right. You're saying that because Rila couldn't remember off the top of her head where she was when she heard about the murder, she's now a more serious suspect?"

The two of us were knee to knee at one of Corner Coffee's small tables. Though the day was bright and sunny, it was also the first of November in northwest lower Michigan, when even the brightest, sunniest day wasn't ever what you'd call warm. By the time we'd left the stadium, it was clear that driving the chill out of my bones would require coffee. Lots of it. Chilson's downtown coffee shop offered not only that but also a cozy atmosphere, complete with maple floors, a map of the USA stuck all over with pins indicating where people had come from, and blueberry muffins large enough to feed a family.

I looked at the love of my life over the top of a mostly demolished muffin. "Were you not paying attention? It was her reaction, not her exact words.

She'd been open and friendly right up until Bob asked the question about where she'd been at the time of Paige's murder. Then she literally distanced herself from us as fast as she could, stammering things that didn't make any sense."

"What do you mean, didn't make sense?"

Using air quotes, I said, "'I guess . . . Sorry, I don't . . . I don't remember.'"

He shrugged. "Your definition of 'doesn't make sense' must be different than mine."

"Again," I said, trying not to use the patient voice, because when it was used on me it felt way condescending and thus incredibly annoying, "it wasn't her words as much as her reaction. And yes, I know I just recited her words, saying that they didn't make sense, and I stand by that. It's just that her physical reaction, backing away like that, holding up her hands like she was being attacked, meant so much more."

"Huh." Rafe pushed the jug of creamer in my direction. "Guess I didn't notice. I must have been too busy figuring out how to get away from Bob Craw without jeopardizing either your career or mine."

I patted his hand. "And that was very well done. You're the best in your row at faking emergency phone calls." I only hoped, next time I ran into Bob, that I'd remember to tell him that the heart attack of Rafe's uncle hadn't been a heart attack at all, but indigestion after eating a double serving of chorizo-and-egg burrito. "Although, it does trouble me a bit that it was so easy for you to tell a blatant lie."

"Not a lie." Rafe wagged a finger at me. "The timing is off, is all. Happened to my uncle Sig."

Uncle Sig, who'd died years ago, had actually been Rafe's great-uncle on his dad's side. According to Niswander family lore, lots of things had happened to him. Some of them might even be true.

"Speaking of timing," I said, "it's November. We should talk about our honeymoon before it turns into a plain old vacation."

"Huh. We can't have that, now can we?"

"We cannot. And I have an idea."

"Wonder if it's the same one I have."

Interesting. "Should we write our idea down independently, so there's no cheating?"

"We're millennials," he said. "We'll text it on the count of three."

I pulled my phone out of my coat pocket and started typing. "Okay. I'm ready. One . . . two . . . three."

Half a second later, our phones dinged simultaneously. I looked at the message he'd sent and nodded. The first step in our honeymoon planning was done.

"Are you serious?"

Kristen looked at me over the top of a crème brûlée drizzled with dark chocolate and caramel, topped with raspberries, and dusted with the sparkliest sugar I'd ever seen. It was just past noon on Sunday, and it was the last dessert Sunday I'd have at Three Seasons until spring. For years, Kristen and I had had a standing May through October weekly dessert time. Once she'd married and now had infant twins, the previously sacred Sunday desserts had naturally shifted to an iffy thing that happened whenever it worked out.

"You're seriously going on a honeymoon over the holidays?" she asked, frowning at me fiercely. "Who does that?"

I shrugged. "It works out for both of us. He's on winter break, the library isn't very busy then, and I have tons of vacation saved up."

Kristen let her spoon clatter to the stainless steel countertop. Since the heat was already off in her office, we'd opted to eat in the kitchen and were surrounded by mostly empty shelves, because almost everything except the dessert implements was packed away for the winter. "That's how you decided?" she asked, eyes narrowed. "Because it was convenient?"

"There are worse reasons."

"But that's not even two months away! Where are you going to find someplace even halfway decent this late?"

"We'll figure something out." I grinned. "I hear the Florida Keys are nice that time of year."

The next day, Kristen, Scruffy, and the babies were driving to New York to deal with *Trock's Troubles* post-production work, after which they'd head south for Key West, Kristen's favorite winter location.

She rolled her eyes. "Like either you or Rafe wants to spend your honeymoon hanging with small humans."

"If we don't," I said, "I won't see Eloise and Lloyd until April. They might forget Auntie Minnie."

"Won't let them." Kristen picked up her spoon and dug in. "There's photographic evidence. And the presents you'll send."

"Speaking of evidence." I studied my dessert

and planned series of spoonfuls that would distribute the raspberries equally, because to have the last bite be custard and no raspberry would be deeply distressing. "I need to catch you up on what I've learned about Paige Ferrer and who might have killed her."

In a roughly linear fashion, I told her the whole kit and caboodle, starting with Honey Hollow and ending with Rila at the cross-country meet. When I finished, Kristen, who'd been nodding thoughtfully throughout my recital, did the one-eyebrow thing. "What's next?"

"Next?" I fished around in my head for my suspect list. "Blaine Callaway is the one I know the least about."

"And what's next?" she asked, still with the eyebrow going on.

"Well." I eyed the remains of my dessert. "If his family has lived in Gainsborough year-round for a long time, that means he went to high school here, in Chilson or in Dooley. If I figure out what school and what year he graduated, I can try to find someone I know that graduated with him, and figure out a way to ask some innocent, yet clever, questions."

"Someone you know," Kristen said. "Or someone Rafe knows, or I know, or your aunt Frances knows, or Julia knows, or for crying out loud, someone that Mitchell Koyne knows. Don't limit yourself, young lady." She thumped the counter with her fist again. "Use your resources!"

I eyed her. "Let me guess. You've been talking to Trock."

"My father-in-law is a wise man," she said, solemnly. "He's also a complete scatterbrain whose success is unfathomable, but who ever said life was fair?"

Absolutely no one, and that night I sat on the couch with my laptop while Rafe watched hockey, trawling the Internet for information about Blaine Callaway. If I didn't find anything, the next morning I'd have a chat with Camille Pomeranz, editor of the *Chilson Gazette*, and ask for access to their shelves of high school yearbooks.

"Huh," I said. "That was easy."

"Yeah?" Rafe didn't look away from the television. "Cool. Wings are on a power play."

"Cool," I said, using the exact same tone he'd used, which he either didn't register or didn't care about. Both were possible.

I scrolled down through the LinkedIn entry for Blaine Callaway. The social media app was business-oriented, with organizations posting all sorts of positive things about their activities. People had their own pages, too—I had one myself, although I hadn't touched it in months—and those individual pages often read like short résumés.

The LinkedIn page for Blaine had the typical information. Current employer, previous employers, education. He was a graduate of Central Michigan University and of Dooley High School. His page said he'd worked at the Petoskey hospital right out of college and was now a pharmacist at Dooley Pharmacy, and had been there since before I'd moved to Chilson.

The dates listed meant he was about ten years older than me, so Rafe wouldn't have crossed paths with him in high school sports. Then I remembered something.

I nudged my beloved with my elbow. "Isn't your friend Tank originally from Dooley?"

"Huh?" Rafe almost focused on something other than hockey. "Yeah. Why?"

"Blaine Callaway graduated from there, about ten years ahead of us. Do you think Tank would know anything about him?"

Instead of wasting time on something like actual conversation, Rafe pulled his cell out of his pocket and started texting. A few *bings* went back and forth, and then Rafe handed me his phone.

Rafe: *Know a Blaine Callaway from Dooley?*

Tank: *My oldest sister dated him back in the day. What's up?*

Rafe: *Background info for a thing. What's he like?*

Tank: *Was kind of a hothead. And always yapping about the weight he could lift, how good his eyesight was, how quick his reflexes. You know the kind.*

Rafe: *Yup. He still like that?*

Tank: *Dunno. Haven't seen him in years*

Rafe: *If you had a chance to hire him, would you?*

Tank: *Not unless he's changed. A lot.*

Rafe: *What I wanted to know. Thx. Go Wings!*

I disregarded the last sentence, which I knew was a reference to the hockey game. "Thanks," I said, returning the phone.

"Anytime."

His attention, which hadn't ever strayed far from the television, returned to it completely, leaving me to think about what I'd learned.

In Blaine Callaway's youth, he'd been proud of his strength, eyesight, and speed.

And he'd been a hothead.

Hmm.

The next day was a library day, and it started out like many library days, with me in my office early catching up with e-mail and undone Friday tasks. As the morning wore on, the time was interspersed with trips to the kitchen for caffeine and conversation with coworkers, most of which on Mondays centered on weekend activities and the week ahead of us.

Josh, muttering mild curses as he slopped coffee over the edge of his insulated mug, which was almost as big as his head, said, "Mia has me going to some downtown meeting tonight."

Holly and I exchanged amused glances. Not so very long ago, anything outside of work or gaming had not been part of Josh's life. Marriage had improved him in many ways, and there was a very slim possibility that someday we'd get tired of telling him so.

"Meeting?" Holly asked. "What kind?"

He shrugged as he snapped the lid on his vat of coffee. "Don't remember. Something environmental, maybe? Could be interesting, could be boring. Either way, it's in the back room at Hoppe's, so we can at least get beer and food."

Holly being Holly, she started making fun of Josh for not knowing what kind of meeting he was headed to. If they really wanted to know, all they had to do was look up the events page on Hoppe's website, so clearly what they preferred to do was argue like siblings.

I eased myself away from the bickering and

headed back to my office, thinking. You could learn a lot about someone by observing their behavior in a meeting. Some people stayed in the background, not saying a word; other people said a lot. Some people were polite, letting others have their say. And some people tried to bully their way through a meeting, controlling it from beginning to end. Verity Gauthier was chair of her township's planning commission, and how she conducted herself would tell me a lot about her, especially if they were still discussing short-term rentals.

Back at my computer, I pulled up Carlow Township's website, clicked around to find their upcoming agendas, and blew out a breath.

"Looks like I'm going to a meeting tonight," I murmured.

The Carlow Township Hall was about what you'd expect for a township that didn't have the financial benefit that came from significant property taxes. It was a building about fifty years old and worn at the edges with the feel of making do as long as possible: white vinyl siding fading into gray, a roof years past its expected life span, and windows that should have been replaced a couple of decades ago.

But it was well-tended, the landscaping was tidy, and, as I stepped inside and out of the blustery November wind, I noted that the interior was spic-and-span clean.

As I took stock of the folding banquet tables and metal folding chairs, my nose caught the distinct smell of burning dust. This almost certainly meant that that hall was only used once or twice a month, that the heat was kept low, and that whoever was first to the meeting turned the thermostat up to Tolerable.

There were maybe twenty folding chairs, about half of them occupied, set up facing the seven people sitting at the front tables. In the center of the middle table was a seventy-something woman that I took to be Verity Gauthier. She sat tall, her silver hair in a pixie cut, wearing a rich purple jacket with a sheer patterned scarf loosely tied around her neck in a way that I could only have achieved if Julia had done it for me.

I picked up an agenda from a small table near the door and sat in the back row, pleased that no one had paid any attention to my arrival. Observe and learn, that was my goal. Learn more about short-term rentals, learn more about Verity. Learn anything that might be useful in figuring out what had happened to Paige Ferrer.

"Can you believe her?" a woman in the row ahead of me said. "She's going to keep this discussion going until she gets what she wants."

The man sitting next to her shrugged. "Oh, I don't know. They've been revising this ordinance for what, a year? Short-term rentals are complicated. It's not just because of Verity that it's taking so long."

I slid forward on my seat. There was no point in missing any of the conversation if I could avoid it by inching closer.

"Really?" His companion made a rude noise. "I'd say it's exactly because of that woman. She's the one who's saying she's ready to take on the State of Michigan if they pass legislation to put STRs in residential districts."

"She's just talking," he said.

"Verity doesn't say anything she doesn't mean." The woman snorted. "Remember Melette and Foster Heubel? Friends of my cousin? Well, they have a summer place at Gainsborough, and they said Verity came door to door out there last summer, talking all about the evils of short-term rentals, not saying anything about the positives, basically threatening people if they started renting out their places."

"Threatening?" He scoffed. "I'm sure it wasn't like that."

"No?" she asked. "What does this sound like? 'If you rent out this place you'll wish you'd never set foot in Gainsborough.'"

I sat back.

What it sounded like was a threat.

Chapter 13

Eddie's yellow eyes studied me with a deep and slightly disturbing intensity. It was the look that meant one thing: He wanted something I didn't want to give him.

I looked straight back. "No. Whatever it is, no. You've had treats. I've played the bird game with you. I've snuggled you, and I've put you down exactly when you wanted. What else could you possibly want?"

His mouth opened and closed in a silent *Mrr*.

"Yeah, well." I flourished the last spoonful of my morning oatmeal. "This is mine and you're not getting any of it."

Eddie's look turned mournful.

"And just so you know, guilting me will not work."

His sides went up and down in a huge kitty sigh.

"Still not going to work," I said, turning my attention back to my phone and the morning news feed. Rafe was already gone, and I was taking my time with breakfast. My work day wouldn't start for hours, as Eddie, yours truly, Hunter, and the book-mobile were scheduled for a noon-to-eight-p.m. day that started at the Lake View Medical Care Facility, winding around the northern half of the county, with a final stop at a convenience store in Williams Township.

The only potential downside to the day was the distinct possibility that Hunter would be telling me he wouldn't be able to work on the bookmobile any longer, but I would deal with that possibility when—and if—the time came. No sense in worrying about things that hadn't happened.

"What do you think about that?" I asked Eddie. "I actually am getting to be more like Aunt Frances."

My cat kept on with the intense gaze.

"Quit," I said. "Not going to . . . Oh, fine." I hopped off the kitchen stool, slid my oatmeal bowl off the counter, and placed it on the floor. "There. You happy? I'm sure you're not, because you were hoping for milk leftovers from a bowl of cereal. You haven't yet grasped that October through April is oatmeal weather and—" I stopped. "What are you doing?"

Instead of moving in on the bowl, Eddie was sitting up, cat statue style, but with one difference. He was holding one front paw out in front of him.

I crouched down and reached for the extended paw. "Did you get an owie? Let me see."

Eddie yanked his paw away, shot me a Look That Should Kill, and stalked off.

"Love you, too," I said after him." I got my winter coat, pulled it on, opened the front door, and called out, "It would be great if you did a couple loads of laundry today. Okay? Thanks!"

I thought I heard a muffled "Mrr," but it could

have been the wind whooshing in. Outside, the November cold wrapped itself around me as I walked
up to the Round Table. It had been a minute since
I'd seen Sophia, and yesterday I'd asked when she'd
have time to hang out. She'd responded quickly that
her schedule was relatively flexible, asked what would
work for me, and sent a thumbs-up emoji when I'd
suggested a midmorning coffee break.

I spotted her blond hair the moment I walked in
the door, a feat easier than it might sound since
there were only three people in the restaurant: Sophia in a booth near the entrance, and an elderly
couple side by side in a booth at the back.

Sliding in across from Sophia, I said, "Sorry I'm
late."

"You're not. I was early." She smiled, her brown
eyes warm. "Court was slow this morning."

"How's life at the boardinghouse?" I turned
over the thick ceramic mug on the table and looked
around. Carol, the restaurant's other forever waitress, was already coming in with a carafe of coffee.

"There," she said, putting it down. "This will save
us all time and trouble. Any food?"

Sophia asked for two scrambled eggs and sourdough toast, and I asked for the smallest blueberry
muffin Cookie had. When Carol had gone, I looked
at Sophia. "Boardinghouse," I prompted. "Anything fun going on?"

"Well." She studied the coffee mug she'd been
holding since I'd walked in. "Not as much as I'd
like, to tell you the truth. I told you we're getting
two more renters after the holidays, right? Right
now it's just Anika and me rattling around in that
big house, and Anika is gone most of the time. She

came north to be with her boyfriend—he has one of those condos on the far side of Janay Lake."

I knew the ones. Built less than ten years ago, they were reported to be bright, airy, spacious, and far outside the price range of assistant library directors and middle school principals.

"She's been spending most of her time with him," Sophia said. "I hardly ever see her. And just last weekend they got engaged, so my guess is she'll be moving out as soon as she works it out with Celeste."

With a guilty jolt, I realized that Sophia had moved Up North without having an Aunt Frances or a Kristen. She didn't have anyone to sit in front of the fireplace with, sharing a huge bowl of popcorn. She didn't have anyone to grumble to about bosses or summer traffic or winter weather. Sophia was lonely.

"Small town life," I said slowly, "isn't quite like those sappy movies, is it?"

Sophia gave a wry smile. "What is?"

I sipped my coffee, thinking. Sophia could use a group of friends, but expanding an existing group of friends to include a newcomer wasn't the easiest thing in the world. Of course, some groups were more accepting than others. Then again, it might be easier to create a new group.

The food came and our conversation shifted to other things, but as I ate the last bite of my muffin, I made a silent vow to help Sophia find a solid circle of friends.

I made it home in time to microwave an early lunch of leftover chicken stir-fry and make a brown bag dinner of peanut butter and jelly. Not that I needed any of it. Carol had insisted that the blueberry muffin she'd brought me was indeed the smallest Cookie had, but it was still the size of a swollen softball. Though I ate it all, as leaving any on the plate would be rude, I was already regretting my actions.

"I suppose I could have brought half of it home," I told Eddie as I buckled his carrier into my car's passenger's seat. "Why didn't I think of that?"

Eddie, still annoyed because I hadn't read his little kitty mind about the oatmeal bowl, or whatever it was he'd really wanted, turned so that the black-and-white fur on his back was sticking out through the wire door.

"So adult of you," I said, buckling my own self in. "Speaking of adults, who do you think would be a good friend fit for Sophia?" Silence from the cat side of the car. "No need for you to talk so fast. I don't have pencil and paper handy."

Smirking at my own humor, I drove us through the streets of Chilson—no traffic to speak of, hooray for November!—with me still thinking out loud.

"First thing you think of is to find friends the same age, but that's not necessarily true." Some of my favorite people were decades older than I was, and some were younger. "Plus there's that personal chemistry thing. Predicting which people are going to connect instantly and which ones never will is a guessing game."

A faint "Mrr" came from the right side of the car.

"Good to hear." I glanced over and saw that his back was still facing me. Rotten cat. "And another thing to think about is my suspect list. I haven't heard anything from Ash in forever, so I'm going to guess that he's making as much progress as I am." Which was none.

"How many suspects do I have now?" I asked a quiet Eddie. "Excellent question." I held up my index finger. "One. Blaine Callaway from Gainsborough, with the temper and reported physical prowess. Two is Verity Gauthier, who is publicly against short-term rentals and has allegedly threatened neighbors. Three and four are Rila and Will Wilcox, who were suing Paige." I stuck out my thumb. "Last is Alec Ferrer, who bow hunts."

Two suspects had motives that dealt with short-term rentals, two had revenge-type motives for a reportedly botched surgery, and her son had a financial motive.

"The next obvious step," I said to an uncaring feline, "is to eliminate suspects. Best way is through alibis. A clarification of motive, or a determination of lack of motive, can also be helpful."

An obvious problem with finding alibis, however, was that I had no good reason to walk up to Blaine Callaway and demand to know what he was doing on the morning Paige was killed. Social media posts could sometimes help, but I'd already done a minor amount of cyberstalking on The Five, and none of them had posted anything that helped.

I thought about next steps the rest of the morning. Luckily, not only was Hunter happy to drive, but he was also not in a talkative mood, and I was left to think my thoughts, moving from Alec to Blaine to Rila to Sophia to Verity to Will in that order, because I was a librarian, and working through things alphabetically gave my world a small sense of order.

We were nearing our first stop of the day—the parking lot of a small fieldstone church—when we came to a stop sign where the road we were traveling teed into a county road. It was a busy intersection in rural Tonedagana County terms, and the corner gas station convenience store was often crowded.

Idly, I glanced at the store's gas pumps and parking lot, looking over the assortment of vehicles, and suddenly sat bolt upright. "Stop!" I yelled. "Pull in!"

Hunter gave me a startled look, but to his great credit nodded and did as I'd asked.

As soon as he'd braked us to a halt, I unbuckled and jumped up. "Be back in a flash," I said. "This will only take a minute. Honest."

I shut the bookmobile door on a very loud "Mrr!" and trotted across the cracked asphalt lot, hoping that I wasn't about to make an idiot of myself. Or that if I did, that no one there knew me and wouldn't be able to spread the story very far.

As I hurried toward the store, I eyed the pickup truck that had made me shriek at poor Hunter. The shiny and new truck had doors that were painted with the name and distinctive logo of Saville Beverages, and Rila Wilcox had said her husband Will was a sales rep for Saville. What were the odds that a truck like that would be driven by anyone other than the regional sales rep? I had no actual idea, but they had to be low.

The truck was empty, and I pushed open the store's glass door, thinking fast about what I could say that might make some semblance of sense.

At the front counter, a purple-haired woman of maybe twenty was ringing up the purchases of an elderly couple. Beyond her, in a small office, a woman in her fifties sat behind a desk, looking up at a man in his thirties who was handing out a stack of what looked like bar coasters.

Will Wilcox. Had to be.

Okay, maybe it didn't *have* to be, but the likelihood was strong.

I wandered around the store, picking up snacks for Hunter, Eddie, and myself, while keeping an eye on the action in the office. Timing here would be critical. It all had to look accidental and serendipitous. All I had to do was stay calm and cool and not come across like—

A door I hadn't noticed swung out fast and banged into me. "Ow!" I said involuntarily, almost dropping everything I was carrying.

"Oh, geez." Will Wilcox came through the doorway. "I'm so sorry, I didn't know you were there. Are you okay?"

"Fine," I said, ignoring the shooting pain in my upper arm. "Don't worry about it."

"You sure?" Will tucked the box he was carrying under his elbow and held out his hand. "Will Wilcox. Just in case you need a name for the police report." He smiled, and I recognized that under the corporate baseball cap and tidy beard, he was a good-looking human being, if you liked rugged and macho. Not my style, but I could see the appeal.

I made a show of peering at his coat's logo. "You work for Saville Beverages?"

"That's me. Sales rep for ten counties." He fished into his coat pocket and held out a business card, still smiling. "If you ever need a wholesale order, give me a call."

"Is Rila your wife?" I asked, taking the card. "I met her just the other day."

At the mention of his wife, his face took on a cautious tinge. "Yeah?"

I nodded. "Sure. I work for the library, and we're always looking for people to talk to groups on almost any subject you can think of."

"Public speaking isn't Rila's thing," he said.

"That was definitely the impression I got." I made myself laugh, hoping it didn't sound as forced as it felt. "But she said you two met while training for the Olympics, that you're an archer. That sounds fascinating. Would you consider talking to a group about your experiences?"

"Sorry, but I haven't touched a bow in years, not since I messed up my rotator cuff." He touched his shoulder. "Kept me out of the Olympics, out of any international competition."

I felt like a jerk for bringing up what must have been an emotionally painful subject. "First your shoulder, then Rila's knee?" I shook my head. "That's tough."

"What's tough is what a mess that surgeon made of both of Rila's surgeries." His voice went loud. "No way should she have been operating on anything that was worth what my wife's knee used to be worth."

"Well," I said after an awkward pause, "I hope, um, that things work out. It was nice meeting you. Tell Rila I said hello."

He headed out, and I went to the register to pay for the snacks none of us needed while mentally reviewing my suspects. Even if Will's anger level at Paige was still high, if he couldn't pull a bow, he couldn't have killed Paige.

The list was down to four.

* * *

That night, Hunter and I hauled crates of returned books back into the library. There were more than normal, because four of the day's total six stops had been to elementary schools or churches that were hosting homeschool group events, and the younger the kids, the larger their appetite for the highest pile of books.

"Thanks for . . . coming along . . . today," I said to Hunter through huffing breaths as we carried in the last of the totes. "Not only gives me a break from driving, but it's nice to have you help with the toting."

Hunter, nearly a foot taller than me, with arms at least that much longer, also had muscles twice as strong. Yes, I was small and mighty, but my body's physiology didn't allow me to do what he did: carry two totes of books at a time.

"No problem," he said, holding the back library door open for me with an elbow. "Happy to do what I can."

We went into the utilitarian room that held the bookmobile's book collection. I plopped my tote on the long table we used for sorting and checking in. "It's late," I said. "Go home to your wife. I'll take care of this in the morning."

"You sure?" He slid his tote boxes onto the table. "I told Abigail I'd be staying late."

"Yep. And I'll delegate. I doubt we'll be busy tomorrow. Donna and Kelsey will get it done in no time."

"Okay, thanks. But, um." He put his hands in the pockets of his jeans and looked at the floor.

Before he said another word, I knew what was coming. "Stop." I held up my palms to ward off the bad news. "You're about to say that you love being on the bookmobile more than life itself, but your welding business is really taking off, and you really want to finish your business degree, and you don't have the time to keep doing all three and still have time to, you know, eat, sleep, and talk to your wife more than once a week."

Hunter half smiled. "Pretty much."

Rats. I'd hoped to be wrong. Yet another instance of Pandora's gift being nothing more than a delay of the inevitable.

"But not for a while," he said.

My ears pricked up. "So five years from now? To be honest, ten would be better, but I'll take five."

"Sorry." He laughed. "I just signed a contract that starts right after the holidays. Hopefully you can find someone in the next couple of months."

That hope thing again. "It's way better than a regular two-week notice," I said, sighing. "So thanks. And I am very happy about your business. Truly."

"No, I get it." Hunter nodded. "Feeling two different ways about the same thing sounds impossible, but I bet everyone does it all the time. We just don't pay enough attention to ourselves to realize it."

I looked at him. "I'm not sure if that's deeply profound or if it's banal."

"Let's go with profound," he said. "Be a good way to end my day."

I thanked him again for the heads-up on his departure date, and we walked outside into the chilly dark. He headed to his pickup truck, and I headed to my car, where Eddie was waiting.

"Did you hear?" I asked. "Hunter is bailing on us. His real job is getting too busy." I glanced at my cat. "At least that's what he said. Maybe that was just a story. Maybe it's something else entirely. Did you do something to upset him? If you did, go apologize right now."

Eddie yawned, the dashboard's dim light just barely illuminating what I knew to be a pink tongue and sharp white teeth.

"Just a joke," I muttered, then started the car and embarked on the short drive home. "Not my fault you didn't find it funny. And it was, by the way. Funny. Anyone with a real sense of humor would say so."

My furry friend didn't say a thing.

"Cat got your tongue?" I smirked. "Hah! That still makes me laugh. No, I won't bother explaining it to you. You're in a mood and—" I stopped short and swiveled my head as we drove past Bianca Koyne's office.

"Mrr?"

I pulled over to the curb, completely empty of cars on a November weeknight. "Be right back. Don't get into any trouble while I'm gone." I hopped out of the car and hurried back half a block.

There, in the middle of the top of new listings, was exactly what I'd thought I'd seen. A full-color photo of Paige Ferrer's house. **Rare Gainsborough listing,** the flyer proclaimed. **The Duvall House, long known as one of the Twin Houses.**

Barely two weeks after Paige had been killed, their sons had listed the house. Interesting. I looked at the price, and my eyes went wide.

"Alec," I said quietly, "your motive for murder just got a lot more real."

Chapter 14

So it's on the market already." Rafe shrugged. "I don't see anything sinister in that."

We were upstairs getting ready for bed, and Rafe was once again putting way more toothpaste on his toothbrush than he needed. I tried to share an exasperated glance with Eddie, but his attention was focused solely on grooming his tail, with no kitty brain space available for the needs of the human who fed and watered him.

"Did you not hear what I said about the listing price? That's more money than we make in"—I did some quick mental math, always a risk—"almost twenty years!"

"Thirty, after taxes."

Whatever. "Either way, it's a serious chunk of change, and money is always a motive for murder. People have been killed for a lot less."

"Yeah, but my guess is that price means that Paige didn't own it free and clear." Rafe stood, toothbrush poised. "Her kids probably can't afford the mortgage payments, is all."

I wasn't convinced. "Doctors make a lot of money. And she was a specialty surgeon. They're bound to earn more."

"More than who?" he asked. "Me, you, or Trock Farrand?"

"Kristen's father-in-law probably owns houses he's never set foot inside, and if you keep talking while you're brushing your teeth you'll end up with toothpaste dripped on the front of your shirt."

He looked down, which created a white drip down the front of his shirt. "Huh," he said. "Was that happenstance or serendipity?"

"Depends on your point of view," I said, trying not to smirk.

"Mine is that your cat is taking up half the bed."

I turned around and saw that a thirteen-pound cat had indeed managed to sprawl himself across fifty percent of a queen-sized mattress, something that should have been physically impossible but clearly wasn't. "How is it that he's my cat when he's a pain and he's your cat when he's all snuggly and purry?"

"Serendipity." Rafe grinned, sending another dribble of toothpaste out of the corner of his mouth.

I grabbed a washcloth and dabbed at his face. He took my hand and gently kissed it, which led to other, more interesting things, and it wasn't long before Eddie got up in disgust and left us alone.

The next morning, though, he was back. At least I hoped it was Eddie who was sitting on my chest. It wasn't Rafe, because I could hear him in the shower humming "Singing in the Rain," so the weight on me was either Eddie or some other cat who'd snuck into our house in the middle of the night.

"Then again," I said out loud, "maybe this weight on my chest isn't a cat at all." The weight started purring, so its catness was a near certainty, but there was always the chance I was still really sleepy, and partially dreaming. "Maybe I'm having a heart attack. Maybe I should call 911. Or go to the hospital. Or at least call a doctor."

Eddie's purrs rumbled even louder.

"Are you saying you agree with me?" That had to be a first for so early in the morning. "What doctor should I call? I know, how about Tucker?"

The purring came to an abrupt halt.

"Kidding," I said, reaching around the covers to give him a long pet. "I deleted his phone number a long time ago." A few years ago, I'd dated Dr. Tucker Kleinow, an emergency room doctor. Though there had been many reasons our relationship hadn't lasted, Tucker's cat allergies hadn't helped. "Last I heard, he'd moved to Atlanta."

"Mrr," Eddie said.

"Good riddance? Really? Gee, why don't you tell me what you really think? It's great that— Oof!"

My fuzzy friend leapt to the floor, using my ribs as a starting block.

"Nice," I groaned, rubbing what were sure to be oddly shaped bruises. "Hope I don't have to explain these to anyone other than Rafe. Good thing I don't have a doctor's appointment any time soon because . . ."

I stopped talking. No one was listening to my ramblings, not even me, because I'd just had a thought. There was another doctor I could contact, one who would surely take my call. Dr. Eric Apney had a boat slip next to mine at Uncle Chip's Marina. Eric of the untidy brown hair was a divorced downstate cardiac surgeon who spent a serious part of the summer on his forty-odd-foot boat. Maybe he wound up tighter when he was in doctor mode, but when he was Up North, he was almost as laid back as Rafe.

A couple of hours later, at a more reasonable time for an out-of-the blue text from someone you haven't seen in weeks, I sent him a *Do you have time for a phone call?* message as I was waiting for the first pot of library coffee to finish brewing. There was no instant response, so I mentally shrugged, filled my mug, and headed to my office. Halfway there, my cell buzzed.

"Yo," Eric said. "What's up in the Up North?"

He spoke over background noise of chatter and public address calls that sounded like Charlie Brown's teacher.

"Are you at work?" I asked. "This isn't urgent. It can wait until you're not busy."

"At the hospital, waiting for some other yahoo surgeon to get out of my operating room," he said cheerfully. "Distract me. Please."

So Doctor Eric sounded just the same as Up North Eric did. The consistency was surprisingly comforting.

I asked if he'd heard about Paige's murder. He had not, so I gave him the short version, ending with "Since you're a doctor, too, I have a couple of questions." Then, not waiting for his agreement, I plunged ahead. "A summer place that Paige recently bought was just listed for more than two million dollars. Do you think she'd be able to write a check for that, or would she have had to get a mortgage?"

"No clue," Eric said promptly. "What, you think doctors share their salary details at conferences? Even if we did, which we don't, she was ortho. I'm cardiac. We don't mix."

"Sure, but you must have some idea."

"What I can tell you is that if it had been me, I'd be in mortgage land."

Hmm. "Okay, that helps. Thanks."

"Anything else?"

I was about to say no, but then I remembered Will and Rila Wilcox. "How common are malpractice suits?"

"Depends," he said, which was what I'd expected, but was irritatingly unhelpful. "For some doctors, it's almost part of the job these days. For a big practice, I'd be more surprised if they didn't have some flavor of litigation going on at some point."

"What about you?" I asked. "Or is that a really inappropriate question for me to ask?"

"You can ask. Doesn't mean I'll tell you." He laughed. "But knock on wood, so far I've escaped any malpractice suits. Tomorrow may be a different story, so . . . Hang on." In the background, the PA system was blaring. "Yep, they're calling my name. If you have more questions, call me in about ten hours. Cheers!"

And he was gone.

The rest of the day, I thought about income levels and second homes and investment properties. I also thought about doctors and malpractice lawsuits and how there were so many things I didn't know.

"It feels like I'm losing ground," I said to Rafe that night. It was his turn to cook, so we were about to have a tossed salad and chicken with Spanish rice instead of the frozen pasties and store-bought coleslaw that I would have served. We could have that next week, easy enough.

"Losing what ground?" Rafe stirred the rice, something I rarely did, which was probably why mine always turned out glumpy and sticky.

"My brain. I feel like I'm getting dumber, not smarter."

He gave me a quick glance. "You don't look any dumber than you did this morning."

"It's incremental." I sighed and turned. The kitchen windows faced the backyard, with its lilac bushes and gazebo. But it was November, and six o'clock, so it was full dark outside and all I could see was my own reflection: a curly-haired thirty-something perched on a stool, her elbows on the kitchen island, looking a little sad.

Wait. What?

Why on earth was I feeling sad? I had a wonderful new husband who was cooking me dinner, the best job in the world, a cat who got birthday cards, a great set of friends and family who loved almost everything about me, and I lived in a gorgeous part of the world.

Maybe it wasn't sadness. Maybe what I was feeling was . . . melancholy. Not flat-out sadness, but a pensive ache without any obvious cause. Then again, maybe the cause was obvious—I wasn't making any progress on figuring out who killed Paige, and that failure was manifesting itself in my mood.

"Hello. Earth to Minnie, come in, Minnie."

I blinked and saw Rafe standing in front of me holding two steaming plates of food. "Where are we eating?" he asked. "Choices abound."

"Dining room." I slid off the stool to gather napkins and utensils. "Kitchen is for breakfast and lunch, dining room for dinner, living room for popcorn while watching TV."

Rafe let me go ahead into the adjacent room. "If those are hard-and-fast rules, we should have had them included in the wedding ceremony."

"Along with a mandate to always hang wet towels where they belong?"

"Good one." He put the plates down. "And to always write down on the grocery list the things that you use up."

"This conversation is getting a little too specific," I said as we sat across from each other.

My husband grinned, and my heart went a little mushy. "Nah. We're just talking. Too specific would be listing the places where I left them."

Well, that was easy: the bed, the kitchen counter, the porch railing, and every doorknob in the house. But I kept the list a mental one. Though reciting them would be temporarily entertaining for me, it wouldn't be in the best interest of our marriage.

"Six weeks," I said.

Rafe, who was usually very good at picking up my non sequiturs, looked at me with a classic deer-in-the-headlights expression. "Um . . ."

"We're going on our honeymoon over the holidays, in about six weeks."

"Your math is excellent."

"Thank you." I nodded modestly. "But if we're leaving in six weeks, we should have some idea of where we're going."

"Mrr."

We looked down at Eddie. "Sorry, pal," I said. "You're not going with us. You wouldn't like it. Honest."

"True fact." Rafe patted Eddie's head, sending a few dozen hairs flying in at least three dimensions. "Remember how you felt about that long drive downstate last Christmas? Imagine that, only multiplied a zillion times."

Eddie sank away from Rafe's touch and stalked off, tail held high.

I watched him go, then returned my attention to my beloved. "We're driving somewhere? When did we make that decision?"

"Didn't." Rafe shrugged. "Just wanted to see what he'd do."

"You do realize that he really can't understand what we're saying, right?"

"Sometimes. Other times, not so much."

Though I knew exactly what he meant, I wasn't sure I wanted to admit it out loud. "What about a ski trip?" I asked. "We both like to ski. We could go out west somewhere. Maybe a smaller resort in Idaho."

Rafe was shaking his head. "Remember a few years back I went to Colorado with Tank and Ash? The trip when I learned I'm prone to altitude sickness?"

"Right. Forgot about that." I'd heard stories, and none of them had been good.

"Now that I know I get altitude sickness," he

said, "I've read up some on treatments. But who knows if any of them would work on me? I don't want to risk feeling that rotten on our honeymoon. What about a cruise?"

This time it was me shaking my head. "Remember when the *Master and Commander* movie came out? Kristen and I went to see it, and I came this close to needing one of those special little bags they have on airplanes."

"You own a houseboat." Rafe frowned. "And we go out on Janay Lake all the time. I've never once seen you anything close to seasick."

"We don't go out on Lake Michigan. Or a great big ocean. I'm fine on little waves that go like this." I tipped my hand front to back. "It's when they start doing this, too, that my problems start." I started tilting my hand from side to side.

"Better put that down," Rafe said. "You're starting to look a little green."

"So a ski trip and a cruise are both out. Any other ideas?"

"Tour of major U.S. breweries?"

"Not unless we pair every brewery tour with two library tours."

"Moving on, then."

"How about a city?" I asked. "Somewhere neither one of us has ever been. We're small-town people. Going to a major metropolitan area could be fun."

"Yes, it could." Rafe nodded solemnly. "Progress, my little apple pie. We have made some serious progress."

I nodded back, just as solemnly, and wished that I felt the same way about finding Paige's killer.

*   *   *

First thing the following morning, I went to the library to pick up a half zillion totes of books. In addition to the books I'd be dropping off to those who qualified for homebound delivery, I had books for a small private elementary school, books for a new substance abuse disorder clinic, books for a tiny library space set up in a township hall, and books for a church senior center.

I used my own car for these types of deliveries. The bookmobile's gas mileage was about the same as a large powerboat—as in abysmal—and its size made getting in and out of the average residential driveway a bigger challenge than I needed at this point in my career.

Loading the books into my car trunk, back seat, and passenger's seat kept me warm and toasty, which was a good thing. A cold north wind was whipping down the back of my neck, and although technically the sun should be just then rising above the horizon, there was enough low, gray, and thick cloud cover to hide the fact that the sun was actually up.

"It's going to be one of those days," I said, buckling my seat belt. There was no answer from Eddie, which surprised me until I remembered that today's copilot was a box of books, not a fuzzy feline.

"You're losing it," I muttered, and started the car. It was bad enough that I talked to an uncaring cat. If I was going to start talking to an imaginary cat, I'd have to tell Rafe about my mental decline. That would be a fun conversation. I played it out in my head, didn't like where it went, and decided to think about something else.

I glanced up at the dark gray sky—the car headlights would be in use all day today, for sure—and decided not to think about the disheartening knowledge that the hours of technical sunlight were still getting shorter and would continue to get shorter for another month and a half. Life in the Up North was not all puppies, kittens, and rainbows, that was for sure.

On the plus side, the short days and long nights meant lots of time for cozy snuggling with my new husband in front of the fireplace, time for huddling under a blanket with a book and a cat, and time for slowing down and relaxing.

At least that was what happened in my fantasy of winter. Real winter meant time would now be spent shoveling the driveway and sidewalks, extra time spent driving on slippery roads, and—

"Quit," I said out loud. Once again, I was drifting down into melancholy and it needed to stop. At this point, I was pretty sure the descent was due to a lack of progress on finding Paige's killer, so clearly what I needed to do was take steps in that direction, the bigger the better. Yes, I'd eliminated Will as a suspect because of his shoulder injury, but I still had four suspects to work through.

Paige's last words were still circling inside my head. *Behind the books.* What had she meant? Was it something truly important, or was it only scattered words she'd strung together from a mind that was starting to shut down?

But I'd been there. I'd seen the tension in her face as she'd clutched at me. I was sure she'd been trying to say something important, something that she'd been trying so very hard to communicate, and I was not getting it.

At all.

My spirits sank another notch.

"You're not that smart," I muttered. "You're not even as smart as Eddie thinks you are, and that's a low bar." I pictured Eddie's expression if he'd been part of the conversation and smiled, because he would have been giving me the equivalent of the one-raised-eyebrow thing.

The simple act of smiling made me feel a bit better, which was good. I was pulling into my first stop of the day, the elementary school, and having a real smile on my face was much better than a fake smile.

Once I got into the groove of distributing books, it was easy to forget everything else and focus on the happy task in front of me. Matching books to people, being a librarian, was the best thing in the world, and being an outreach librarian was somehow even better. I wasn't sure exactly how it was better, I just knew that it was.

By late afternoon, the totes had been emptied and refilled with returned books, and my body ached with the pleasant fatigue of a job well done. It had been a good day, and the senior group in the church behind me had been so enthusiastic that I was trying to figure out how to add it to the bookmobile's regular schedule.

I started my car and pulled out of the church's parking lot, thinking about bookmobile routes. If I combined the Dooley-area stops with Honey Hollow Adult Foster Care, this church wouldn't be too far out of the way. I just wasn't sure if the road between here and Honey Hollow was bookmobile-suitable.

There was only one way to find out. I imagined

myself behind the wheel of the bookmobile and started driving.

By the time I approached Honey Hollow, I'd decided to add the church to the route. The half-dozen miles of roads were all asphalt and in reasonably good condition, so the only problem was to make the timing work. It would be best if I could get more hours added to each day, but I wasn't sure how to do that.

Of course, there were lots of things I wasn't sure about and I still managed to get things done. At least most of the time. And when I wasn't sure, how did I figure things out?

"By doing something," I said to myself. Something was always better than nothing. Even if it ended up being the wrong thing, at least there were things to be learned in the process.

"So do something," I murmured.

I glanced up at the gray sky. The little daylight the cloud cover had allowed through was already fading. It would be full dark in another half an hour. Gainsborough was only a hop, skip, and a jump away. Would I learn anything by driving in and looking at the Duvall house? Maybe, maybe not. But it wouldn't hurt to try, and I was practically there already.

Five minutes later, I was driving down the shallow bluff by the summer resort. Here, under the tall trees mostly empty of leaves, there was no light in the sky at all. One house, far down, had lights on inside, and I wondered if it was the Gauthier or the Callaway place.

Paige's whisper came back to me. *Behind the books.*

I drove around, parked in the long empty lot on the far side of the grassy oval, and got out of the car, slipping my phone into my coat pocket.

The Duvall house was for sale. Not that you could tell, because there wasn't a sign posted in the lawn, but there were probably rules against that in a place like this. Still, it was on the market. I'd seen it advertised in Bianca's window, and I had recognized it. What was the harm in walking up to it and taking a quick peek inside?

None, that's what. And there was always the chance I'd see books. Maybe they'd jog something loose in my memory, and maybe I'd finally understand the meaning behind Paige's last words.

I climbed up the wide wooden steps and onto the porch, where I saw one obvious sign that the house was for sale—a real estate agent's lockbox on the front door handle. The lace curtains on the inside of the door's window were pretty enough, but I found them annoying because they kept me from seeing anything inside. Moving right, I tried to peer inside the double-hung windows next to the door.

Lace curtains there, too, but they were looped back. I pulled out my cell phone, turned on the flashlight, and aimed it inside. An overstuffed sofa, end tables, lamps, and—movement.

The skin on the back of my neck went tight before my brain fully registered what I was seeing.

Someone was inside the house.

And with no car out front, and with no lights on, it couldn't be someone who had a right to be there.

I flicked off the flashlight and backed away, my heart pounding hard and my breaths coming fast, because who else could it be, other than the killer?

My feet found the porch steps. As I whirled to start a flat-out sprint to my car, I heard and felt the slam of a door. Running footsteps faded away into the woods and in seconds the night was as quiet as it had been when I'd arrived.

Huh.

I made no attempt to chase after whoever it was, but after I got into my car and made sure the doors were locked, I pulled out my phone.

"Hey, Ash. It's Minnie."

Chapter 15

A billion years later—or more accurately, four hours—Ash and Chelsea and Rafe and I were sitting at the Bridge Street Tap Room in Charlevoix. We had adult beverages in front of us and were waiting for our food to arrive. I was itching to hear what had happened at the Duvall house, but if I pestered Ash to tell me, he'd punish me by repeatedly changing the subject, so I was trying to be patient.

I must not have been doing a very good job, because Chelsea elbowed her fiancé and said, "Put the poor girl out of her misery, Wolverson. Tell her what you learned out there."

Ash grinned. "Not sure now is the time. It can wait."

Through gritted teeth I did my best to smile and felt my molars lose a layer of enamel. "Whenever you're ready," I said in an excruciatingly polite voice. "The last thing I want to do is rush you."

All three of the other people at the table knew

that was a total lie, and they all had different reactions. Rafe, who'd been studying the beer list to prepare for his next selection and so was oblivious to the entire conversation, turned the page of the menu. Ash's grin slid into a smirk. Chelsea glared at him.

"You can be such a pain," she said, then turned to face me. "I was standing over him when he wrote up the report. I'll tell you what happened." Ash gave her a startled look, which she ignored.

"When you called," she said, "you reported an intruder at the home owned by Paige Ferrer, murder victim. You were advised to leave the premises, which you did after a short conversation."

That was an interesting summary. I'd told Ash that the intruder was long gone, adding that since I'd been the last one to talk to Paige, it might be helpful if he could let me inside the house to look around. With no hesitation, he'd said absolutely not. When I'd tried to change his mind, he'd repeated his "No" response and hung up before I could say another word. I'd stayed a few minutes longer, keeping an eye out in case the intruder came back, and left before Ash arrived.

"Mr. Almost-a-Detective Wolverson," Chelsea said, "contacted Bianca Koyne and they both drove out to the house. Ash had been through it a couple of times during the murder investigation, and Bianca had been through it a couple of times before she listed it the other day. There was no sign of a break-in, neither one of them saw anything missing, and neither one saw anything that had been disturbed."

"That's . . . weird." I sat back, then thought of something. "Did he"—I nodded at Ash—"contact Paige's sons? The younger one lives out west, but the oldest lives downstate. Maybe it was one of them?" Not that I could come up with a good reason why Alec or Logan would have run off into the woods, but people could be funny creatures.

"That idea did occur to Mr. Wolverson." Chelsea slid her gaze at Ash, who was now reviewing the beer list with Rafe. "There have been instances in which family members have illegally tried to remove items of real or perceived value from homes that are on the market."

So maybe not a good reason, but one that was conceivable. "Was he able to figure it out?"

Chelsea nodded. "The younger son was in Vancouver on a business trip. Alec was at work all day, according to his boss, so it couldn't have been either one of them."

I leaned forward again. "Does Ash think it was the killer?"

"Could be." She shrugged. "But maybe not. The house is in an isolated area and it was just put on the market. Could have been someone who watches for upscale listings, who knows how to pick a lock and was looking for a quick sale of whatever he could grab."

Huh. I hadn't thought of that.

She tipped her head at her fiancé. "He's having a deputy cruise past a couple of times a night, if that makes you feel any better."

"It does." I nodded. "Thanks for letting me know."

"Of course, if we have any more deputies quit,

that'll stop in a heartbeat." She sighed. "It's hard to keep people these days, let alone find anyone who has the certifications we need. Does the library have that problem?"

We were just finishing our discussion about employee attraction and retention when Rafe and Ash finished their beer selection discussion and the existence of their significant others returned to their awareness.

"Minnie's all caught up," Chelsea said. "And now you're going to tell her a few things about the Ferrer murder investigation."

"I am?"

"Unless you want me to." She smiled, and I caught a slightly evil glint in her eye.

Ash looked from her to me and back. "Why do I get the feeling I missed something?"

"Every day, babe," Chelsea said, patting his shoulder.

Rafe shrugged. "Truth hurts, Wolverson."

"With friends like this, I should go out and get some new friends," Ash muttered.

"Investigation," Chelsea prompted.

Giving off a clear vibe of let's-get-this-over-with, Ash spoke quickly. "As is typical with murder investigations, we first looked into family members. The ex-husband, both sons, and Dr. Ferrer's siblings all have confirmed alibis."

I hadn't once thought about siblings. Good to know the sheriff's office had been on top of that. "Okay," I said. "Thanks for letting me know."

A waiter approached, laden with a tray of food. Our dinners were distributed, Chelsea asked for malt vinegar, Rafe and Ash ordered a second beer, and I was quiet, because I was mentally revising my suspect list.

Two had now been eliminated. Three to go.

It was a cold, wet, dark, and windy Saturday morning, the kind of day that anyone with any sense would avoid venturing out into. Julia, Eddie, and I were out in the bookmobile, but with this weather, I was pretty sure people were going to stay inside their cozy homes and binge-watch *The Last Kingdom* instead of coming out for books.

Then again, you never knew. Today might be the day a child picked up a copy of *Frindle* and fell permanently in love with reading, changing their life forever.

So with hope in my heart, I drove us to the first stop of the day and told Julia about my stop at the Duvall house and what I'd learned from Chelsea and Ash, with an emphasis on Chelsea.

"To summarize." Julia held up her index finger. "One. Verity Gauthier, chair of the Carlow Township Planning Commission, who has a virulent hatred of short-term rentals, and therefore, one has to believe, Paige Ferrer."

She held up her middle finger. "Two. Blaine Callaway, same reason as Ms. Gauthier." A third finger went up. "Alec Ferrer, who is in line for a significant financial windfall now that his mother is dead. Four is Norris Wilcox, known as Will because no one would stick with Norris if they had a choice, who along his wife Rila was suing Dr. Ferrer for a surgery that, if it had gone well, would have salvaged Rila's promising and financially lucrative career as a professional soccer player. That makes how many?"

I had no idea. I'd dropped into bed in the wee hours of the morning after a little too much fun for three of the four people that had gone out to dinner the previous night. I'd been designated driver, and my need to get home at a reasonable hour had not been taken as seriously as it should have been.

My brain and motor reflexes were fine, but I was short three hours of sleep, and that made me even less inclined to do mental math than usual, which was a trick because my normal inclination was close to zero. "Lost track," I said.

"Five." Julia waved her splayed hand around in front of her, then folded her thumb into her palm. "Will, however, suffered a shoulder injury that kept him from pulling a bow ever again, so we're down to four. And we've been told that Alec has a rock-solid alibi, so it's down to three." She tucked her pinky finger under her thumb."

"Mrr!"

"Exactly." Julia tapped her toes on the cat carrier. "Progress, my young friend. Three is a much more manageable number."

"MRR!"

She frowned and leaned down to peer in through the wire door. "What's with him?"

"Do you want the list?"

Julia gave the carrier a soft pat and sat up. "Some things are best left to the imagination, don't you think?"

"Listing all the things that might be wrong with Eddie would take time, and we need to start planning the scavenger hunt."

"Ooo, I love a good plan!" She clapped her hands,

then stopped, midclap. "Wait. We don't have to actually stick to the plan, do we?"

I eyed her. "What's the point of having a plan if you don't?"

"Oh, dear heart." She heaved a dramatic sigh. "Plans are mere suggestions. They're a basic framework. What makes a plan a success is its capacity for improvisation."

"Right," I said. "When you were acting, that's what a script was? A suggestion?"

She twirled an imaginary mustache. "Every good actor," she drawled, "knows when dialogue needs improving."

I doubted the playwrights felt the same way, and was about to say so, when I had an idea. "Speaking of improving, maybe we should do a smaller-version scavenger hunt first, just to work out details."

"You realize what that would be, yes?" Julia snickered. "Minnie's Mini Scavenger Hunt."

"Please don't ever say that again." I flicked on the blinker and took my foot off the accelerator, getting reading to turn into our first stop, a farmers' market. This particular market took place in a parking lot when weather cooperated and was held inside the Williams Township Historic Hall when it didn't. In spite of the inclement weather, there were a number of cars in the parking lot, so maybe we'd get more people in the bookmobile than I'd thought. "Do you think it's a good idea?" I asked. "Kind of a test version?"

"Sure," Julia said. "What are you thinking, just fewer locations where we show up? Or have it inside, maybe, with those adorable cardboard bookmobiles from ABOS? How about Lake View?"

"That might work." I liked the idea of involving residents of the nursing home. "But it could be a lot of work for staff. I know they're shorthanded and . . ." My voice trailed off, because I'd just had the best idea ever.

Julia's eyebrows went sky high. "That's your Grinch smile. I don't know what you just dreamed up, but it's going to be a tiny bit evil, so I love it already."

Evil? Not even close. But it would be a payback of sorts. I just needed to make one phone call.

"You want me to do what?" my beloved asked.

My cell phone was sitting on the bookmobile console, set to speaker. Julia was smirking, Eddie was snoring, and I could feel a Grinch-type smile on my face. I'd called Rafe after coming to a stop at the farmers' market, and I was sure he looked as bleary-eyed as he sounded.

Perfect.

"Talk to your English teachers," I said. "I'm sure they'll be thrilled to take part in a bookmobile scavenger hunt pilot project."

"You're using the bookmobile to go hunting?"

I crossed my eyes at the phone. "I told you about this a couple of weeks ago," I said patiently. "People find the bookmobile, not the other way around. Duffy Ulrich from the Friends proposed it and the library board has approved it. But it's something way different from what we normally do, so I want to run a smaller one first."

"Now?"

His voice sounded gravelly and tired. I squashed the teensy bit of sympathy that was inside me and said, laughing, "Well, not today, silly. It's Saturday. But within a week or two." Right after the holidays we'd have to start prepping for the full-fledged version, and I wanted to do the pilot version as soon as possible.

"So next week, or the week after," he said.

I crossed my eyes again. Yes, because that was what I'd just told him. "The only thing the English teachers will have to do," I said, "is rearrange their lesson plans for an hour. Two hours, maximum."

Rafe's groaning sigh indicated that the world's weight had been on his shoulders and had suddenly doubled. "You know not what you ask."

"It'll be like a partial snow day," I said. "A little time off from teaching. And the kids will have a good time."

The love of my life made another groany noise. "That's the problem," he muttered.

I told him we'd talk about it later, turned the phone off, and grinned at Julia. "Consider it done. I'll get him to schedule it for week after next, and we'll do the planning next week at the library. We'll do it on a non-bookmobile day, of course, so we won't have to cancel anything. And you won't need to come in for it."

Julia puffed up. "In what world," she said in what might have been an Eastern European accent but also might have been a completely made-up accent, "do you think I'd let you have this fun all for yourself?"

"Yep," I said, nodding. "That's what I do. I hog all the fun jobs. It's in my job description. But if you're good, just this once I'll let you have a little bit of that fun for yourself."

"Hooray!" Accent gone, Julia clapped her hands, then stopped, midclap. "Um, how good, exactly, do I have to be?"

I smiled, and there might have been a bit of Grinch inside that one, too. "You'll have to wait and see."

"Help me out here, Eddie," she said in a loud whisper, leaning down toward the cat carrier. "What will I have to do to be put in the 'Good' category?"

By this time we were parked and I was unbuckled and starting our opening routine. "Like he'd know. He hasn't landed on the Good side of the page since the day he was born."

"Aww, did you hear what your momma said about you?" Julia crooned. "What kind of mother would say such horrible things about her baby?"

"Anyone who had an Eddie," I muttered, but not very loudly, just in case he could understand more words than "no" and "treat"; I didn't want to hurt his fuzzy feelings.

We woke up the computers, unhitched the back chair, and tidied the few books that had bounced around on the way over, and sat down to wait.

And wait.

And wait.

Fifteen minutes after we arrived, the parking lot was half full of cars, but we hadn't had a single person climb aboard.

"Do we smell?" Julia took a series of small sniffs.

"It's the weather," I said dourly. "People are focused on chores and heading home as soon as they can."

"Tell you what." Julia slapped her hands on the computer desk and stood. "I'll go in and fetch people. All they need is a little encouragement and I know just how to—" Her cell phone rang. She slid it out of her pocket. "Hubby," she said, her tone shifting from playful to dead serious in a heartbeat. Her husband had never once, in all the time she'd been on the bookmobile, called her during work hours.

I jumped to my feet. "Um, I'll head over and see what I can do."

Julia nodded vaguely as she thumbed the Answer button. "Honey? What's wrong?"

I was outside and closing the door before I heard anything else. Whatever it was, Julia needed privacy. She'd tell me what I needed to know soon enough; about the last thing I wanted was to unintentionally eavesdrop on family drama.

Dodging the opaque puddles that pocked the gravel parking lot, I hurried through the biting wind, trotted up the hall's concrete stairs, and went inside.

I looked around with curiosity. In spite of the fact that we'd been stopping here once a month for almost a year, this was the first time I'd set foot inside the Williams Township Historic Hall. It hadn't functioned as a township hall in almost three decades, when the township government had built a smaller, easier-to-heat building that more easily accommodated things like computers, the Internet, and air-conditioning.

After ten or fifteen years of abandonment, a group of residents had banded together, formed a nonprofit, bought the building for next to nothing from the township, and spent years of sweat equity bringing it back to life as a community center.

According to the nonprofit's website, the building had originally been a Depression-era WPA project, made with federal dollars, local labor, and local materials. The fieldstone exterior, interior maple floor, and maple ceiling all had come from nearby fields and woodlots, and the current volunteers were doing an outstanding job keeping it polished and ready for future generations.

I moved through the lobby and into the main high-ceilinged hall. A broad stage at the far end was empty, but the room itself was occupied by maybe a dozen vendors, all of whom had portable tables teeming with goods. Most of the goods were produce or food-related items such as maple syrup, honey, and jam, but some tables had craft goods in red and green, reminding me that the holidays—and my totally unplanned honeymoon—were not that far off.

But I was here to drum up business for the bookmobile, not ponder my lack of planning ability or the lovingly restored building around me. I looked around, hoping to see someone—anyone—that I recognized, because I wasn't sure I had it in me to channel my inner Julia by jumping up on that empty stage and making some sort of entertaining announcement that would have people flocking to the bookmobile.

"Do you need help?"

I turned, but the fiftyish man wasn't talking to me, he was talking to a woman standing a few yards from me. She had sharply styled salt-and-pepper hair and was wearing a long down coat in a deep brown, sleek black boots, and a cream-colored beret. She also had two lovely wooden canes, one in each hand, and was trying to manage two cloth bags bulging with purchases.

"Does it look like I need help?" she snapped.

I inched closer. The voice sounded familiar, but I couldn't place her.

"Yes," he said. "It does, Verity. It's not a character flaw, you know."

Verity Gauthier. Gainsborough resident, hater of short-term rentals, and chair of the Carlow Township Planning Commission. When I'd seen her at the meeting the other night, she'd been sitting ramrod straight, chin up, looking as if she could take on the world. To see her hobbling across the floor in obvious pain was unexpected—and sad.

"When's your operation scheduled?" the man asked.

"First week of December." She reluctantly handed her bags to him. "That's assuming my surgical team can agree on what to do with these hips. 'Never seen such rapid deterioration,' they say. All those degrees and no one knows what's what. The ninnies want me to use those hideous forearm crutches, or a walker." She scoffed. "My papa's canes worked just fine for him, and they'll work for me."

"Well," the man said, "sometimes it takes a while to get the right diagnosis. And you do have good days, right?"

"Don't patronize me, young man. I knew you when you were still in diapers and I remember how you screamed like a hyena when a spider dropped into your lap at the church picnic."

"I was four years old," he said, laughing. "And that spider was huge."

"Well, I suppose it was." She nodded as they walked off. "And I do thank you for taking care of my leaves this fall. Not sure what I would have done. Maybe next year I can get back to raking."

I watched her hobble across the room. With pain like she was obviously in, there was no way she could have run out of the Duvall house and across the lawn less than twenty-four hours ago. But what if yesterday had been one of her good days, and today was a bad one because of her efforts last night?

Verity was still on the three-count suspect list.

Chapter 16

Late the next morning, I was sitting in my favorite booth at the Round Table, a steaming cup of coffee in front of me, my favorite husband next to me, and Sophia Aguilar across from me. Breakfast had been ordered and would be arriving soon, and almost all was right with the world. The sun was shining, the roads were dry, and yesterday's scary phone call from Julia's husband had turned out to be an easily solved problem.

The mild panic on his end had been because he couldn't remember what time the two of them were scheduled for dinner at her sister's house and he wanted to make sure he had time to drive to Petoskey. "To pick up some fancy spice from Toski Sands," she'd said. "Apparently it'll be perfect for the dry rub my sister is making."

I'd breathed a sigh of relief, as I'd anticipated everything from a heart attack to a burning house. "At least it wasn't a real emergency."

"We'll see about that when I get home," she'd growled, then put on a bright smile and moved forward to help the people I'd towed over from the historic hall.

All in all, it had been a successful day or two. Ash had helped me cross a suspect off my list, I'd overtly manipulated Rafe into offering up the middle school English classes for a pilot scavenger hunt, and I'd signed up three people from the farmers' market for library cards.

Sunday, however, might not end up as big a success. At my casual suggestion that Sophia think about joining the Friends of the Library, she'd instantly started making excuses about being too busy and too tired.

"Too Tuesday," Rafe said, nodding.

Sophia and I gave him puzzled looks. "What are you talking about?" I asked.

"Best excuse for not doing something on a Tuesday night is that it's too Tuesday." He shrugged. "No one can argue with that, right?"

The two adults at the table exchanged a glance. "Anyway," Sophia said, "I appreciate the idea, but my mom was in a library Friends group when I was a kid, and it always seemed to me like that group did a lot of talking and not much doing. That's how I feel about most of my days. I don't want to keep doing it at night."

"We have a new president," I said, "and she's super enthusiastic. Lots of good ideas."

Sophia scrunched her face. "So a good chance of a lot of work for the handful of people who are willing to step up, is what you're saying."

What I was thinking was that it was time to move

to another subject. "Well, if you ever change your mind about the Friends, let me know and I'll connect you with Duffy Ulrich, the president."

"Duly noted," Sophia said.

Footfalls came our way. "Breakfast for three," Sabrina announced, and three fully occupied plates landed on our table. My order of cinnamon French toast and sausage had been dictated to me; same with Rafe's full breakfast of eggs, bacon, and hash browns. Though Sophia had been allowed to order off the menu, Sabrina's pursed mouth indicated that this privilege wouldn't last long.

We picked up forks, and a few bites later I looked across at Sophia. "You said you're doing a lot of talking and not much else. Is that how the job goes?"

Sophia swallowed, then took a sip of water. "I shouldn't have said that. It's just . . . some weeks are harder than others. Sometimes you feel like you're making a difference, other times not so much."

"Know what you mean," Rafe said. "Middle school administration is more reading contracts and signing invoices than helping kids."

"Exactly." Sophia nodded, her blond curls bobbing along a fraction of a second afterward. "If I'm going to stay in this field, I need to find a way to remember that all parts of the job are important, even the boring stuff."

"When you figure it out, let me know." Rafe toasted her with his mug.

"The most boring part of my job," I said, "is tracking the magazine subscriptions to make sure nothing expires."

Sophia squeezed half a bottle of sriracha sauce over her eggs. "Most boring thing has to be populating the data on the court docket. One of these days it'll show up automatically through the state software, but they're still shifting court systems to full electronic filing, and smaller systems are at the bottom of the heap."

"This is data that's available to the public?" I was trying to remember what she'd said the other day.

"Sure. The software is a little, um, opaque to the uninitiated, but if you spend some time using it, and especially if you learn the case codes, you can parse out a fair amount of information about cases without too much trouble." She stopped. "I've told you some of this already, haven't I? Sorry for repeating myself."

"If you did, I've forgotten the details, so pretend I don't know anything."

She nodded. "In a nutshell, most court records are public documents. It's a matter of knowing how to get at the data, is all."

Huh.

Right then and there, I decided that the laundry I'd planned to do that day could wait. I needed to learn more about what court data I could access.

Rafe and I had walked to the Round Table mostly because it would be embarrassing to be caught driving to a restaurant that was a short walk from our house, so we also had to walk home.

Hand in swinging hand, we decided that since the sun was still shining, we should take advantage of that rare November fact and spend as much time as possible in it. Which meant some sort of physical activity, because sun or not, it was still barely forty degrees, and we hadn't brought along the thick blankets, wool socks, fleece hats, and coffee-filled thermoses we'd need to stay warm while sitting on a bench.

Rafe was whistling as we walked, and I tried to guess the tune. Not an easy task, because song identification was not my thing, and his whistling expertise was on par with my song identifying skills.

"'Stairway to Heaven'?" I asked. "No, wait. 'If I Had a Million Dollars.'"

"Nope, and nope."

"'Shake It Off'? 'Pinball Wizard'? 'Supercalifragilisticexpialidocious'?"

After a short pause, he asked, with suspicion thick in his voice, "You're just naming random songs, aren't you?"

I nodded happily. "And given enough time, I'll get the right one."

"Not sure I want to spend the rest of my life waiting for that. It was 'Surfin' USA.'"

"My next guess."

He laughed, and contentment spread through me from head to toes. I made my husband laugh. I made him happy. Maybe I didn't know how to fry an egg without burning something, and maybe I wasn't sure what I was going to do about finding Paige's killer other than poking around the district court's website, but right that second, life was good.

Rafe swung our hands forward and back. "Speaking of guessing."

"A hundred and twenty-eight," I said promptly.

"Nice try, but no. Do you want to guess where I'm thinking about for our holiday honeymoon?"

"Disney World."

"Not even close."

"Okay." I thought for half a second. "Disneyland, then. Going with the original. Nice. Always worth doing."

"Last time I checked you said any Disney-ward expedition would have to include your brother. Family time is nice, but that's not how I want to spend my honeymoon."

"Reasonable." And he was right about my brother. Matt was an Imagineer, and if we included him on a Disney trip, we'd get into all sorts of places that we wouldn't otherwise. "Okay then," I said. "Legoland it is."

Rafe snorted. "How old are you? Ten?"

"Fine." My nose went up into the air. "I've made three suggestions and you've made none. Let's hear your ideas, my friend. Wait, what's that I hear?" I cupped my free hand against my ear. "Crickets? No, less than crickets. I'm hearing a total of zero possibilities from the male side of this team."

"Hang on," he said. "I'm just . . . thinking."

"Really. Let's go back to your earlier question, when you asked, what was it? 'What I'm thinking about for our holiday honeymoon.' And now that I'm actually asking what you're thinking, you have nothing."

"Yeah. And?"

I stabbed him in the arm with a mittened index finger. "And that means you weren't thinking anything. That you were depending on me to come up with ideas. That you were abdicating responsibility for all of this."

"Happy wife, happy life," he said.

"What, you think me having to do all the thinking, decision making, and planning for this trip is going to make me happy?"

"I was hoping."

Stabbing at his arm again, I said, "Nice try, bucko, but no such luck."

After we'd walked in companiable silence for half a block, he said, "I do have one idea. Your aunt planned our wedding for us. The honeymoon is an extension of the wedding, so Frances should have had this all figured out for us months ago."

I felt a slow smile spread over my face. "Young man, I like the way you think."

After we got home, I fired off a text message to Aunt Frances that was guaranteed to have her pick up her phone and call me back.

I stared at my unchanging screen for a full minute. "Nothing. Not even a series of dots that disappeared."

Rafe, who was by now settling onto the couch and picking up the TV remote, said, "There are lots of people who aren't glued to their phones. Most, even. Especially those above the age of, you know, us."

"Sure, but . . ." I made a mean face at the screen, willing a response and getting nothing. "I texted that her role as our wedding planner wasn't done, and that she needed to get on the stick and finish the job."

"Uh-huh."

I could tell that his attention was not on the other person in the room, and was almost completely on the pregame commentary for the day's football matchups. Why anyone would want to watch people talk for hours about something that hadn't happened yet I did not know, but my husband was living proof that people would and did.

Then again, with him occupied for hours to come, I wouldn't have to be entertainment director and was therefore free to do whatever I wanted.

I hunted down my personal laptop—in the study, of all places, poised and ready for bill paying—and took it into the kitchen. To get started properly, I brewed a pot of coffee, took a mug to Rafe, and poured a nice big one for myself.

When I turned around, Eddie was on the island, sitting next to the computer as if he belonged there and peering at the keyboard.

"Get down!"

My cat ignored me.

"Hey!" I put my mug on the counter and clapped loudly, the cue that he absolutely knew meant he was doing something wrong. "Get! Down!"

Eddie looked up, gave me the stink eye, and jumped all the way down to the adjacent stool, leaving behind a few floating cat hairs.

"Do you do that on command?" I asked. "The cat hair thing? Because it sure seems like you have the power to shed when and where you feel like it."

My furry friend settled into the cat statue pose, wrapped his tail around his feet, and said nothing.

Such a surprise.

My coffee and I sat down, and I pulled the laptop close, getting ready to learn more about Tonedagana County's District Court in general, and the lawsuit between Will and Rila Wilcox and Dr. Paige Ferrer in particular.

A couple of bleary-eyed hours later, I felt as if I'd

stepped through the looking glass and into an alternate world, one with a different language, different titles, different customs, and a vastly different way of doing things.

Arraignments, pretrial, sentencing. Filing fees, civil fees, small claims fees, landlord and tenant fees. Traffic violations ranging from speeding to failure to signal to improper lane use, whatever that was. Judges, including a chief judge, court administrators, community corrections managers. Court decorum and expectations for juror candidates and empaneled jurors.

Then there were the acronyms, many of which didn't mean anything to me even when I could figure out what the letters stood for.

DSC for District Court System. SCAO for State Court Administrative Office. MCL for Michigan Compiled Law. MCR for Michigan Court Rules. JIS for Judicial Information Systems, JSR for Jury Statistics Report, MCAP for Michigan Court Application Portal, EDMS for Electronic Documents Management Systems, and CMS for Case Management Systems.

If the person who'd first invented acronyms had been in the room with me, I would have given them an Eddie-strength death glare.

After way too much time spent staring at the screen, I flipped my laptop shut. Though I'd found the court docket and the Wilcox name on one of the cases, there was no information attached, and the case was noted as Pending.

"Along with five zillion other pending cases," I said, rubbing my eyes.

"Five zillion is a lot."

I looked at Rafe through eyes still a bit blurry. "Didn't know I'd married a mathematical genius."

"I'm full of surprises," he said. "And so are the Lions. Take me away from the pain, my pumpkin spice. Let's go do something."

Thanks to a football team that was having a bad day, I was back to being the family entertainment director. Nice. "How about a brisk run along the waterfront?"

He leaned his elbows on the kitchen island. "Try a real idea."

So much for my tactic to offer only dumb suggestions in hopes that he'd step up and assume the entertainment director role. I tapped my laptop, thinking. "Weelll," I said slowly, "there is one thing . . ."

Fifteen minutes later, we were on the road out of Chilson. I'd texted Bianca, asked if Rafe and I could walk through the Duvall house, and gotten an enthusiastic thumbs-up, the code to the lockbox, and a comment that we'd be the first potential buyers to take a tour. Rafe was behind the wheel of his truck; I was riding shotgun and parceling out the snacks and drinks we'd picked up at the convenience store on the edge of town.

"Lunch of champions," Rafe said, digging into the bag of seasoned tortilla chips sitting on his side of the console.

I looked at the white cheddar popcorn in my hand. "Tonight we'll eat healthy."

"We will?" Rafe frowned.

"Yes," I said firmly. "I want us to live to a ripe old age. Eating like we're still in college won't help that, so yes, tonight we will eat something that's good for us." I had no idea what that might be, but there was plenty of time to figure it out.

Just after we finished round two of snacks—Oreo cookies for Rafe, caramel M&Ms for me—we trundled down the Gainsborough bluff, around the park oval, and to the forest-edged parking area.

The cold air was still, and there wasn't a soul in sight. The noise of the truck doors shutting felt almost obscene. I took Rafe's hand and held it tight all the way across the park and up onto the steps of the Duvall house, and only let go when I needed both of my hands to enter the lockbox's code and take out the house key.

"What are we looking for?" Rafe asked as the front door squeaked open.

I felt around on the wall for a light switch and flicked it on, illuminating the scene I'd viewed through the lace-curtained window two days ago. Ash had told us the house wasn't being considered a crime scene, so there was no reason not to be there, but I still felt as if we were doing something a little bit . . . wrong.

"Not sure," I said, looking around at the overstuffed furniture and wood end tables, and I wondered what it had been like living here when the house was new. There wouldn't have been any trees outside to speak of, because everything had been logged off back then. Our trees were all second growth, or maybe even third.

"Earth to Minnie." Rafe snapped his fingers in front of my face.

"Stop that," I said automatically. "And I'm not

sure I'm looking for anything. It's more that spending time in a place where Paige lived might help me connect some dots. Or . . . something."

Rafe didn't make fun of my vagueness, proving once again how correct I'd been in my choice of husband. "Okay, but if this was also a short-term rental, she probably didn't leave much here in the way of personal possessions."

"Yeah." I started wandering around the room. "It is kind of hotel-ish, isn't it?" Everything was very nice, but at a foundational level, not at all personal. Even the WELCOME TO THE LAKE sign gave off the distinct sense of impersonality.

"It's all about the same age," Rafe said.

"Hmm?" I'd drifted to a set of bookshelves that had been cleverly built into the triangular area below the stairs, taller on the right and shorter on the left. The shelves held mostly books, but also driftwood, pinecones, and a glass bowl full of Petoskey stones. The books were a mix of fiction and nonfiction, serious and not, adult, juvenile, and children's, many by Michigan authors or set in Michigan. I'd just started thumbing through a copy of *Vintage Views of the Mackinac Straits Region*, a book we had at home, when Rafe said, "Everything in here is the same age. Rugs, furniture, lamps, everything. That's why this feels like a hotel."

I looked around. He was right. "Makes sense, though. The family she bought it from probably either took everything or took all the good stuff." I hefted a copy of *Let's Hike in Northwest Michigan*. "This has only been in print a couple of years."

A memory burst into focus. Eddie in our dining

room, squirming behind our books, knocking them onto the floor.

Behind the books.

I moved closer to the shelf and looked into the gap I'd left after pulling the book out. Nothing looked out of the ordinary. I turned my head sideways and peered over the top of each shelf, but didn't see anything. I even started reaching behind the books. Still nothing out of the ordinary, unless you counted a lack of dust as unusual.

So maybe Paige's last words hadn't meant anything. Maybe she hadn't been trying to tell me something, and as I knelt on the floor to check behind the books on the bottom shelf, I wondered why it made me sad.

"You know," I said, sitting back on my heels after a fruitless search, "maybe we should plan our final words now. Just so we're prepared."

"Sure," said the love of my life. "I'll add it to my list."

As far as I knew, Rafe had never created a to-do list in his life. But I gave him points for playing along with me. I turned to look up at him, thinking once again how lucky I was, overbalanced, and fell to the floor with a *thump*.

"If you'd warned me ahead of time," Rafe said, "I would have had video of that."

"Sorry to disappoint." I lay there for a quiet moment, then started to push myself up, but stopped abruptly.

"You're okay, right?"

"Fine," I said. "It's just . . . there's something under the couch."

Rafe got on the floor beside me and turned on his cell phone's flashlight. "It's bright green. And not very big. Maybe the size of a utility knife." He reached out. "Got it . . . and . . . huh."

I frowned at the green object in his hand, which looked kind of like a utility knife, but kind of not. "Do you know what it is?"

"Not a clue," he said. "You?"

I did not. But I knew how to find out.

Chapter 17

First thing the next morning, I dropped the object, now in a rumpled paper lunch bag Rafe had found in the back seat of his truck, onto the desk of Detective Hal Inwood. After taking a photo, using available resources—otherwise known as the Internet—we'd discovered that what we'd found was a fletching tool, used to make and repair arrows.

He sighed, put down his coffee mug, and gave the bag a long baleful look. Only then did he gaze up at me. "Good morning, Ms. Niswander. What can I do for you so early in the day?"

I took that as an invitation to sit, so I did. "We found this at the Duvall house. You know, the Gainsborough house owned by Paige Ferrer that her sons have already put up for sale? Yesterday afternoon, Rafe and I decided to go through the house. The Realtor gave us the lockbox code, and we found this." I nodded at the bag, which Hal hadn't touched.

He rubbed his chin. "The real estate agent is Bianca Koyne, I believe."

"Um." Rats. Was I going to get Bianca in trouble? But I didn't see how. We'd done nothing wrong, and she sure hadn't done anything wrong. She was just trying to sell a house. "That's right."

The detective rubbed his chin with one hand and picked up a pen with the other, poising it above a yellow legal pad.

"Go on," he said.

I watched the tip of his pen, but it didn't make a single mark on the page, not even to write down a name and date. It would have been so much easier to talk to Ash, but Chelsea had told me he was at the shooting range all morning, helping the undersheriff work with the newest group of deputies.

"This was under the couch." I slid to the front edge of my seat, leaned forward, opened the bag, and let the tool tumble to the desktop.

Hal studied it. "That's a fletching remover. Takes the feathers off arrows."

I smiled stiffly, trying not to be annoyed that he'd identified it so fast. "Correct. And it must have been left behind by whoever was in the house on Friday night."

"Must have?" Hal leaned back in his chair. "What makes you say that?"

So many reasons. "Paige was using the Duvall house as a short-term rental. Cleanliness is key for rentals. And it's an unlikely object to have in a rental at all. Plus, you can see that this has seen a lot of use. See the scratches? Nothing else in that house was more than a year or two old. This looks way older than that."

He slowly reached for his pen and paper. I tried to keep deep satisfaction from showing on my face, failed, and didn't care.

"Plus," I went on, "what Paige was trying to say, about being behind books, maybe it was something important to the killer, too. Maybe he—or she—was trying to find it. Maybe that's why he—or she—was in the house in the first place."

The detective glanced up. "There are a lot of maybes in there."

I wasn't sure that three qualified as a lot, but whatever. "Do you want to hear my original list of suspects, who I've eliminated, and why?"

His expression said absolutely not, but what he said was "Might as well. I don't have any appointments until nine."

"Love the enthusiasm," I said. "Here's who I had at first. Feel free to nod if you suspected them, too. To make things easier for both of us, I'm going to go alphabetically, by first name."

"Easier," he murmured. "What an interesting viewpoint."

Ignoring him, I got started.

"Alec Ferrer, because he and his brother stand in line to inherit a significant amount of money. I hear he's been cleared due to having a boss give him an alibi, so he's off the list."

Hal squinted at me. "And who, exactly, told you that?"

"Does that really matter? Moving on, we have Blaine Callaway, a year-round resident at Gains-borough. He hates short-term rentals, and it stands to reason that he hated Paige, too. He's a bow hunter. Last summer he bought an expensive bow. He told the store owner that he was going to hunt with it this fall."

I was watching his pen carefully, but it wasn't moving. Seriously? I firmed my convictions and continued.

"Next is Rila Wilcox," I said. "She was Rila Shutleff before she got married, an up-and-coming pro soccer player, when a knee injury took her out of the game. Paige operated a couple of times, but Rila never healed enough to get back to playing. Rila and her husband are suing Paige for malpractice. Rila is still a suspect."

As I'd talked about Rila, the pen had made some small movements. This pleased me, but when I sat up straight, I could see that he was drawing squiggly circles with the pen, trying to get it to write.

"Next," I said loudly, "is Verity Gauthier, another year-round Gainsborough resident, and another person who despises short-term rentals. But she has something wrong with her hips, and she can only walk with the help of two canes, so she can't be the person I saw running away from the house Friday night."

"And she's seventy-two years old," Hal Inwood said.

"Meaning what?" I asked, my ire rising. "Are you saying older women can't be athletic? Because Donna Beene, one of our library clerks, is a year older than Verity, and Donna regularly runs marathons. Bet she could run circles around you and half the deputies in this office."

Hal sighed. "Anything else?"

"It's possible that whoever was in the house on

Friday isn't the killer, so I shouldn't eliminate Verity just yet."

"Heaven forbid."

"Lastly," I said, putting some steel into my voice, "is Will Wilcox, Norris on his birth certificate. He was a suspect for the same reason as Rila, getting revenge on Paige for a bad surgery."

Hal shook his head. "Not a valid motive. If they were suing Dr. Ferrer, it would be to their benefit to have her alive and making more money for them to get in a lawsuit."

"The suit will continue, even with Paige dead. They'll be suing the estate, is all. And malpractice insurance would cover the payout as the suit was started before Paige's death." At least I was pretty sure that was the case, given the tiny bit of Internet research I'd done that morning.

"Hmm." The detective tossed his pen into a wastebasket and pulled another one out of a "World's Greatest Boss" coffee mug, something that had surely been given to him as a joke.

"Anyway," I said, "Will Wilcox used to do archery in a big way but seriously injured his shoulder. He had to drop out of competition permanently, so he couldn't have killed Paige." Although, now that I was thinking it through, Olympic-level archery and recreational archery were two vastly different levels of the sport. Maybe he could still pull a bow enough to—

Hal tapped his paper with the pen. "Mr. Callaway is working to establish a Gainsborough homeowners' association, whose primary purpose would be to restrict short-term rentals."

I frowned. "Since he's doing that, he wouldn't have killed Paige, is that what you're saying?"

"Not necessarily. Typically in cases like that, an activity that is ongoing would be grandfathered in and allowed to continue."

I glanced at the mug, then back at Hal. "If you ask me, that just increases his motive."

"If I ever want to ask you, I have your number. Now," he said, standing, "I have to prepare for my nine o'clock. Thank you for coming in."

"So you're looking into Callaway?" I stood slowly. "And Rila Wilcox?"

"All avenues of investigation are being explored," he said mechanically, and I found myself on the outside of his office, staring at his closed door.

When I'd walked into the sheriff's office, I'd planned to talk to Ash, drop off the tool, then head up to the library to get a head start on the week's work.

Now my morning plan was out of whack. A one-sided talk with Hal Inwood was not anything close to the same as a discussion with Ash. If I wanted to make sure someone in the sheriff's office paid attention to the significance of the fletching tool, I needed to do more.

I walked down the hallway and opened the door into the lobby. Through the glass I could see Chelsea on the phone. I caught her eye and she waved, but she also gave off the distinct air of being deep in a conversation that was going to take a while.

Outside on the sidewalk, I stood, hands in my coat pockets, looking up at the sky. Mostly clouds, because it was November, but there were a few teensy bits of blue sky up there. I feasted my eyes upon them, willing them to grow, and considered what to do next.

But there was only one realistic option available to me.

Instead of turning right and walking to the library, I turned left. Ten minutes later, I was in my car and headed to the shooting range.

A year or three earlier, soon after I'd started driving the bookmobile, I'd taken self-defense classes, one of which included lessons on shooting firearms and firearm safety.

I'd spent a fair amount of time at the shooting range and had been surprised to learn that not only did I enjoy target shooting, but I wasn't half bad. But it was an expensive hobby, so once the classes were over I hadn't returned to the range.

There was a county-owned shooting range at an old gravel pit north of Chilson where local law enforcement practiced outdoor shooting. The indoor range was owned by a private sportsman's club and was used by club members, law enforcement, and anyone else willing to pay for time.

I pulled into the gravel parking lot. Five of the six parked vehicles were from the sheriff's office: three SUVs and two patrol cars. I was pretty sure the SUVs were the newer vehicles and the cars were the older ones, but it could have been the other way around. Ash and Chelsea had talked about the shift in vehicle types way more than once, but those kinds of details didn't stick in my brain, and asking for clarification at this late date would earn me looks of incredulity if not outright concern for my mental capacity.

The Northern Sportsman's Club was a no-frills, single-story, flat-roofed, concrete block building. The only thing that kept it from being one hundred percent utilitarian was the bright yellow sign that hung next to the front door that had an image of a handgun and the words CAN YOU MAKE IT TO THE BACK DOOR IN .00023 SECONDS? I CAN.

I went inside, walking through the large empty room that the club used for meeting space and banquets. At the back of the room was a metal door. On the door was a sign that had been flipped from RANGE NOT IN USE to RANGE IN USE—KNOCK!

Since I didn't want to get accidentally hit by a stray bullet, I knocked, waited, and eventually the door opened.

"The range is full up—Oh. It's you." A frowning Ash glanced behind me, saw nothing but empty room, and turned his attention back to me. "What are you doing here?"

"Can you talk for a minute?"

He studied my face, clearly trying to come up with a reason to say no, then sighed. "Hang on," he said, and for a second time in the space of an hour, a door was shut in my face.

I waited patiently, not taking it personally, because I knew he was securing range safety. The range itself was not close to anything I'd ever seen on television. There was no long line of booths with fancy pulley systems and targets. Instead, there was an open area to stand and shoot against a solid wall of clay, where targets were pinned. Protocol was to shoot, and then every shooter secured their gun and walked as a group to the wall to check their targets. Low-tech, but functional.

"Okay," Ash said, shutting the door behind him. "I have five minutes. "What's up?"

When Ash said he had five minutes, he meant five minutes and not a second longer, so I talked fast and concisely. I finished with "And I know Hal's not going to be happy that I talked to you after talking to him, but I think this could be really important."

Ash nodded, smiling a little. "Not the first time Hal won't be pleased with you."

"Went past the finger and toe count on that a long time ago. Anyway, I just want to make sure you knew about this. You have my fingerprints on file, right?"

He nodded again. "I'll look into it. Talk to you later." He opened the range door and I could see past him where a cluster of uniformed officers were standing together, comparing targets. Beyond them, just before the door closed, I caught a glimpse of someone else, a female not in uniform.

That was unusual but not unheard of. It had happened to me, once or twice when I'd been taking my classes. You took range time when you could get it, and law enforcement was typically happy to share their range time with members of the public. "Helps build relationships," Sheriff Richardson had told me once, which made a lot of sense.

It was now time to get to the library or be late, so I hurried out and discovered that in the few minutes I'd been inside the club, the weather had turned from not bad at all to blustery with a spattering of massive raindrops.

Putting my head down, I hurried across the parking lot, dodging the puddles that were already starting to form. I was almost to my car when I stopped.

And turned around.

Five of the six cars in the lot were sheriff's vehicles. The sixth was a slightly battered SUV with a bumper sticker: "Chilson X-C."

Rila Wilcox was at the shooting range.

Chapter 18

My drive to the library was free of rain, snow, traffic, deer, and squirrels, which was a good thing because though I was trying valiantly to stay focused on the road, large parts of my mind were thinking about possible implications about what I'd seen at the shooting range.

Rila Wilcox had been there.

She was shooting a gun.

Practicing.

Trying to get better at shooting a gun.

What did it mean? Did it mean anything?

By the time I pulled into the library parking lot, I'd arrived at the conclusion that Rila's comfort level with firearms didn't necessarily relate to a familiarity with using a bow and arrow. After all, I knew how to shoot handguns, rifles, and shotguns, but I'd never drawn a bow in my life. Maybe Rila just liked shooting at targets. Or maybe she was doing her own version of self-defense.

There was no direct connection between range

practice and Paige's death, and Ash obviously knew about it, so why was I still turning it over in my head?

"Because," I said to myself, as I reached the library's back door. "Just . . . because."

"What's that?" Graydon, who'd come in just ahead of me and pushed it open for me to walk through, tilted his head. "Just because you're not an hour and half early, you think you're late?"

I smiled. "Something like that." Or not anything close to that. One of those.

"Did you have a good weekend?"

"Um." My morning had been so full that the events of Friday night, Saturday, and Sunday had been purged from my mind. It took me a moment to remember. Dinner with Chelsea and Ash. Farmers' market. Breakfast with Sophia. Duvall house. Fletching tool.

By the time I'd brought it all to the front of my brain we were in the break room, and my boss had started talking about the week ahead.

"I'm meeting with Russell and Barb McCade," he said. "What's your schedule? They'd like to see you."

"They're still in town?" The fifty-something Mc-Cades summered in Chilson and wintered in Arizona, "winter" being a loose term for them. It usually meant they disappeared the first time the thermometer dropped down anywhere close to forty degrees, and they didn't return north until the apple and cherry trees were blooming.

"Something to do with drying time." Graydon spooned coffee into the filter I'd handed him. "Does that make sense to you?"

It did. To hundreds of thousands, if not millions

of people, Russell was better known as the artist Cade. He painted comforting scenes of cottages, flowers, and garden gates, work that was panned by critics as complete schlock. His work appeared on posters, greeting cards, T-shirts, and hooked rugs for all I knew. "Appeals only to the common folk," he often said, quoting one of his harshest critics and toasting himself with a coffee mug that had one of his new fairy garden paintings. "My bank balance seems just fine with that."

I'd met Barb and Cade a while back when he'd suffered a stroke. With luck and lots of physical therapy, he'd recovered fully, and my friendship with the older couple had been cemented when I'd willingly played along with their game of using words that started with a given letter. The day I'd visited Cade in the hospital it had been the letter D, always a good option.

"Definitely," I said to Graydon. Cade wouldn't ship a painting until it was fully dried, and he also wouldn't let anyone else package them for shipping. It wasn't really a matter of trust, more that if something went wrong, he didn't want anyone else to be held responsible.

What their late departure date almost certainly meant was that Cade had promised a series of new paintings to someone and that he'd ignored Barb's reminders until the last possible minute.

"Speaking of last minutes," I said. This earned a surprised look from Graydon because he hadn't been in on my internal monologue. "Rather, to avoid last-minute problems with next year's book-mobile scavenger hunt, I talked Rafe into hosting a sort of pilot project over at the middle school."

"Sounds like a good idea," Graydon said. "But I'm not quite sure how closely a November event at a middle school will correlate with a public city-wide event."

When he said it like that, it did sound kind of dumb. "Have to start somewhere." I added double cream to my coffee, because it was turning out to be that kind of day. "And if nothing else, it'll be a new outreach opportunity."

"Opportunity for making an idiot out of yourself?" Josh came in. "I don't think you need more of those." At that point, Josh noticed our boss sitting at the far side of the break room's circular table, and though he might have colored slightly, he didn't blink an eye. "Morning."

Graydon nodded. "Good morning, Josh. Minnie here is going to do a middle school scavenger hunt with the bookmobile."

"Yeah? What did Rafe do to deserve that?"

Holly walked in. "Wait, the honeymoon is over before you even went anywhere? Must be a new record. Morning, everyone."

For what felt like the umpteenth time, I explained the concept of a bookmobile scavenger hunt pilot project. As she squinched up her face, I said, "I know, I know. It doesn't scale, but the point isn't to replicate what we're going to do in the summer; that wouldn't work here. The point is to run a proof of concept, to see if we can get kids interested in something that's scavenger hunt adjacent."

"Huh." Josh finished filling his vat of coffee, emptying the pot, and pulled out another filter to start pot number two. "How would that work in a school?"

I sketched out the idea of using miniature cardboard bookmobiles and using clues for the kids to find them. "We could put minis in the gym, the cafeteria, the principal's office, an unused classroom. Four or five should do it. The teachers can send the kids out in small groups."

"Or instead of models, you could hunt"—Holly snorted with laughter, put her hands over her mouth, and talked through her fingers—"librarians."

Josh rolled his eyes, but Graydon and I exchanged a thoughtful glance.

"You know," I said slowly, "that just might work."

Cade, Barb, Graydon, and I pulled up chairs to the table in the small upstairs conference room, which was a space I used so infrequently I tended to forget it was even there. Graydon's office was plenty big enough for meetings of two or three people, but it got crowded with four, so we'd landed here, directly across from the big scary boardroom.

It had the same stolid feel as the boardroom—darkly stained wood trim, coffered ceiling, and carpet of a serious color—but it was a corner room, and it had two outside walls replete with windows. Even on this dim November day, there was enough natural light that the overhead lights didn't truly need to be on. I'd still flicked on the switch, though, because the Craftsman-style light fixtures looked prettier that way.

"Finally meet your deadline, did you?" I asked.

Cade waggled his bushy eyebrows. "The game is on, I see," he said, then sighed heavily. "Deadline. Worst D word in the entire English language."

"His own darn fault," his wife said, using yet

another D word. Barb was a stocky woman whose formerly shoulder-length graying brown hair was now cut in a pixie that framed her face, showing off her cheekbones and highlighting her strong jaw.

Graydon looked from Barb to Cade to me and back around. "Should I ask?"

"You mean, *dare* you ask?" Barb asked.

Cade put a hand to his chest. "Woman, please. I'm exhausted. Spent. Empty of creative energy. I am not up to the game today. Please allow me this one day of recovery before launching me into another round."

She said something under her breath that sounded a lot like "One day, my aunt Fanny," but then smiled at Graydon and me. "Anyway. What we're here for today is a discussion of planned giving."

"That's right." Cade folded his hands on the tabletop, giving an excellent impression of a successful artist with a solid head for business. The artistic success was correct, but the business part was all Barb. She had more skill at making the most of connections and opportunities than I'd known could exist in a single person. They were an amazing team, and if they wanted to take over the world, they probably could.

I spent a quick moment imagining a world created by the McCades. Art on every wall in every shape, size, and color. Plenty of books. Public sculpture, just for fun. And not a single critic anywhere.

Barb nudged me with her elbow. "You're thinking something funny. Are you going to share?"

"Nope," I said. "A team of wild Eddies couldn't drag it out of me."

"As if there's any other kind of Eddie," Cade said. "How is the little rascal these days?"

"Stay on target," Barb said firmly.

"Me?" Her husband looked affronted. "You're the one palavering with Minnie over there."

Barb looked at him severely. "In case you didn't notice, we're doing D words today. Write down your fancy P word and save it for some other time."

He made a motion of writing it on the palm of his hand, tightened his hand into a fist, and tapped it against his chest. "Got it."

"If only you made the same sort of effort when I send you to the grocery store for one single thing."

"You wound me, my love. Deeply wound me. When was the last time I forgot an item? Other than yesterday, of course."

Barb held out her forefinger and tapped the oak table. "Two days ago when you forgot the sliced provolone." Tap. "Last Friday when you forgot the broccoli." Tap. "Three days before that, you brought back baking soda instead of baking powder." Tap. "And either one day, or maybe it was two days before that, I asked you to pick up redskin potatoes and you came home with red tortilla chips."

Graydon, who'd been watching the Barb and Cade Show with interest, asked me in a stage whisper, "Do you think that's all true, or is she making it up?"

"Fifty-fifty odds," I said, shrugging. "But even if she's making it up, it's probably close enough to reality that he's not going to call her on it."

"And now we're back to planned giving," Barb said. "We've talked to our attorney, and we're putting our lake house into a Lady Bird deed, with the library as the inheritor. That way when we're gone, the property doesn't go into probate, and the library will get to do what it wants with it, no fuss, no muss."

Graydon and I blinked. "That's incredibly generous," my boss said. "Thank you." I nodded, rubbing my eyes, which were suddenly watery.

Cade gave a crooked smile. "Not that we plan on dying for another thirty years. Things to do, places to go. All that. It'll probably turn out that both of you have moved to warmer pastures or retired when this comes to fruition, and this will come as a huge surprise to your successors. Ah, you think that's amusing, don't you, my dear Minnie?"

Though I thought it was hilarious, I could tell by Graydon's expression that he was seeing potential problems, and not the humor, showing once again the benefits of being an assistant library director and not the director.

Then a thought occurred to me. "Do you have a problem with short-term rentals on Five Mile Lake?"

Barb shook her head. "Almost all of the cottages on our stretch are generationally owned. Very few newcomers."

"It's an issue on other lakes," Cade said. "Janay Lake not so much, because that's been slowly going that way for decades. What's that place where that woman was killed. Elk Lake? No, Deer Lake, that's it."

I got a tingly feeling at the back of my neck. "Are you talking about Gainsborough?"

Cade nodded. "We've heard there's a resident,

can't remember his name, who's going around to all the other residents and telling them that if they start renting short-term he's going to sue them for everything from a repeated violation of the noise ordinance to breach of peace." He turned to his wife. "What was his name? Not a D word, sadly. Maybe B. Possibly a C."

"Blaine?" I asked.

"That's it!" Cade beamed. "Blaine Callaway. How did you know?"

I murmured something reasonably sane and shifted the discussion back to the change in their deed.

But on the inside, I was moving Callaway to the top of the suspect list.

That night Rafe and I met Aunt Frances and Otto for dinner. Many of Chilson's restaurants were closed on Monday and Tuesday nights this time of year, so our options were limited to the Round Table, Hoppe's Brewing, Fat Boys Pizza, or the Wood Shed, a bar that was almost as nice on the inside as it sounded.

It had taken a remarkably long round of texting to decide on a place and time. In the end Rafe pushed for Hoppe's, the rest of us went along, and it wasn't until Tony, our waiter for the evening, handed out the menus and started listing the beers on tap that I realized what was going on.

After our drinks were ordered, I looked at the love of my life accusingly. "You wanted to come here so you could try that new Shark Free Stout."

"Is that a problem?"

"No, but why didn't you just say so?"

He shrugged. "Not a big deal. Would have been okay to go somewhere else."

My aunt folded her hands on the table and looked across at us. "I begin to see why you two haven't made any decisions about your honeymoon."

"Yes, we have," I said.

"That's right." Rafe put his arm around my shoulders and gave me a smushing hug. "Me and my favorite wife have set a date all by ourselves."

"Just to clarify," my aunt said, "the statute of limitations has long since expired on my wedding planning services. Honeymoon planning is for your travel agent to work out."

I wriggled far enough away from Rafe to allow for ease of breathing. "Speaking of wedding planning, do you think you'll keep on doing that, as a business?"

"Haven't decided. Anya Bennethum contacted me the other day, asking about prices."

"Anya's engaged?" I'd met Anya and her twin brother Collier a couple of years ago. Good kids, both of them. "To Bax Tousely?"

My aunt nodded. "Just a couple of weeks ago. He's had some success with his video business and finally felt like he had something to offer her."

The deep love that was inherent in that sentiment made my eyes sting. I sent the young couple a wish of love and laughter and put my head against Rafe's shoulder. Then I sat up straight and grinned. "Wait until I tell you what happened today!"

I told them about the McCades, their Five Mile Lake property, and the deeding thing.

Otto, who'd been quiet, nodded approvingly.

"Lady Bird deeds are an excellent vehicle for handing down property. It's a pity that not all states allow them."

I wondered if Paige had used a Lady Bird for her property, and if that could have anything to do with her death. I didn't see how, but I put it in the back of my head to think about later. Sometimes ideas swirled around in my head, coalescing into a fully formed concept that popped me awake at three in the morning.

I'd been hoping that would happen with a honeymoon location, but it hadn't happened yet. Well, unless you counted the dream I'd had about spending our honeymoon at my parents' house in Dearborn and playing tourist, which I did not. Nothing against my hometown, but since my mom had worked at Greenfield Village since before I was born, I'd practically been raised there, a circumstance that to my mind automatically disqualified it as a honeymoon destination.

"So, ideas?" I asked.

The other three people at the table looked at me blankly, and I realized that my discussion had been internal. And silent. "Locations," I said quickly. "For our honeymoon. That's why we're here, right?"

"It was my impression," my loving aunt said dryly, "that we were here to enjoy the company of each other."

"Sure, but we could have done that on a Friday. This is kind of an emergency family meeting. I mean, Rafe's Christmas break starts in . . . um"—surreptitiously, I counted my fingers—"in six and a half weeks. If we want to go anywhere real, we need to decide fast."

"Real?" Otto asked curiously.

"A grown-up place," I said. "One that requires reservations and stuff."

"'And stuff'?" Aunt Frances echoed. "You mean planning, the thing you two should have done months ago?"

Rafe and I looked at each other and gave a mutual shrug.

"We've been busy," he said. "Besides, if nothing else works out, we have a fallback plan."

I peered at him. "We do?"

"Sure. We can drive to Chicago. There's bound to be things to do there over the holidays. Hey, thanks, bud," he said, accepting his beer from Tony, then studying it with great intensity.

I looked at the man I'd volunteered to spend the rest of my life with and tried to think of an appropriate response. Yes, he was right, there were surely things in Chicago to do, but we went there once or twice a year already. Honeymooning there would be just like another trip and . . .

. . . and three tables away from us, Will and Rila Wilcox were sitting at a high two-top table. Will was trying to hand Tony the waiter a small piece of paper; Tony kept shaking his head no and Will kept insisting. After some to-and-froing, Tony took the paper, shoved it in his pocket, and gave them a tight nod.

He tucked his serving tray underneath his arm and headed our way. I stood, catching his attention, and pulled him aside.

"What was that about?" I asked quietly, nodding sideways at the Wilcoxes. "Seemed like he was giving you a hard time."

Tony smiled. "No worries. He was trying to hand me a coupon that expired at the end of October. I said I'd check with management, but there's no way they'll honor it." He shrugged. "Some people don't think the rules apply to them, you know?"

I did. And I knew that Rila and her husband did not look like a happy couple. Their body language was louder than anything they could have been saying to each other. Her arms were crossed, her fingers tapping, and her attention firmly focused anywhere but on her husband. For Will's part, his mouth was a firm horizontal line, and he was gripping his menu hard enough to make the thick cardboard crumple.

"Malpractice is malpractice, even if she's dead," Will said, just loudly enough for me to hear. "The estate will pay what we're owed. We need to keep going. We need to finish this. And we need those records."

And I also knew that Will Wilcox was now tied for my number one suspect.

Chapter 19

Was it fair to Will Wilcox that I was comparing a small scam with a restaurant coupon to murder? Absolutely not. And I'd never ever mention to a single human soul that I'd put those two things together in my head.

"Hang on," I said. "You're not human, are you?"

Eddie, who'd been staring at me intently, shut one yellow eye, then opened it again.

"Okay, good. Just checking."

We were on the bookmobile, and I was strapping his carrier onto the floor of the passenger's seat. Julia hadn't shown up yet, so I was mulling over the events of the previous night.

I knew that seeing one small slice of a person's life and making all sorts of conclusions about their personality was ridiculous, if not downright irresponsible. After all, everyone had bad days, and who wanted to be judged by that kind of standard?

But I couldn't seem to stop thinking about it.

"It wasn't a bad-day sort of thing," I said to Eddie.

"Trying to get a discount when it was past its expiration date isn't something you do because your boss was mean to you. That kind of thing is more a personality trait."

Another thing from that episode that had given off the flavor of habit was Rila's behavior. Soon after the coupon caper, Will had gone to the restroom. The second he was out of sight, Rila had jumped up and rushed over to a nearby table, where Tony was taking an order. I couldn't hear what she was saying, but her body language spoke volumes.

"She was apologizing," I told Eddie. "Top-to-bottom and left-to-right apologizing."

Tony had smiled and even my minimalist lip-reading skills picked out what he'd said: "No worries."

Rila had breathed a huge sigh, thanked him, and slid back into her seat just as her husband returned to the table, and she didn't so much as glance at Tony.

I wondered how many years she'd spent cleaning up after Will. Then I wondered if he'd always been like that, or if his bullying behavior could be a recent phenomenon?

"Mrr," Eddie said sharply.

"Tend to agree with you, pal." I tugged on his carrier straps, making sure they were snug. "Though there are circumstances that can induce personality change. Tragedy. Physical trauma. Some medical conditions."

"Mrr!"

"Well, sure. All those have to be pretty rare. I mean, how many people do you know who have ever had a massive change in personality? None. And just for the record, I agree with you."

I also wasn't sure how Eddie could know anyone I didn't, but he did occasionally go out on the book-mobile without me, so it was possible.

"You agree with me?" Julia's voice was silky and warm. "What a lovely way to start the day." She trotted up the stairs, shut the door, and rubbed her gloved hands together. "Are we ready to rock and roll?"

We were, and in moments the bookmobile was on the road, headed out to the southeast part of the county, ending with Honey Hollow Adult Foster Care.

When we walked into Honey Hollow, it was Eddie, of course, who got the biggest smiles from the half-dozen residents who were already waiting for us in the dining room. Even Wanda, today in scrubs of dark blue pants and a light blue shirt decorated with smiling suns, barely looked at the humans who were lugging in not only the cat carrier but also totes of books and magazines.

"It's Eddie!" Wanda said, grinning from ear to ear. "Good to see you, young sir."

"Mrr!"

Everyone laughed. I kept my eye roll internal and set the carrier on a dining room chair. "Do you want him out?" I asked Wanda. "He's been pretty active today, so he might fall asleep on a lap."

She laughed. "Go right ahead. That would make someone's day."

"Okay, ready or not, here he comes." I opened the wire door, and Eddie, ham that he was, stood, then hesitated.

"Come on, Eddie," one woman cooed, rubbing her fingers together.

"Over here." A man patted his lap.

"Puss, puss, puss!" another woman called.

I lifted the back end of the carrier an encouraging amount. Eddie jumped onto the floor and began his tour of the room.

"Knows how to work a crowd, that one."

I turned. Alicia Gwaltny, the elderly woman who'd told me so much about Gainsborough, stood at my elbow. "To the manor born," I said, smiling wryly.

Eddie began to work his magic and Julia started to unpack the totes. I could see a pile of books on a table under the windows that was bound to be the returning books. I started to move that way, but Alicia snagged my sleeve.

"You're the one who found that doctor out there," she said in her raspy voice. "The one who died."

"That's right," I said. "We called 911, and they got her to the hospital, but the arrow had done too much damage."

Alicia nodded. "Nasty bit of business. Sorry for her. Sorry for you, too."

It was only then that I remembered what Alicia had told me weeks ago, that she used to clean houses at Gainsborough. Sometimes it was hard to believe how stupid I could be. "Did you ever take care of either one of the twin houses?"

She peered up at me. "Isn't a square inch of those houses I haven't cleaned a thousand times over. Why?"

"Um, it's . . ." I pulled her away from the others. "Dr. Ferrer said something to me before the ambulance got there."

Alicia's gaze, already focused, went even tighter. "Last words, you're saying. What was it?"

"She said, 'Behind the books,' but I have no idea if it meant anything or if she was in so much pain that it was just . . . words. Does it mean anything to you?"

Alicia smiled. "Course it does. Like I said, there isn't anything about those houses I don't know, or at least did up until twenty years ago. Could be something changed inside, but things don't change fast out there."

"What did she mean?"

"Suppose I can't guarantee that it really meant something, but what I know is this." Her voice, already low, had dropped low enough that I tipped my head close to hers.

"Under the main stairway," she said, "there's a set of bookcases. You've seen it? Good. There's a latch on the left side, at the back near the top. Toggle that little puppy and the shelves swing out, like a big door."

My mouth gaped open. "You mean . . ."

Alicia snorted. "Should see the look on your face. Yep, there's a hidden room back there. Story is they used it to store rum during Prohibition days, weed during the marijuana days. Tiny place," she said reflectively. "Spiders love it."

She talked more about the hazards of cleaning old houses. I tried to listen, but my brain was off and racing.

Paige had put something in the hidden room, something that would point to the identity of her killer. The killer had learned about it, had been trying to retrieve it on Friday night, and that was when the fletching tool had been left behind.

I needed to get back in the house.

"Don't go back into that house," Ash said.

I took my cell phone away from my ear, crossed my eyes at his tiny picture, and put the phone back against my head. "Why not?" I asked. "It's for sale, remember? Bianca said we could go back any time we wanted, as long as we checked with her first to make sure no one else was scheduled."

"Because," he said, and I heard the so-very-patient tone start to creep into his voice, "if a hidden room is still back there, and if there actually is something that Dr. Ferrer put in there, it should be examined by law enforcement. That way chain of custody is clear, which is vitally important if something is discovered that turns out to be pivotal in a murder trial."

"Sure, but—"

"But nothing."

His tone was now I've Had Enough of Minnie's Interference. I couldn't decide which one irritated me more and called it a tie. "What if—"

"Stay out of the house," he ordered. "In ten minutes, the undersheriff and I are heading downstate for a conference. I'll go out to Gainsborough when I get back. But if that snowstorm comes in like they're saying, I might stay another night."

To my mind, it was way too early for a snowstorm, but no matter how often I pleaded with the weather to check with me before planning a large event, it never did.

"There are two detectives at the sheriff's office," I said. "Hal could go."

"You really want Hal to investigate one of your hunches?"

Not particularly. I also didn't particularly like Ash calling my new and very solid information a hunch. "What if the guy who broke into the house comes back? What if he gets in, finds whatever it is, takes it, and destroys it? What if we can't ever convict the killer because he was able to destroy the evidence?"

I let my very good questions hang in the air, letting them speak for themselves.

"Friday night," Ash said, "you couldn't say if the intruder was male or female. Did you remember something?"

I blinked. "Oh. Um, no. At least I don't think so." Was I making a gender assumption, simply because most crimes were committed by men? Or had a quiet part of my brain retained a piece of information that it wasn't keen on sharing?

"Okay. Well, if anything surfaces in that weird head of yours, let me know. Otherwise I'll check out the house on Friday, Saturday at the latest.

"Nice to know you think my head is weird."

He laughed. "Everybody thinks so. I'm just the only one who has the courage to say it out loud."

The phone went quiet. I put it onto my car's console and looked over at Eddie. "He's wrong, you know. Lots of people have told me I'm weird. My mom. Dad. Brother. Sister-in-law. Nieces. Nephew. Every boss I've ever had. Every coworker. Aunt Frances. Kristen. Rafe. Most of the downtown

business owners and workers. The McCades. The
marina people. Half the sheriff's staff. Neighbors.
Most of the library patrons and all the bookmobile
people. If you include incredulous looks, every person I've ever spoken to for more than thirty seconds
in a row." I paused. "There. I think I got everyone."

"Mrr!"

"And you, obviously. Didn't think I needed to
say that out loud."

"Mrr."

"Glad we got that straightened out." I tapped my
mittened fingers on the steering wheel and thought
about what to do next, now that I'd been forbidden
to enter the house that I was sure held the biggest
clue to finding Paige's killer. Yes, I absolutely understood why Ash didn't want me in there, and it
made sense, but that didn't mean I had to like it.
Even a little.

"What do you think I should do?"

Now that I wanted his opinion, he was silent.

Which just figured, because at this point I would
have welcomed any suggestions whatsoever. If I
didn't do something, my sleep would become even
more plagued with dreams of being chased by books
that had been lurking in tiny rooms. Or behind
shelves. Or maybe behind couches, desks, trees, cars,
or shrubbery, because dreams were weird things and
rarely made any true sense, and truth was—

I tapped the steering wheel again. "Verity," I
said. The word itself meant truth, a true belief. She
was mostly off the suspect list because of her health
issues, but maybe there was something I could do
to eliminate her completely. Not a huge step, but it
would be something.

"But how do I do that?" I murmured, starting the car, and by the time I'd pulled into the garage and carried Eddie inside, I had a plan. Sort of.

"What do you think?" I asked Eddie as I opened the carrier door. He gave me a sour look and didn't move.

"If this is such a horrible idea, I'm all ears for better ones," I said. "What's that? None from the cat side of the room? Well, thank you so much for your help. Send me a bill for your time and I'll put it on the bottom of the pile."

Eddie rotated, showing me his back.

"Nice. Love you, too."

I hung my coat on the hooks Rafe had recently installed next to the back door, sat at the kitchen island, and opened my laptop, typing "Williams Township Historic Hall" into the search engine. The website popped up, and their Events calendar was front and center. I clicked on Saturday's farmers' market . . . and got nothing except the hours.

Undaunted, I went to Facebook. "Hah!" I pointed at the screen. "The farmers' market has a Facebook page, and look, that's the guy who was talking to Verity."

Eddie, still in his carrier, didn't care at all.

Whatever. I peered at the photo, and sure enough, it was tagged with the guy's name: Graham Barrett. One additional use of the search engine and I found Barrett Farms' address and phone number.

I pulled out my phone and called.

"Barrett Farms," a man said.

"Is this Graham Barrett?" I asked.

"That's me," he said, his tone now a bit cautious.

"I'm Minnie Hamil . . . Minnie Niswander, with

the bookmobile. We were at the farmers' market on Saturday."

"Sure. I remember. What can I do for you?" Now less cautious, but puzzled.

"Well, I saw you were talking to Verity Gauthier. She seems to be having health issues, and one of our outreach services is home delivery. I wasn't comfortable approaching her directly, but you seemed to know her. Do you think she'd be interested?"

"In getting books delivered straight to her front door? Hard saying. She likes doing for herself."

"From what I overheard, I definitely got that feeling." I laughed. "So maybe she doesn't really need home delivery? I heard you say she has good days."

"Well, her good days aren't that good. Haven't been since August. She still drives, but it takes a lot out of her. If that operation in December doesn't help, she'll be in real trouble."

We chatted a bit longer, and when I hung up, I looked at Eddie, who had exited the carrier and was now sitting on the floor next to me, waiting with an expectant look on his little kitty face.

"Verity's off the suspect list," I said.

He heaved a massive sigh that reeked of *I told you so* and stalked out of the room.

Cats.

Eddie kept up his attitude of irritation the entire evening, giving Rafe and me the cold shoulder during the process of cooking dinner, while we ate, throughout post-dinner cleanup, and continuing the surly attitude as we did a few household chores.

He demonstrated his emotion by following first me, then Rafe, then me around the house, plonking himself down ten feet away, and turning his back to us, his tail sticking straight out in an exclamation point of protest.

"You're missing the dot at the bottom," I said, which made him turn to give me the stinkiest stink eye in the history of the universe, then turn back around to study the fascinating wall.

"He's doing the same thing to me." Rafe stood in the doorway of our small study, where I was pretty sure he hadn't been playing video games but rather reconciling the credit card statement. That was usually my job, but we'd decided to trade off every month, just to make sure we both knew what we were paying for things. "What did I do?" Rafe asked.

I had no idea. "Guilt by association. That, or he's paying you back for something you did weeks ago."

"That doesn't seem fair. Hey, bud." He leaned down, reaching out for a pet, but Eddie oozed away from his hand, rematerializing a few feet away. "Okay," Rafe said, shrugging. "Be that way."

I didn't know if Eddie's mood was becoming contagious or if I was starting to suffer from too many nights of poor sleep, but as Rafe went back into the study, I decided I'd had enough of chores for the night. Would anyone but me notice that the living room hadn't been dusted for a couple of weeks? They would not. Which meant I could go back to being irritated with Ash for not rushing over to the Duvall house. And being irritated with Ash meant that I suddenly didn't trust anything he'd told me about the investigation. Which, admittedly, wasn't much, but there had to be something I could call into question, something I could double-check.

What had he said the other night after Chelsea had goaded him into it? That they'd looked into family members, and found that Paige's siblings, ex-husband, and sons all had alibis.

Interesting, that so many possible suspects were eliminated because of confirmed alibis. You'd think that at least one of them would have said, "Gee, well, I was at home, but it's not like anyone saw me or anything."

On the other hand, Paige had been killed during the day, when people were at work, so maybe it wasn't so surprising that alibis had been easy to establish.

Then again, lots of people worked remotely these days, and just because they were logged into their computer didn't mean they were actually at the computer.

Hmm.

Ash had mentioned alibis for Paige's siblings. Good for him, I supposed, but they hadn't popped up in anything I'd come across. And I'd found out myself that Paige's ex-husband and youngest son weren't even in Michigan at the time. Which left her oldest son, Alec. Chelsea had said that Alec's boss confirmed him being at work all day, but how solid was that, really?

I pulled out my phone and started texting.

Minnie to Chelsea: *Quick question. The other night you said Alec Ferrer's boss confirmed his alibi. Do you remember where he works?*

Chelsea (after a few moments): *Sure. In Kalamazoo.*

Minnie (after rolling her eyes): *Do you know the name of the place?*

Chelsea: *Should I ask why?*

Minnie: *Not really.*

Chelsea: *OK. He's a respiratory therapist at one of the hospitals. Can't remember which one. If it matters I can find out.*

Minnie: *Nope. All good. Thanks!*

And that was that. No way could a respiratory therapist be anything other than an onsite worker. Alec was in the clear and doubly off the suspect list.

"Looks like Ash was right," I said.

Eddie was sitting in the exact middle of the coffee table and paying a total of zero attention to me. That was what I thought at first anyway, until I saw one of his ears give a smidgen of a twitch.

Hah. Got him.

"Want to know what you were right about? Thought you might. It was about Alec, Paige's oldest son. Ash said that he, meaning Alec, was working that day and since he's a—"

In one long fluid ooze, Eddie jumped off the table. Two seconds later, I heard the ascending *thump-thump* of a sulking cat going up the stairs and making enough noise for a creature ten times his size, something only cats had the ability to do as I was pretty sure they had the ability to turn gravity on and off at will. Or maybe it was just Eddie. Because of my dad's allergies, I hadn't known cats as a child and Eddie was my first.

"Nice talking to you!" I called.

And as expected, his response was a very loud silence.

Chapter 20

I'd never been someone who remembered my dreams. Or maybe I'd never been someone who dreamed in the first place. When you didn't have any memory of nighttime scenes it was hard to know which one it actually was. But something had changed.

Since Paige's murder, my sleep had been increasingly plagued with books flying at me from all directions, along with the occasional arrow. I was always dressed in long skirts, white high-necked long-sleeved shirts, shiny black high-buttoned boots, and a wide-brimmed hat topped with a spray of flowers and a massive bow.

At first I'd been amused, but the dreams were getting creepier and creepier, and after an evening of enduring Eddie's standoffishness, the dreams that night were downright scary.

I woke up into a pitch-black bedroom, gasping, heart pounding hard. The flying books had invaded the bookmobile. Eddie had been trying to escape by clawing his way into the cabinet, howling his kitty lungs out. Julia had been on her knees, head down, arms up in front of her face, screaming, "Turn it off! Turn it off!" And I'd been standing there, frozen as a Popsicle in January, unable to do anything to help them. Unable to save them.

"Breathe," I whispered. "Breathe. It was just a dream. A silly old dream."

"Hmm?" Rafe rolled over and put his arm around my waist. "You 'kay?"

I patted around on the bed and found Eddie on top of the comforter, just below my knees. All must have been forgiven, because he started purring.

"Fine," I said softly. "Go back to sleep."

Soon I was surrounded by snores, one whistling set from Rafe, one snuffling set from my cat. Their sleepy presence calmed me, soothed me, and I fell into a dreamless sleep.

When my phone's alarm went off, I came awake in a single blink. Rafe was already up and in the shower. When I padded into the bathroom to brush my teeth and take my own turn in the shower, I called out, "It's Wednesday. Two days later than Monday."

Rafe turned off the water, opened the door, and took the towel I was holding out. "Good to get something right first thing in the morning, I always say."

I ignored him. "It was Monday night that we said we were going to make a final honeymoon decision within the week."

"Means we have until Sunday night. Lots of time."

"You do realize we could decide ahead of Sunday, right?"

"What, and set a precedent?" He shook his head, scattering water droplets from his hair into the air surrounding him, which included me. "Raising expectations like that seems like a bad idea."

Sometimes he could be a real pain. "What we need is more ideas. If we hear the right one, maybe we'll just know."

Rafe shrugged. "We could ask around."

"Around where?" I looked left and right. "Not sure Eddie is going to be any help."

"Leave it to me, my little scented soap. I'll have ten new ideas by breakfast."

"And if you don't, you're going to drop that new nickname permanently, aren't you?"

He grinned, which made my heart go a little mushy. "Time will tell, my little indigo bunting. Time will tell."

Indigo bunting? Why on earth had the name of a bird rarely seen in Chilson been in a part of Rafe's brain that he could extract it at six fifteen on a dark November morning?

I grinned back, because if a good marriage was based on the level of brain weirdness, we were rock solid.

When I went downstairs, clean and clothed, I sat at the kitchen island and pulled my already-filled coffee mug across the counter toward me, murmuring a thank-you to the best husband in the world.

The microwave dinged. Rafe served our oatmeal and came around to sit next to me. "Guess how many?" he asked.

"How many what?" I peered at my breakfast. "Raisins? Blueberries?"

He tapped my temple with his index finger. "Memory much? I said I'd have ten new honeymoon locations by breakfast, and I have eleven."

"Any good ones?"

"Oh, sure, now you add qualifiers." He pulled out his phone. "I texted the guys and asked, is all. Different people, I figured they'd have different ideas than we'd been thinking."

Although I'd never been sure exactly who participated in the group text labeled "The Guys," it wasn't a bad idea. "Hit me," I said.

"Niagara Falls."

"In January? Pass."

"Agreed. Barefoot windjammer cruise in the Caribbean. I know, seasick. Next was"—he scrolled his phone—"a trip to New York City."

"If we did that," I said, "we'd have to spend time with Trock."

"Moving on. Trip to the Seychelles?"

The idea was appealing, especially in the darkness of winter. "Maybe. But isn't that where Mitchell and Bianca are headed right after Christmas?"

"And moving on once again," Rafe said, scrolling. "We have Hawaii, Thailand, Venice, Athens, Paris, New Zealand, Bali, and that's it."

"I'd like to go to all of them. Someday."

"Places to go, things to do, sure. But a little narrowing down would be best for the honeymoon thing."

"You know," I said. "Where we go doesn't matter that much. We'll be on a trip together, and that's what counts."

"Yes, but no." Rafe aimed his spoon at his oatmeal. "What really matters is that we go some-where much cooler than Ash and Chelsea."

"That's what matters?" I asked.

"It's not a contest, but we have to win." Then, before I could roll my eyes, he said, "One thing about a lot of those suggestions is that they're in different countries. Is that what we want to do?"

"If it is, we'd better check to see if our passports are up to date. Although," I said, realizing something that I should have thought about months ago, since Canada was a day trip for us, and somewhere we went a couple of times a year, "I should get a new one anyway, now that I have a different last name."

Rafe leaned over and kissed my head. "I'll leave the whole thing up to my little palm tree."

At eight thirty sharp, the front doors of the Toned-agana County Building unlocked. I entered the hundred-plus-year-old building, walking around on the black, white, and sage green mosaic tile floor until I found the treasurer's office, which was where the county's website said I should go for passport applications.

A tall, slender fiftyish woman came to the glassed-in front counter. "Hi," she said, and pushed her wire-frame glasses up on her nose. "How can I help you this fine morning?"

I looked over my shoulder, at a window that was just barely showing daylight, even though the sun had technically been up for an hour. "Your defini-tion of 'fine' must be different than mine."

Her laugh was a delightful waterfall of sound,

and I found myself laughing along with her. "It's what I always say to people," she said. "Most don't pay any attention."

"Well, silly them. I'm here about passports."

"Are you getting new or renewing?"

"One renew, one renew with a new last name."

She nodded and slid two packets under the glass that separated us. "There are lots of pages there, but the directions are clear enough, if you go slow." She glanced at my left hand. "Did you just get married?"

"In September."

My new friend Wendy, at least that's what the name plate on the nearby desk said her name was, smiled. "Such a nice month to get married. Do you live here? Then maybe you saw a lovely wedding at that little private marina. They must have some connection to the library, because the bookmobile was there, too."

I laughed. "That was us!"

"Really?" Wendy's eyes were wide.

"Truly." I pulled out my phone, showed her some pictures, and introduced myself and Rafe.

"That sure explains why half the town was down there," she said, laughing again. "The bookmobile cat lady and the middle school principal. You two should have a song written about you."

"I'd be happy to have a honeymoon destination." I tapped the paperwork. "We're going somewhere over the holidays, we just don't know where."

"Oh, dear." Wendy's mouth pursed. "Right now, the wait to get a passport is going on two months."

My entire self deflated. Why hadn't I thought about this earlier? Why was I so stupid? Why hadn't I—

"Unless you don't mind driving," she said. "You can apply for an urgent passport, but you have to go to Chicago or Detroit."

I perked right back up. "Detroit it is. My parents live in Dearborn."

Wendy recommended taking a look at the timing requirements and added that we probably needed to make an appointment. "And don't forget to get passport photos ahead of time," she said. "There are a couple of places in Petoskey."

"Thanks so much," I said, meaning it. "You've been extremely helpful."

She smiled. "Happy to help Eddie's mom. Can't wait to tell my dad about this. He's at Lake View and a big fan."

I stopped, midturn, and started to ask her dad's name. Eddie and Julia and I had spent many a story hour at Lake View Medical Care Facility and knew many of the residents by name. The irrepressible Max Compton for one, but many others, as well. But someone else was approaching the window, and I'd already taken up a lot of Wendy's time, so I nodded and eased away.

But since I was in the county building, I might as well pop into Sophia's office and say good morning. Two floors and three hallways later, I dinged the bell sitting on the district court's countertop.

A bright and chipper twenty-something left her computer and came to the window. "Good morning! How can I help you?"

"Good morning. Is Sophia Aguilar available? I happened to be in the building, so I thought I'd stop by. I'm a friend of hers."

"A friend? Really?" The youngster leaned back,

looking over her shoulder. "Um, hang on, okay?" She hurried off and returned seconds later. "Sophia said if your name is Minnie, you can come on back."

I laughed. "Do I need to show photo ID?"

"No, I know who you are." She grinned. "You're the bookmobile cat librarian. Can't get more trustworthy than that."

Her offhand comment warmed my heart. "Thanks," I said, blushing a tiny bit as she opened the door and led me into the district court's inner sanctum. "I'll tell Eddie you think he's deserving of trust."

Giggling, she knocked on Sophia's doorway, right next to the ATTORNEY MAGISTRATE nameplate. "It's Minnie," she said, and left us alone in the large corner office, lit even on this gray day by the natural light that poured in from the tall windows.

Sophia pushed herself away from her computer and stood. "To what do I owe the pleasure? And do you want coffee?" Her index finger hovered over the Start button of a single-serving coffee maker.

"Yes, please, and passport applications."

"That makes me, what?" She pushed the button and the lovely dark liquid dribbled into a paper cup almost instantaneously. "Collateral damage?"

"Something like that," I said, sitting in the chair she indicated. "But I was also wondering about the Wilcox malpractice suit, if you've . . . Never mind. I can see by that deer-in-the-headlights look that you don't have anything new."

"I am so sorry, Minnie. I meant to talk to the judge about it, but I completely forgot."

Her expression was so full of abject apology that I had to laugh. "Don't worry about it. But"—I put on my best shark smile—"there is a way you can make it up to me."

My sharkish capacity was clearly lacking, because Sophia didn't look frightened in the least. "What's that?" she asked.

"The museum is looking for volunteers and I was wondering if you'd be interested." I knew this because they were always looking for volunteers.

"Museum?" Her nose wrinkled. "I don't do well with dust."

"Okay, what about that trail group, the one that's trying to get a nonmotorized trail from Chilson to Petoskey? They're a new group, and I bet they'd love to have an attorney in their midst."

"Pass," she said, shaking her head. "This job is enough lawyering for me. I don't want to work in my downtime, too."

"Got it. How about—"

Sophia's eyes went wide. "Gosh, look at the time! I need to get ready for court. Thanks for stopping by, Minnie. I'll look into that malpractice case as soon as I can."

And before I could blink, I was outside in the hallway, a paper cup of steaming coffee in my hand.

"Sounds like she doesn't want your help," Holly said.

We were in the library's break room, ten minutes before the library opened its doors, and if I hadn't been about to bite into one of Holly's amazing brownies, I would have winced at the truth of her comment. However, since I was sinking my teeth into a still-warm chunk of nutty chocolate just-shy-of-gooeyness, I focused on the task at hand until I'd swallowed. "You're probably right. But I was just trying to help."

Holly handed me a napkin. "Help comes in all shapes and sizes. And sometimes you can help the most by backing off."

I made a face into the napkin.

"Saw that," Holly said. "And don't stick your tongue out at me, it'll be covered in chocolate and I see that enough with my kids, I don't need it from you, too, and Sophia will be fine. From what you've said, she's smart, funny, and cute. She'll find her way, so stop worrying about her."

"I'm not worrying."

"You are such a bad liar." Holly sighed. "How did you get to be this old and still be so horrible at lying?"

Though I knew it was a rhetorical question, I also knew the answer—it was the way I was made. That, and a childhood in which I'd been caught out the one time I'd lied. I could still see the sadness on my mother's face when she'd checked the floor under my bed and found all the books I said I'd put back on my bookshelves, which was worse than any punishment I could have received. Only in the last few years had I started to wonder if she'd put on the expression intentionally. One of these days I might ask her. Or not. One of those.

Holly finished cutting the brownies and started washing the knife. "Anyway," she said over the noise of running water, "she's not from here, but she fits in. Like you. Just give her time and things will work out."

I used my napkin to wipe off the smears of chocolate that, even though I couldn't feel them, were sure to be on my face. "You sound like my aunt Frances."

"She's a wise woman, so thank you."

As Holly nodded, Josh came in. I escaped before I could get drawn into their perennial bickering and spent the rest of the morning at my computer, diving deep into employee vacation requests, grant applications, and lecture programming.

When lunchtime came, I stood, rubbed my face with my hands, and turned to look out the window.

"Eww," I said. The sky, which all morning had had that feeling of being gray with no purpose, had changed its mind and was now pouring down rain. Or mostly rain, because I was pretty sure there were bits of white mixed in.

I'd been looking forward to walking downtown for a turkey avocado wrap from Shomin's Deli and popping into Pam Fazio's fun Older Than Dirt retail store. I hadn't seen Pam in what felt like forever, and I could use a dose of her offbeat humor. Plus, I needed to start thinking about Christmas presents, and Pam's eccentric mix of old and new was always good for a gift or three.

But I wasn't about to soak myself with thirty-seven-degree rain, so all that would have to wait. I opened my bottom desk drawer and pulled out my emergency lunch—a can of chicken noodle soup.

Five minutes later, I was back at my deck, trying not to slurp as I opened the district court website. I looked for new information about the Wilcox case, but it looked just the same as before. Pending.

I took in a couple more spoonfuls of soup, then thought of something I should have thought about way earlier. Why was I restricting my court search to the Wilcoxes? Why hadn't I looked up all my suspects?

Growling at my own stupidity, I ran a search for Verity Gauthier. Nothing turned up for her name, or for anyone with the last name of Gauthier. Entering Alec Ferrer also resulted in a total of zero returns. There was a case involving a Ferrer, but the first name was Belinda. The case was an escheat, whatever that was. I looked it up, read a few paragraphs, and decided I would have to live my life without ever fully understanding the concept.

Then I typed in Blaine Callaway's name.

Chapter 21

Sleety rain slashed against the window while I read the decision in the circuit court case *David R. Poston and Ramona A. Poston, Plaintiffs v. Blaine Callaway and Vanessa Johnson Callaway, Defendants, and Driscoll Reagor and Maria Reagor, Third-party Defendants, and Oak Meadow Association, Defendant.*

It took me three readings—and numerous side trips to Google to look up legal terms—but by the time the last unspoonable bits of my soup had dried into a hard-to-wash-out film, I was pretty sure I'd gotten the gist of things, and it had me shaking my head all afternoon.

"For decades, the Postons and Reagors owned Lake Michigan summer places next door to each other, just outside of Chilson," I told Pam Fazio when I stopped by Older Than Dirt on my way home. "The Postons own a downstate landscaping company, and over the years they've made their backyard into a real showpiece. Outdoor kitchen, patio, pergola, pond with a waterfall, fancy plants, the whole nine yards."

Pam nodded, loosening her short shiny black hair from behind her ears. She absent-mindedly tucked it back into place. "What changed?"

"The Reagors sold their place to the Callaways seven years ago. And the Callaways said some of the Postons' landscaping was on their property."

"And that leads to a court case how, exactly?"

"Without a trial transcript, it's hard to know for sure what happened, but from what I could gather out of the decisions—and there ended up being three of them, one trial court and two appeals, which I didn't know you could even do—it sounded the Callaways put up a new fence right in the middle of some really expensive plants. The Postons called the police and wanted the Callaways cited for trespassing, but the Callaways said it was the Postons who were trespassing."

Pam laughed. "Bet that was a fun time."

"No doubt all the other neighbors came out to see the show. The sheriff's deputies told them it was a civil matter, and that's probably when everyone started calling their attorneys." I'd almost called Ash about it, to see if he'd been involved with the case, or if he remembered it, but decided the gory details didn't matter right now.

"The Callaways sound like a piece of work," Pam said. "How did the homeowners' association get dragged into the lawsuit? And the Reagors? They were long gone, right?"

I'd wondered the same things. "My guess is their bylaws include something that says the association board has to approve any large projects."

"The Reagors?"

"That had something to do with, um"—I squinted, trying to remember the term—"acquiescence. From what I could tell, they should have been more aware of their property line and defended their right to it."

"So who won?"

"Nobody except the attorneys. Irony, right? At the end of it all, the appeals court ordered a brand-new property line that split the contested property down the middle."

"What a huge waste of time and money," Pam said. "The Postons and the Callaways should have spent it on good coffee and talked things over like adults instead of calling in the lawyers."

I smiled. Pam took her caffeine seriously, something I deeply respected. When she'd moved north a few years ago, she'd vowed to have a cup of coffee outside every morning for the rest of her life. As far as I knew, she'd done just that, if you allowed her to consider her glassed-in front porch outside.

"Is there more to the story? No? All righty then." She grinned. "If you come into the back, I can show you the socks that came in today."

I left with three pairs for future gifts. One for my brother that said "Selective Hearing Specialist," one for my oldest niece that said "I'm complicated, thank you," and the third pair for my dad that said "I almost died, but it was just a cold."

The rain had stopped before I'd left the library, but the wind had picked up. I was wearing my in-between coat, not my winter coat because it wasn't even the middle of November for crying out loud, so I was shivering and miserable in a minor way.

Which made this a perfect time to stop at Fat

Boys. It was my turn to make dinner, and sub sandwiches were a perfectly fine meal as far as I was concerned.

I stepped inside and was surprised at the number of people milling about, and at the high noise level. Then I realized that the vast majority of them were of high school age, and that they all wore Chilson High School Cross-Country jackets.

"Pizza is up." Brendan, the evening manager, slid a stack of boxes across the counter.

Rila Wilcox grabbed the pile and brought it to the large back table, the kids trailing after her like she was the pied piper. "Eat up, you monsters," she said, laughing. "You earned it."

"To us!" one of the girls called out, raising her fist high. "For pounding Petoskey into the ground!"

A cheer rang out, the boxes were flung open, and Rila sat with her team to eat.

I walked home, thinking about Rila. There'd been good reasons to consider her a murder suspect. She and her husband had been suing Paige. And at the cross-country meet, when Bob Craw asked her where she was when Paige had been killed, she'd stammered an awkward reply and slid away from the conversation. And I'd seen her at the shooting range.

But now she was happily treating her team to pizza after a victory over a rival school.

"There's no way she killed Paige," I said, putting the plastic bag on the kitchen island. "There's no reason for it. Maybe the surgery was botched and maybe it wasn't. Either way she's moved on with her life. Besides, remember that way uncomfortable scene at Hoppe's, when she apologized to the waiter for her husband? She's a . . . a conciliator, not a provocateur." I was fairly sure those were both actual words, and if they were, that I'd absolutely used them correctly.

Eddie, who'd been sitting in the middle of the floor looking up at me, opened his mouth in a huge yawn.

"Please cover your mouth when you do that," I said. "The roof of your mouth is not your most attractive feature. All those weird ridges, for one thing. But that black spot is creepy."

Sighing, he wrapped his tail around his feet and continued to sit.

Whatever.

I took off my coat and hung it up, still thinking. What I hadn't told Pam, because I could tell she'd been getting bored with my lawsuit story, was what I'd found when I'd looked up the Callaway property on the county's website. It was now owned by Vanessa Johnson, whose mailing address was down in Grosse Pointe. Which led me to look up ownership of the Gainsborough properties. Blaine Callaway didn't own anything, but the Callaway Trust did.

"Not that I want to jump to conclusions," I said, taking off my damp shoes, "because that would be wrong, but it seems reasonable to assume that Blaine and Vanessa are now divorced, and that Blaine moved to the family property after the divorce. Something like that can really mess with you, and if years ago when that lawsuit stuff started, he was already the kind of person who was combative and antagonistic, having Paige run a short-term rental could have tipped him over the edge, and—"

"MRR!"

I winced at the decibel level of his complaint. "What's the matter now? I told you, we capped the well. There's no way Timmy could have fallen in."

This earned me a look of disdain followed by a sigh so heavy that I was surprised I couldn't feel his kibble-laden breath on my face from across the room.

"Anyway," I said, "Blaine is my top contender for Paige's killer. Look at the . . . well, maybe not evidence that would hold up in a court of law, but certainly points that make him a person of interest." At least to me. "He gets angry, and then he does something about it."

"Mrr!"

"What has he done, you ask? Excellent question." I glanced at the microwave clock. There were probably ten minutes before Rafe got home. More than enough time for me to run upstairs, change into fleecy comfort, and get back downstairs to plate our fancy dinners.

"One thing," I said as I climbed the stairs, puffing only a very tiny bit, "is that lawsuit over the property line. Yes, he was a defendant, but having that fence installed was what sent it into litigation in the first place. And he was the one who fired up the appeals process."

Though I suppose it could have been Vanessa who was the mastermind behind the whole thing; the court decision's narrative only mentioned Mr. Callaway.

"And Blaine did all those Facebook posts about the short-term rentals." I slipped out of office clothes and started pulling on loose leggings and a fleece hoodie of Rafe's so old that the Chilson Middle School lettering looked more like a graphic design than text. "I know, I know, Facebook posts are keyboard courage, not an indication of actual action. But Blaine, according to Barb and Cade, is basically threatening other residents with lawsuits if they go the short-term rental route."

An odd pattering sort of noise hit the carpet. My head emerged from the top of the sweatshirt. "What are you doing?"

"Mrr!"

"Don't know if you noticed, but I don't speak cat." Or at least I didn't speak Eddie. "What did you do? Because it sure sounded like you pushed . . ."

My foot had hit something that wasn't carpet. I looked down. It was a small, scattered pile of loose change that Rafe must have left on top of his dresser. I knew this because Eddie was sitting on the dresser's corner, looking exceedingly pleased with himself.

"Nice." I picked up the change and dropped it into the massive glass jug in the corner. "Blaine is top suspect for all those reasons. The only other one left is Will Wilcox," I said, "and it doesn't make sense. If Rila isn't wound up tight, looking for vengeance, what could he have for a motive?"

Eddie gave me a long look. Sighed. Looked away. And said nothing.

Thursday was an uneventful bookmobile day, which was good because thanks to Rafe's leadership, powers of persuasion, and promises of library swag for all participants, the mini scavenger hunt had been scheduled for Friday afternoon. A calm day on the road meant Julia and I spent a large chunk of the drive time talking through hunt plans.

Why I hadn't figured out any of these details as

soon as I'd known the mini event was going to happen, I had no idea. The only thing I really knew was that if I made it through Friday without looking like an idiot, I'd be more than pleased, I'd also be shocked and amazed.

Julia, naturally, hadn't expressed any concern about having to fly by the seat of our pants.

"It'll be like being back on Broadway," she'd said, rubbing her palms together gleefully, "only without the stress."

"How's that?" I'd asked. "Because personally, I'm feeling all sorts of stressors."

She'd twiddled her fingers. "You have butterflies. It'll pass. This will be like a play because something will go horrifically wrong, but the show must go on, so you'll jump in and save the day. Standing ovations and curtain calls will result."

I'd doubted that any middle school English class ever had given a standing ovation to anyone. I also wondered why it had to be me who saved the day, not someone else, but left that small detail alone in favor of getting back to the last-minute planning.

Friday morning passed in a blur of even more last-minute planning, and just after lunch, I drove the staff-laden bookmobile up to the middle school.

I parked where Rafe had just that morning told me to leave it ("Oh, right. Just park in the bus stop zone, next to the main entrance. It'll probably be fine.") and we all tumbled out, each of us carrying a box of previously stuffed swag bags.

Rafe, waiting at the front door, greeted everyone by name. "Good to see you, Graydon. Kelsey, how's the coffee? Donna, looking good. Morning, Shilah. Hunter, my man. Julia, always a pleasure."

We stood in the entry in a football-team-like huddle. Rafe looked around, scanning the faces, and said, "Okay, I have to ask. Who's left at the library?"

I blew out a breath. "Josh and Gareth."

"Talk about a skeleton crew." Rafe grinned. "Think the building will still be there when you get back?"

"It'll be fine," I said, projecting a confidence I didn't feel, and very intentionally did not look at my boss. Getting him to approve leaving the IT guy and the maintenance guy to staff the library had been the hardest part of the whole enterprise. "We'll only be gone a couple of hours. And it's mid-November, not exactly our busy time."

Though Rafe was typically oblivious to the cues I tried to send him, this time he picked up right away and moved on. "All right, people, here's the plan. There's seven of you, and seven English classes, which made the math easy, so thanks for that. Everyone is in their rooms, ready and waiting for their first clue. Soon as we get you into position, we'll let them loose."

"Um . . ." I glanced at the suddenly cautious faces of my coworkers. "Let them loose? What does that mean, exactly?"

Rafe gave a crooked smile. "Are you telling me you're scared about hordes of screaming preteens coming toward you at a dead run?"

"Yes," Graydon said simply.

My husband laughed. "Wise man. But I think we have that figured out." He led the way to the gym, and I outlined the plan to everybody one last time. The kids would be getting the clues and working out the destinations. When they had the destination, their teacher would lead them there, where a librarian would be waiting with the next clue. Final destination was the gym, where I'd be waiting with the swag bags of used books, library pencils, bookmarks, and pens.

Rafe had given me the destinations the day before, and Julia and I had written the clues, most of which involved children's book titles and their authors. We'd paired the principal's office destination with the clue of *Front Desk* by Kelly Yang and the school's kitchen with *Lasagna Means I Love You* by Kate O'Shaughnessy. The remaining clues pointed to the library, the swimming pool, the auditorium, the nurse's office, and of course the gym.

"It'll be fine," I said. "Ready, set, go, okay?"

All but one of the library staff fanned out, heading to their assigned destinations. The sole survivor was Graydon, who'd never before set foot in the building. He went with Rafe back to the principal's office, and I moved bags from boxes to the tables some kind soul had set up for us.

Soon I heard the chatter of excited middle schoolers, accompanied by a number of adult calls to "Slow down, kids! This isn't a race. No one's getting extra points for being first!"

I smiled. Of course it was a race. In my experience almost everything was, especially if boys were involved.

In less than half an hour, running footsteps pounded in my direction and a pile of youngsters poured through the doorway.

"We're first!"

"We're number one! We're number one!"

"Mrs. Ryan's class gets the prize!"

Laughing, I said, "Everyone gets a prize," and started handing out the bags.

"Um, Mrs. Niswander?" A square-faced girl with impossibly smooth skin looked up at me. "Where's the bookmobile cat?"

"Yeah," the boy behind her said. "Where's Eddie?"

He was home, of course. Probably curled up on the back of our expensive couch, squashing the cushions into an Eddie-shaped dent. "He couldn't make it," I said, pushing two bags across the table. "Nice job with the scavenger hunt. Congratulations on being first."

"But I thought he'd be here," the girl said. "The bookmobile is here. Why isn't the bookmobile cat here, too?"

"Um." My gaze darted around. Where were my fellow librarians? Especially ones who had female offspring? Or Rafe? "How about . . . this?" I whipped out my phone and opened it to a recent picture of Eddie.

"He looks mad," the boy said.

I looked at the screen and saw a close-up of his expression when he'd been denied treats after already getting more than he needed. "More disappointed than mad."

The girl crossed her arms. "Me, too. I thought I'd get to pet the bookmobile cat."

"Yeah." Her sidekick nodded. "We had expectations."

I did my best to hide my smile. "You had . . ."

Just then a tiny metaphorical light bulb went off in the back of my head as the word settled in.

Expectations.

* * *

"And that's what I've been missing," I said. "Expectations."

We were back at the library. Five librarians had returned to their normal duties, and Julia was helping me put the bookmobile back into order. After the scavenger hunt, the kids had come aboard on a class-by-class basis for a quick tour. Even still, the din had been tremendous, and they'd managed to pull all sorts of books that now needed to be reshelved.

Julia looked at me over the top of a stack of Goosebumps books. "You do realize that I have no idea what you're talking about, yes?"

"Oh?" I tried to do the one-eyebrow thing. "Because I was thinking really really loud about Paige's murder. That when I've been working through motives, I wasn't considering expectations. Well, outside of the inheritance expectations Paige's sons might have had."

"You're going to have to spell this out for me." Julia shelved R. L. Stine's books. "In small words, please. No more than two syllables."

"Blaine Callaway had expectations of what life in Gainsborough would be like," I said. "He didn't want it to be any different than it had been since the place was born. Same families up year after year, cottages handed down for generations. Paige using her place as a short-term rental changed that."

"But did it?" Julia asked. "Gainsborough has what, twenty cottages? Would who stays in one of them make that much of a difference?"

"Probably not. But if more and more people rented their places out, then yeah, it would absolutely change things."

She opened her mouth, then shut it. "Okay. What about Will Wilcox?"

"Will expected that his wife would become a professional soccer player. He probably expected a certain level of fame, and the kind of money librarians only read about in books."

"But he wouldn't have been the famous one," Julia pointed out. "Rila would. And it would be her money."

"Fame by association," I said confidently. "He couldn't get it any other way because of his shoulder injury. And unless there was a prenup, her money is his money."

"And we're back to the shoulder thing. How could he kill Paige if he couldn't pull a bow?"

Now that was an excellent question. "Maybe he lied. Maybe he never had an injury. Maybe . . ."

Julia looked over. "Uh-oh. She's got that look."

Though I wanted to say *What look?* I knew she was talking about the vague blank expression that I got when I was working through what might be a brilliant idea.

I glanced around the bookmobile. "And we're done, right? Right. Off you go. See you next week." I shooed her out the door, locked up, and hurried home.

My laptop was on the kitchen island, so I plopped down in front of it and pulled up the search engine. "National archery competition winners," I said out loud, typing, and added the year of a decade earlier.

Eddie materialized on the stool next to me, craning his neck around to look at the screen. "Mrr," he said.

"Yeah, I'm not sure why I didn't think of this

earlier, either," I murmured. "Sometimes I can't believe how . . . Ah, there we go." A long list of names popped up. I scrolled down a bit, and there was Norris Wilcox, in twenty-fourth place.

Huh.

I typed in the name of the same competition for other years, further back in the past, and moving to more recent dates. Will had never finished in the top ten. And there was only one time that he'd finished in the top twenty.

"Look at that," I said, nodding. "That last year he competed he came in fifty-second. Maybe he did have a shoulder thing going on, but you know what I think?"

"Mrr!"

"Exactly. He just wasn't good enough to compete at that level." Not national, and certainly not international. Going to the Olympics had been nothing but a pipe dream for him.

Had he grown up thinking he'd go to the Olympics? Had his personality been formed around that? And when he'd been forced to acknowledge that he would never make it, did he latch on to his wife's athletic prowess, make it a part of him? And when her knee injury smashed those dreams, too, had it twisted him up inside?

"Yes," I said, looking at that fifty-second placing and comparing it against the man I'd met in the convenience store, a man who'd exuded an air of I'm Smarter Than Everyone Else in the Room.

"Mrr."

"Glad you agree." I patted him on the head, sending a handful of Eddie hairs flying. "But that doesn't mean he killed Paige."

"Mrr!"

"Sure, it seems likely, but Blaine is still a strong possibility. What I really need is proof. And you know where that is? In the Duvall house, behind that bookcase." What was it Ash had said, other than the flat and unequivocal "Stay out of the house"? That he'd be home from his conference either tonight or tomorrow, depending on whether the snow came in.

Hmm.

I opened my weather app, entered a Grand Rapids zip code, and blinked. It was currently snowing down there, with an eight-inch storm total predicted. Which was weird, because the Chilson forecast was for a dusting.

My phone was in my pocket. I slipped it out and started texting.

Minnie: *Weather in GR looks nasty. You driving or staying?*

Ash (after a minute): *Driving. I'm playing passenger princess. We're north of Big Rapids already. Thought about getting some tickets to the Griffins game and staying another night, but they're out of town.*

Minnie (after remembering that the Griffins were a minor league hockey team and not the name of a band): *So . . . the Duvall house?*

Ash: *Tomorrow. After lunch. I can meet you out there.*

Minnie: *How about I go out there tonight and the deputy cruising past can do the chain-of-custody thing?*

Ash: *About that. We had another deputy quit day before yesterday. The sheriff had to pull road patrol in that part of the county.*

Minnie (her eyes wide): *No one's keeping an eye on the house?*

Ash (after a slight pause): *I'll meet you out there tomorrow.*

I stared at the words.

Tomorrow. He wouldn't go out there for more than twelve hours from now.

The entire time between the break-in and now, there'd been some police presence at the Duvall house. There'd been none for the past two days. What if Will—or maybe Blaine—had figured that out and was going to take advantage of it? What if tonight was the night? What if tonight was the night the evidence was stolen and destroyed? What if this was the one night I could go behind the books and find proof of the killer's identity?

"What do you think?" I asked.

"Mrr."

Unless Eddie had learned ventriloquism, he'd jumped off the stool and wandered over to the door. I turned around and saw that he'd pulled my winter scarf from its hook, and was sitting in the middle of it.

"How thoughtful." I got up and gently encouraged Eddie off to the side. "Cat hair on my scarf is exactly what I needed."

"Mrr!"

"You want me to put it on? Sure. Whatever makes you happy." I draped it around my neck, pulled on my coat, and texted Rafe that I was headed out to Gainsborough and would be home for dinner.

Then I grabbed my car keys and headed out, closing the back door on a howling "Mrr!"

Chapter 22

The digital clock in my car's dashboard, which had taken me only a week to update after the time change, was telling me it was almost five o'clock. I squinted, but the hour stayed the same. How had it gotten so late? Well, it didn't matter. A twenty-minute drive time to Gainsborough and twenty minutes back still gave me twenty minutes to find a way into the secret bookcase and be home by six, which was the time Rafe had said he'd be home with pizza in hand.

I smiled, remembering, because he'd whispered it into my ear as the troop of librarians was leaving the middle school. He'd also whispered details about what he'd like to do after the pizza was gone, and not all of them had to with what movie he wanted to watch.

"You'll have to hide your eyes," I said, then felt my face heat up because I was talking to a cat who wasn't there. Then I wasn't sure which was sillier:

talking to a cat at all, talking to a cat who was miles away, or getting embarrassed when there was no one to see how stupid I was being. It was along the lines of the question about whether a tree falling in the forest made noise if there was no one to hear it, only not quite.

I shook my head, trying to clear it of the nonsense. Though thinking nonsensical thoughts when I was anxious about my imminent future was a basic coping mechanism for me, it wasn't always the smartest thing.

"Figure it out," I muttered to myself. Break it down into steps. Take the big task at hand and outline it into smaller tasks, just like a school paper.

First thing was to get to Gainsborough, something that almost didn't need to be listed as a task, but things could happen. I could swerve for a deer and hit a tree. Or the car could break down. Or the gas gauge could be off and I could run out of gas. Or the weather could take a hard turn for the worse. It could start to snow, or far worse, my least-favorite weather could show up: freezing rain.

I glanced at my car's outside temperature reading. Well, that was interesting. Earlier that day it had been in the high thirties, and it was now sitting right at thirty-two.

The ground wasn't anywhere close to being frozen, so if it snowed just a little, it would melt on the above-freezing asphalt. But if it snowed a lot, like the inches they were getting downstate, the roads would turn into a slushy slippery mess that had a decided penchant for pulling cars into ditches.

Though I'd seen the forecast for tonight—hovering around freezing, twenty percent chance of mixed precipitation—I hadn't looked at the radar. Northwest lower Michigan was a region buffeted by multiple competing weather influencers: three Great Lakes, Canada, prevailing westerlies, and the occasional hurricane. All of which meant that what actually showed up on the weather radar didn't always match the forecast.

I looked over the steering wheel, peering into the headlight beams. Was that snow? I squinted, squinted some more, then sat back, nodding to myself. Bugs. It had to be bugs. Not that there should be bugs flying around after the hard freezes we'd had, but unprecedented times and all that.

A few minutes later, I was driving over the bluff and down into Gainsborough. My headlights brushed across a mix of bare maple tree branches and the dark green of cedar trees. It was now as good as full dark, and down at the south end of the cottages, dim lights from inside Verity Gauthier's house were just barely visible. If she was home, she'd pulled her drapes and hunkered down.

Not that I could blame her. Who wanted to be out on a junky November night, wind rising and—because I couldn't deny any longer what was smattering onto my windshield—snow coming down.

On the other hand, Blaine Callaway's house, up toward the north end, was fully dark. It was the start of the weekend, after all. Lots of people did fun things on Friday nights. Went out to dinner. Saw a movie. Hung out with friends.

I sat there, my car engine idling.

If Blaine was the killer, he would have had oodles of opportunities to remove any and all evidence from the twin Duvall house. So if Blaine was the killer, and if I went into the house, there was no risk to my personal health and safety. Well, minimal risk. There was always the chance of me tripping and falling over my own feet. It had happened before, and I was sure it would happen again.

I drove around to the far side of the open grassy area and backed under a huge cedar tree. With a little bit of fussing, I wedged in so far that the tree's green fronds were brushing the front windshield and hood, hiding my car completely. Nicely done, Minnie! I typed Bianca a quick message that I wanted to take another look inside the house and sent it off with a quiet *whoosh*.

"Behind the books," I said, and opened the car door.

The weather had flipped since I'd left Chilson. Precipitation, now unequivocally snow, was pelting down, and the wind gusted great cold breaths down my neck.

I pulled off my mittens, turned on my phone's flashlight app, and aimed it at the lockbox's keypad. More like tried to aim it, because my hands were shaking from the wind-and-cold combo. The light was dancing every which way but the way I wanted it to go.

Multiple muttered tries later, the box clicked open. I took out the key, unlocked the door, and slipped inside, shutting the door with a soft thud.

"So-oo-o c-c-old out th-there," I said to the house, tucking my hands under my armpits. The house didn't answer, which was just as well. Having a cat who answered me back was bad enough.

I slid my phone into my coat pocket and walked

around in small circles until the feeling in my hands warmed past blocks-of-ice status while I was trying to remember everything I could about the theoretical secret bookcase. What was it that Alicia Gwaltny had said? There was a latch. On the left side, at the top.

I waited until the pain of thawing tingled out of my fingers, then looked around for a light source. The sofa had a nearby end table with a lamp atop. After unzipping my coat and putting it on the couch, I turned the three-way switch to full bright and pulled the whole kit and caboodle near the bookcase.

It was still supercool, tucked under the stairs all cozy and tidy, with its shelves of so many different lengths, and as far as I could tell, no one had moved any of the books since Rafe and I had been there. The children's books were still on the bottom two shelves, left to right in order of age, and up higher, *Station Eleven* was still next to *A Cold Day in Paradise*.

But there was one big question. Had the shelving been renovated since the last time Alicia had cleaned the Duvall house? I gripped the edge of one shelf, wiggled it around, but couldn't budge it.

Hmm.

I tried moving the other shelves and found the same thing. All of them were permanently fixed in place. I scanned the room, eyeing the woodwork, and looked back at the shelves. White paint covered the doors, trim, and shelving. If my eye was any judge—and I considered myself an educated amateur after becoming full partner in owning an old house—it was original woodwork.

With the flats of my hands, I felt along the left side of the next-to-highest bookshelf, figuring that Alicia's definition of "top" might be very different than mine. I found nothing but wood, so I went to the next shelf up. Nothing on the side of the bookcase, nothing on the bottom of the shelf, nothing on the top, and—

A wide smile spread across my face. My fingers had found a latch, right where the back of the bookcase met up with its left side. A toggle, Alicia had said.

My home improvement experience had led me to understand that a toggle was a kind of on-off switch, not a latch, but my experience was limited. And maybe Alicia was remembering wrong, or maybe she didn't know what a toggle was, or maybe she'd been wrong about the whole thing and the latch I was trying to open didn't do anything.

Taking a deep breath that was more sigh than anything else, I felt around to see what I could feel. It was metal, and about the size of the latches that closed double-hung windows, but different. Not a half circle of metal. A short arm, that if I pushed hard enough, it would go—

Click.

My smile went wider and I almost said *Ta-da!* out loud. Instead, I grabbed the edge of a bookshelf and pulled firmly.

Nothing moved.

Well, to be absolutely correct, *I* moved.

A lot.

I'd pulled on the bookcase hard enough to dislodge a heavy object after months of inactivity, and as every action has an equal and opposite reaction,

I ended up stumbling backward, flailing my arms, thumping back against the end table, and crashing to the floor.

I spent a few winded seconds on the oval braided area rug, taking stock, establishing that I wasn't hurt, and happy that I was all by myself and that no one had witnessed my ungainly acrobatics.

"Nice," I muttered, then rolled to my side and gazed up at the bookcase, which was still in place and looking as if it hadn't moved since the Eisenhower administration.

I put my elbow on the floor and propped my head on my hand. Alicia hadn't cleaned this house in years. There'd been at least one new owner since then, maybe more. It was very possible that the hidden bookcase was long gone, renovated away, that this was all a wild-goose chase, and that Paige's last words hadn't held any deep meaning.

"Then again . . ." I said softly. Because down there on the floor, I'd caught sight of a second latch. One at the bottom left corner. Alicia's recollection of one latch in the middle suddenly made sense. Back then, there had been only one, but at some point, someone had replaced the one with two. For additional support? To spread the bookcase's weight? I had no idea, and someday I'd ask my engineer father or engineer brother, if I wanted to get a lecture on stress points and angles and other things that I hadn't thought about since I'd managed to pass my high school physics class.

I scrambled to my hands and knees, flipped the latch's arm, and stood. This time my deep breath was far more preparation than sigh. Then I gripped a shelf and pulled.

With a long *crr-eeeee-eak*, the bookcase swung open.

For a moment, I didn't—couldn't—breathe. There actually was a *behind the books*. Paige's final whispered words, Alicia's reminiscences: They had all been true.

But had it meant something? Had it meant anything?

After my heart rate dropped back to normal from "beating hard enough to freak out a cardiologist," I took another breath and reached out. The bookcase was heavy, and it hadn't opened far. I took a firm grip and pulled. Just past the halfway point, an inside light turned on, refrigerator-like, and I poked my head around to peer into the secret room.

I'd mentally prepared myself for a tight space of unfinished wood darkened with age and festooned with cobwebs that hung heavy with the dust of decades. The reality was not that. On the contrary, the contents got me thinking about a future home renovation.

Tucked under the stairway was the cutest little built-in home office imaginable. Tight space, yes, but the wood had been painted a warm buttery white. On the wall facing me was a bulletin board covered with photos, a calendar, and Post-it notes of various sizes. On my right, at the tall end of the stairway, was a built-in cabinet with bookshelves above, and on my left, at the bottom end of the stairway, was a desk that was just my size, maybe three feet wide, with a narrow set of drawers on its right side and a castered stool for a chair, a stool that looked like what you'd see in a doctor's office. It also had a laptop computer on its surface.

I nodded. It made sense. Paige used the house as a short-term rental, but not all the time. Sometimes she stayed here, too, and this was a part of the house off-limits to renters. She'd only owned it for a short time. It was possible her sons didn't even know about the secret room, and so didn't know to tell the detectives to look inside.

Putting it into words made the corners of my mouth turn up. A secret room. So. Very. Cool. My only complaint was the amount of light. The only illumination was coming from the living room, so it was more shadow than anything. I went out and dragged the end table closer, getting the lamp's light deeper into the room. Either Paige had installed some lighting too clever for me to figure out, or she'd done the same thing I was doing now when she sat down to work at the desk.

But . . . Alicia hadn't said anything about a desk or bookcase. I ran my fingers over the desktop, then turned and did the same to the shelving and cabinets. Plywood. Which hadn't been used widely until the late 1930s, and to my eye, the built-ins looked brand new. No scratches, no gouges.

Huh.

The stool's cushion gave a small fluffy *whoosh* as I sat down.

First things first. Paige had bought standard fare for the shelves out in the public living room. Beach reads, airport stuff. Carefully curated tomes that contained nothing in the least objectionable.

I scootered myself over to the books, turned my head sideways to read the titles, and started smiling.

Here, tucked away in the hidden room (in alphabetical order by last name), were many of the same tattered books that were on my own bookshelves, running the gamut from middle grade to adult.

Lloyd Alexander. L. Frank Baum. Judy Blume. Nancy Bond. Susan Cooper. Walter Farley. John D. Fitzgerald. Dick Francis. Bette Greene. Robert Heinlein. James Herriot. Carolyn Keene. Laurie R. King. Ursula Le Guin. Madeline L'Engle. Lois Lowry. Robin McKinley. L. M. Montgomery. Mary O'Hara. Dodie Smith. Elizabeth George Speare. D. E. Stevenson. Mary Stewart. Albert Payson Terhune. Angela Thirkell. Laura Ingalls Wilder.

Some of the authors were still popular, some were now out of favor for one reason or other, but that clearly hadn't mattered to Paige. She'd kept the books that had meant something to her, kept the books that had touched her, perhaps had formed her, helping her become the woman she'd been.

I ran a fingertip over the book spines, feeling grief for a woman I'd never met. I ached, wishing our paths had crossed years earlier, that we'd had the chance to become friends, because anyone who could dream up this amazing little space was someone I wanted in my life.

But I wasn't here to mourn; I was here to search for the reason Paige had tried so hard to tell me about the hidden room, because no matter how much you loved the books of your youth, I wasn't sure anyone's dying words would be their location. Even what's-his-name in *Citizen Kane* just said Rosebud, not where the sled had ended up.

I gazed at Paige's books one last time, then rolled back to the desk and flipped open the laptop.

Even though I crossed my fingers on both hands and repeated the single-word incantation of "Please, please, please," under my breath, the computer didn't boot up. I sighed, but the computer would undoubtedly be password protected anyway. Paige was a doctor. No way would anyone in the medical profession leave a laptop lying around that could be simply opened up to prying eyes like mine. It probably had two-factor authentication. Or three.

I stared at the screen and wondered if four-factor authentication was a thing. Probably was. Far as I knew, five-factor might be something used by people deeply concerned about cybersecurity.

"Stop it." I was wasting time, sitting here staring at a computer I couldn't access. Then again . . .

I opened the narrow drawers, got up and studied the bulletin board, knelt and peered up at the desk's underside, looked under the computer, looked behind the bulletin board, all the obvious places Josh had warned me over and over again were the dumbest places ever to put a computer password.

Nothing.

Clearly, Paige was not dumb, something I'd suspected all along what with the "Doctor" in front of her name, but it was nice to see that she was smart about other things, too.

Back on the comfy stool and feeling a teensy bit of what a real doctor might feel like when about to examine a patient, I rolled over to the cabinet, used its glass knobs to open both doors, and sucked in a quick breath as I stared at the contents.

Notebooks. Stacks and stacks of notebooks.

This absolutely had to be what Paige had been trying to communicate to me.

I gazed at the piles. At the bottom, closest to the toes of my boots, were composition notebooks in the classic speckled black-and-white covers. The next layer was spiral-bound notebooks in primary colors, the kind my parents had bought in college to take notes. Paige had stored lots and lots of those.

The next stratum up was high-quality spiral-bound notebooks: thicker covers in understated hues with the spiral in a warm gold color. Above those were cloth-bound notebooks in various shades, and the final series were leather, with marbled edges. I picked up one of the top volumes. **Dr. Paige Ferrer** was stamped into the cover in gold lettering.

It was an obvious progression. The notebooks on the bottom, the cheapest ones, were from college and medical school. Then came internship and residency, when she could afford to pay upward of two dollars for a notebook instead of fifty cents. After that came her first real job as a doctor and the accompanying funds, part of which she used to buy the super nice spiral notebooks. Then partnership and the engraved notebooks.

But what was in them? Were they full of class notes, then medical case notes? Or were they personal journals, with nothing doctorlike at all?

Whispering an apology to Paige for the intrusion on her privacy, I opened the book in my hand . . . and landed inside a vocabulary so strange it might have been a different language. Well, except for the date at the top, August 24 of this year. That part I got. The rest, not so much.

"Scott Opeta, male, 73, total knee arthroplasty. Meniscus deterioration beyond expectations; TKA proceeded. Follow up soon as possible regarding concerns for pneumonitis, pulmonary embolism, thrombosis, DVT, infection, heart attack, arrhythmia. Confirm that home health aide is aware of all concerns."

Right.

I flipped pages to an entry dated in January.

"Aurora Han, female, age 37, repaired complete rupture of the UCL. Dynamic transfer of adductor pollicis from its insertion on ulnar sesamoid to ulnar base of proximal phalanx. Given the patient's propensity for skiing moguls, concerns regarding wound care and inflammation. Many concerns."

Huh.

Gently returning that notebook, I pulled out a sage-green spiral-bound version and opened to a random page, dated almost thirty years ago.

"John Blint, 62, total hip arthroplasty, lateral approach, cement on the femoral stem, uncemented attachment on the socket. Hip incision 30 cm, removed damaged joint, replaced with metal alloy joint. No complications; 94 minute surgery. Dr. Andrews noted concerns about deep vein thrombosis and pulmonary embolus."

It was the same format as the other entries. Date, patient's name, description of the surgery, and a list of things she was worrying about, post-surgery.

Hmm.

Next layer of notebooks down, the entries were structured the same, but I started noting a shift. The earlier notebooks were heavy on the surgery descriptions and lighter on the questions, while the most recent notebooks were the opposite.

Interesting. I would have thought it would go the other way around. More surgeries meant more successes meant more confidence which meant fewer questions. What kind of person, the further she went in her highly skilled and technical career, had more questions the older she got, rather than fewer?

"A driven one," I murmured, and decided that Paige must have been an extremely good surgeon. Anyone this dedicated to writing out case notes that questioned her skills—and laid out paths for improvement—had to be good at what she did.

It was easy to imagine. I could almost see the Paige in the photo on her practice's website, sitting at that very desk, writing and thinking through what went right and what went wrong. Thinking about how to do better and writing out ways to make it happen.

These notebooks had to be what Will Wilcox was after. That night at Hoppe's, he'd said they needed the records. Thanks to the hundreds of court cases I'd watched on television, it was easy to picture an attorney standing in front of a jury, citing every word of the entry for Rila's surgery out loud, voice level rising as the questions were read, coming almost to a shout at Paige's vow to do better next time.

"This, ladies and gentlemen of the jury," the attorney would say, waving the notebook, "is a clear admission of guilt!"

I was pretty sure the law didn't work that way, but if Will Wilcox was bent on getting money out of Paige, it probably wouldn't have taken him long to convince an attorney to take the case.

Only . . .

Frowning, I reinserted the spiral-bound book

into its place in the pile and shut the cabinet doors. The notebook in question had to be part of the lawsuit. Paige would have turned it over during—what did they call it?—discovery, so why would Will care about old case notes?

The world went black. Suddenly dizzy, I reached out for the cabinet, unsure which way was up and which was down.

Clunk.

Hang on. That was the bookcase. It must have swung shut. That's why the light went off. Silly me. All I had to do was push it back open, and—

Click.

My body recognized the threat before my brain did, sending that awful metallic taste of adrenaline into my mouth.

No. No-no-no—

Click.

The second latch dropped into place.

Someone had locked me in.

Chapter 23

I pushed at the back of the bookcase. Nothing moved.

Pushed again. Still nothing.

"Hey!" I shouted. "There's someone in here! Let me out!"

Again with the nothing.

"Hey!"

The continued response of nothing was troubling. A distinct feeling of uneasiness began taking me over, so I did what I always did when feeling uncomfortable. I started to babble.

"It's Minnie Hamil—Minnie Niswander. You know, the bookmobile librarian? With the cat? Not that either the bookmobile or Eddie, that's my cat's name, are here. You'd have seen the bookmobile, of course. Hard missing that, right?"

I paused, heard less than crickets, and went back at it.

"Hello? Is anyone out there? Anyone?" That was stupid. Of course there was someone out there.

Or at least there had been, a few seconds ago. I pushed away the fear that was starting to clench my stomach into one big knot—because my cell phone was in my coat pocket, a million miles away on the sofa on the other side of the bookcase—and pounded on the bookcase.

"Hey! Let me out! Open this door, bookcase, whatever, and we'll call it even. No harm, no foul, right? Just an accident."

I put my ear against the bookcase, listening, but couldn't hear anything over my heaving breaths and the pounding of my heart. I closed my eyes—which made no sense because there was nothing but black dark surrounding me, but habits are hard to break—and tried to be still.

Three seconds later, I gave up and went back to shouting and pounding the bookcase with the sides of my fists. Three seconds after that, the cognitive part of my brain woke up, which quieted the frantic panicking lizard part of my brain.

Why was I pretending not to know who had locked me in? It was Will Wilcox. He was looking for the notebooks, just like I was. And acting as if I didn't know it was him wasn't helping me. Or . . . could I play it to my advantage?

I thought about that, then shook my head.

Nope. Didn't see how. Maybe someone skilled at negotiations could do that, but librarians didn't get that kind of training, and I certainly hadn't been born with that kind of skill set. If I had, I probably wouldn't have become a librarian in the first place. Which meant I wouldn't have moved to Chilson, wouldn't have reconnected with Kristen and Rafe, wouldn't have married Rafe, wouldn't have met my coworkers, wouldn't have pushed for the library to get a bookmobile, wouldn't have found Eddie, wouldn't—

I blew out a breath and closed my eyes again.

Stop that. Do something. Something different that might help you get out of this.

"Will?" I called. "Will Wilcox? I know it's you out there, okay?"

I paused, and the dark silence rang in my ears. Onward.

"Hey, Will? You do realize this isn't going to help, right? I know it's the case notes you want and they're in here with me. How about this? You open the bookcase a teensy little bit and I'll slip the notebooks out one by one. When you get the one you're looking for, just say the word and . . ."

And what? There was no way he was going to let me out. Ever. Why would he?

My voice was already getting raw from shouting. I rubbed my throat and thought about dehydration and how long a human could go without water. I also thought about how I'd been so pleased about finding the perfect hiding place for my car, and how I never would have hidden my presence if I'd known I was going to get locked into a hidden room. And I thought about how Will could turn down the heat, and about hypothermia. Then I thought about possible impacts of dehydration combined with hypothermia, the possible deadlier impacts.

That was when I stopped thinking and started listening again.

Because I'd heard . . . something. I wasn't sure what, but Will was out there doing something noisy. I put my ear to the bookcase.

Clanking noises. Metallic clanking. Tools? Pipes?

I imagined Will loosening water pipes upstairs, letting water run all over the house, turning down the heat. Eventually the water would run through the floorboards, drip down light fixtures, stream down the stairs, and the house would become one of those Internet memes, with a frozen Minnie hidden behind the bookcase.

But he wouldn't need tools to do that. All he had to do was turn on the upstairs taps, adjust the thermostat, and walk away.

So what was he doing?

I turned my head and put my other ear to the bookcase, just in case that one had better hearing.

A distant final-sounding *thud*, then nothing.

I held my breath and tried to still my heart, hoping that the concept of losing one sense meant gaining capacity with the others was actually true, and listened hard.

Footsteps.

Coming my way.

The heavy treads stopped just outside the bookcase. Though I couldn't hear his breathing, I could almost feel it.

"Will?" I asked, and was pleased that my voice hardly trembled at all. Brave Minnie! "What were you doing out there? With the tools," I added quickly, just to clarify. "It sounded like something with pipes."

Back to silence.

I'd just decided that it was going to stay that way when his voice seeped through the bookcase.

"This is your fault," he said conversationally. "If you'd minded your own business, I wouldn't have had to do this. It's not on me. It's on you. Just like it was for Paige Ferrer. What happened to her was her own fault. Remember that."

My brain flooded with so many responses to his illogic that my mouth opened and closed soundlessly half a dozen times before any words came out.

"This is absolutely my business," I said, trying to stay calm. "And, by the way, my husband knows exactly where I am." Sort of. "He'll find me soon enough and he knows that you're at the top of my suspect list and—"

Slam!

The house shuddered as the front door shut hard.

Well.

I felt around for the rolling stool and sat down as the quiet settled down around me.

This would be fine. I'd be fine. Rafe more or less knew where I was, all I had to do was wait.

So I waited.

Waited some more.

Got extremely bored while I waited a little longer.

"This is stupid," I muttered to myself, and stood. Rafe would eventually show up, but I'd rather be found doing my best to escape my hidden prison than be found sitting meekly, hands folded, waiting like a good little girl for someone to ride to my rescue.

I felt along the edge of the bookcase, checking again for a safety trigger, and once again found nothing. I ran my fingers along the top, looking for a gap, looking for anything. Found nothing. Did the same thing on the other side of the bookcase and found nothing but woodwork.

I dropped to my knees, pried at the tiny gap between the bookcase and the floor, and found nothing except gritty dust.

"Rats," I said, sitting back on my heels. Now what?

Continuing to pointlessly pound on the back of the bookcase would do nothing but bruise my fists even more. Going back to shouting would just turn my throat even more raw.

Aunt Frances had told me many times that when all else fails, take a deep breath. And if that didn't help, take another. And if you still don't know what to do, take another.

So that was what I did.

On my fifth, or maybe sixth, breath my nose twitched. Something didn't smell right. It was something I'd smelled before, but when? And where?

I sniffed at the air, trying to remember, trying to pin it down. This was a slightly organic smell. Skunk? No, not quite. More like a rotting smell. Cabbage? But that didn't make any sense. Or was it . . . rotten eggs? Which also didn't make any sense. There wasn't any food in the house. The kitchen was empty; Bianca had said she'd cleared everything out. Nothing in the fridge, nothing on the stove—

The tumblers in my head fell into place. The smell. I knew what it was. I'd smelled it in my aunt's house when I was a child, back before natural gas had been piped into town.

It was propane.

An extremely explosive gas.

Chapter 24

That was the noise Will had been making with the tools. He'd been loosening the nuts that connected the propane fuel line to the gas cooktop. And, I had to assume, did the same thing at the furnace. All sorts of propane was likely spewing into the house, turning the air more and more flammable.

Or was it *in*flammable? Did they mean the same thing? Or was there a difference? If there was a difference, which one was right in this particular situation? I was a librarian, how could I not know? What was wrong with me? Why—

"Stop it," I said, and pushed away the inane thoughts that wanted to take over my brain in lieu of panic. Time to focus on getting out of here without blowing myself into mini pieces of Minnie.

I scrabbled my way back to sitting on the stool, opened the desk drawers, and rummaged around, hoping for a letter opener. I could maybe wedge that into the side of the bookcase, lift up the latches, and be home before Rafe.

The top drawer held pens, pencils, yellow sticky notes, and what felt like highlighters. The next drawer down was envelopes and stamps, and the bottom drawer was printer paper, all of which was a total of zero help.

I sat back and tried to think clearly.

There was no letter opener. Also no screwdriver, or even a three-hole punch that I could have pried apart and used as a makeshift tool. A total of zero help. So much for easy. Now what did I do?

The rotten-egg gas smell was getting stronger. That might have been psychosomatic, because I now knew it was there, but it could also be real. How long would it take before the house filled with enough propane that the slightest spark of static electricity would start the reaction?

If my dad or brother were there, I could ask them. If they were both there, they'd be pulling out their phones and starting calculations, racing to be the first one to get the answer.

Which honestly wouldn't be all that helpful. Far more useful would be a way to get out of this hidden room, a space that half an hour ago I'd considered so adorable I'd wanted one in my own house. Now? Not so much.

"Think," I said, and the sound of my own voice was startling. I'd sounded . . . small. Insignificant. And scared. So very scared.

Darkness, already all around, pressed in so hard I couldn't breathe. The panic I'd barely been keeping at bay consumed me and stole all my strength.

I slid off the stool and onto the floor, wrapping

my arms around my knees, tears streaming down my face, teeth chattering with fear, sobs racking my entire body.

"There's no way out," I whispered. I'd never see Kristen's twins grow up. Would never know if my nieces and nephew grew up into fully functioning adults. Would never have my own children. Would never see if I managed to become library director. Wouldn't grow old with Rafe.

This was the end.

I rested my forehead against my knees and felt empty of everything except a deep sense of shame at the abject fear that had taken me over.

Then, slowly, I sat up straight.

Of course I was scared. Anyone who wasn't scared in a situation like this either was not fully aware of the circumstances or was self-deluded. Thanks to a lifetime of being overlooked by many because of my age, height, and/or gender, not only was I fully aware of my limitations, but I was also aware of my capabilities. And, on a good day, I knew full well that I had far more capabilities than limitations.

I could do this. I could find a way out. No, I would find a way out. All my fault, he'd said. As if. No way was I going to let a bully like Will Wilcox get away with killing the both of us. Not a chance in the world. I'd find a way to escape and I'd point a finger at Mr. Wilcox and say out to a jury in a firm voice, "He did it. He killed Paige Ferrer."

I scrubbed the tears from my face, clambered to my feet, and took stock.

The gas smell was now, without a doubt, growing stronger and stronger. Since there was nothing I could do about that, I decided to ignore the source of my pending doom and focus on escape strategies.

So. What were my assets? My strengths?

A mental SWOT analysis popped into my head, just like something out of graduate school.

Strengths? My ingenuity, efficient size, relative youth, and health.

Weaknesses? Imminent panic.

Opportunities? Hmm. I'd have to get back to that category.

Threats? The threat of going kaboom at any moment.

Well, that wasn't so bad. Lots more strengths than weaknesses and threats combined. Sure, the opportunities were limited, but—

My heart thudded as I thought of an ancillary threat, one that was sending my panic closer to the surface. What if Wilcox had turned the thermostat up, expecting that the spark of electricity lighting the furnace would set off a massive explosion.

Breaths heaved in and out of me, panting as if I'd run a race, as my mind rushed through those fun possibilities, and then I shrugged. There was nothing I could do about that other than get out of here as quickly as possible.

"Come on, Minnie," I said out loud, and this time the sound of my voice was almost reassuring, because I'd managed to sound like I wasn't riding the far edge of fear. Maybe that fake-it-until-you-make-it thing was real. Who knew? "Think," I murmured. "Inside the box, outside the box, doesn't matter. Just come up with options."

I reached around in the inky blackness, making

sure to not run into the stool, and stood. No static, no sparks, no boom—all good and happy things for yours truly—and I tried to think what Paige would do if she were me. Other than not be in this situation in the first place, of course.

Ten seconds of that got me nothing new. No surprise, because if Paige had been me, she'd be me and I was here, trapped in a room with no apparent way out. What I needed to do was think like Paige.

An internal light bulb flashed so bright I was almost able to see it.

That was it! Think like Paige!

The trick, of course, was how to do that since I'd never known her, but . . .

I took a deep breath, trying to calm my overactive brain.

Be still. Be quiet. You can do this.

And then I remembered how much I did know about Dr. Paige Ferrer. From what I'd been able to tell, she'd been well-liked by her coworkers and staff. She'd been supportive of Sharrow's efforts to build her own business. She'd had the courage to move Up North by herself, without the backup of friends or family. She'd bought this house, paying for much of it through short-term rentals. She tucked away her personal things into a hidden place. And for her entire medical career, she'd written meticulous case notes that clearly had a goal of constant improvement.

What did all of that tell me? That she was smart, brave, and resourceful. And that she left little to chance.

"There's another way out," I said, gasping a little, because the gas smell was so strong. But I was sure I was right. A woman like Paige wouldn't have created a space where someone could have been locked in. She would have an escape.

But where was it? And would I be able to find it in a darkness impregnated with explosive gas fumes?

"Yes," I said.

The bookcase itself was clearly not the way, so I ignored that side of my prison altogether. Gently but firmly, I pushed and heaved at the built-in desk with hands, arms, legs, and hips. Nothing budged. Not even a little.

Okay. If that had been the escape, if there'd been another latching door, something would have racked out of plumb at least a tiny bit.

So. Not there.

I put my palms against the back wall and pushed. The wall moved even less than the desk had, something I wouldn't have thought possible. The wall's texture was that of plaster, not drywall. Thick and old plaster, probably. Quality materials, dried now to what felt like concrete.

My hands moved to the side and—

Thump!

No no no . . . the bulletin board. I'd forgotten all about the bulletin board, hanging from a nail, full of photos and notes and pushpins that were metal and if I'd knocked out a bunch of them, they might fall in a heap to the floor, sparking, sparking, sparking . . .

Nothing happened.

Blowing out a long breath, I steadied the still-swinging corkboard and moved on, trying to visualize what I'd seen for a few short minutes, wishing I was better at that memory board game.

My fluttering fingers found the edge of the built-ins, cabinet below and bookshelves above. I sank to my knees and pulled the cabinet doors wide open.

As fast and carefully as I could, I shifted the stacks of journals out of the interior shelves and behind me, without igniting a single spark from the spiral-bound versions. Slowly, so very slowly, I removed the single shelf and put it on top of the journals, fixing its location in my head.

I inched forward, placed my hands against the cabinet's back wall, pushed, and . . . felt a slight movement.

Hope flared inside me, so bright I was afraid it could ignite the gas.

I pushed again. And again. And again. But no matter how hard I shoved, nothing else moved.

The headache that had been climbing the back of my neck reached inside my skull. I rubbed at my temples and stood, trying to think, trying not to panic, trying not to think about the small space I was trapped in, trying to be intrepid and brave.

Okay. The cabinet back wall had moved. Just a little, but it had moved. What if . . . what if what? I had no idea.

Another long breath gusted out of me. I leaned forward and rested my head against the books. Paige's books. I had so many of these same books on my own bookshelves. It was nice to know that I was in good company.

I ran my fingertips across the volumes. Surely that was the slipcovered two-book set of Mary O'Hara's *My Friend Flicka* and *Thunderhead*. And that was absolutely a copy of *A Wrinkle in Time*. And there on the end, a series of books all feeling the same, had to be the Nancy Drews, ostensibly written by Carolyn Keene. Paige's copies had been the original 1930s versions, hardbound with the paper slipcovers. My mom had gifted hers to me, the 1960s edition, with the yellow covers.

My fingers lingered on the books. It had been my Nancy Drews that Eddie had squirmed behind the other night. He'd kicked a copy of *The Hidden Staircase* to the floor, and I'd told him how weird he was.

I made a sound that sounded almost like a whimper. I'd never see Eddie again. Never feel his rumbling purr, never pick his hairs off my clothes, never snuggle up with—

Hang on.

The Hidden Staircase. That was the book I'd seen on this very bookshelf, all the way against the left side of the bookcase, left of *The Secret of the Old Clock*. But *The Secret of the Old Clock* was the first book in the series. *Hidden Staircase* was the second. No way would anyone who'd grown up with Nancy Drew put the books in that order. And hadn't *The Hidden Staircase* involved twin houses?

Barely breathing, I removed *The Hidden Staircase* from the shelf, put it horizontally on top of the other books, and reached into the gap, feeling for a latch, a knob, something . . . anything . . . wait. What was that? It felt like one of those ancient push-button light switches. If I pushed, would it . . . what would . . .

I swallowed, and pushed.

Click.

The entire bookcase rotated slightly, as if it were on a spindle.

Gently, oh so gently, I pushed. It moved a few inches.

I pushed again. It moved a few more inches, letting in a half-hearted light, the most beautiful thing I'd ever seen in my life, but it was accompanied by an even stronger smell of gas. Stopping was not an option, though, so I kept encouraging the bookcase forward in its circular arc, inching it along. Carefully, so very carefully . . .

And then I could make out vague shapes. Brooms. Mops. Vacuum cleaner. The rotating bookcase opened up into the back of a utility closet.

Not breathing at all, I edged forward. All I had to do was get out of the house, and I'd be safe. Easy peasy. Just get out.

Practically tiptoeing, I reached the door of the closet. Held the knob tight and rotated.

Click.

The closet door opened into the kitchen—no explosion—and my eyes drank in the dim light, the shapes of counters and appliances and hanging pots and utensils. I'd never been so happy to see a kitchen in my life.

My eyes were watering from the stench of the gas, and my head was pounding. No way could I take the time to get my phone. I had to get out of there.

Carefully, slow-fast, I eased myself to the kitchen's side door.

One more door. Just one more. Get outside and all will be well. You'll have saved yourself, none the worse for wear. Just one more.

The handle was cold in my hand. I pulled in a quiet breath and turned.

Click.

So far, so good.

Breath held tight, I cracked open the door, and a rush of winter-cold wind whooshed over me. I sucked in the life-giving stuff. Never ever had I smelled anything so good as the scentless air that was filling my lungs.

I was going to live. I'd escaped. Made it out. And I was going to make sure Will Wilcox paid the price for what he'd done.

Leaving the door wide open to let the propane gas dissipate, I hurried down the steps and into six inches of snow. Honey Hollow was only a couple of miles away, close enough that I could get there if I had no other choice, but I'd seen faint lights at Verity Gauthier's house. All I needed was a phone. Just one phone call, and soon this would all be over.

Wet and heavy snow, my least favorite kind, trickled down the insides of my low boots as I hurried down the sidewalk, or at least the approximation of the sidewalk. With the snow cover it was impossible to tell.

What I could tell, however, was that I was the first person to walk across the snow. Will was gone. With luck, he was long gone. I'd call law enforcement, they'd find him, I'd give a statement, and my job would be done.

The only thing I heard as I struggled through the snow was the sound of my breathing and the beating of my heart. Nothing of me had been blown up, all was fine, life was good.

My legs, though, were starting to get tired, and Verity's house seemed just as distant now as it had been when I'd started, which didn't seem possible, but was clearly true.

I turned my head to see how far I'd come. My gaze followed my empty footsteps backward . . . okay. There was the house. I'd walked about a hundred yards. Maybe a hundred yards to go. I could do this.

Nodding, I gave the Duvall house one last look, and everything inside and outside of me clutched hard and tight with fear. Behind that tree. I'd seen movement. Human-shaped movement. And there was only one person it could be.

Panic. There was no stopping it this time. Not with a large potentially armed male fifty yards away who was intent on killing me.

I charged into a run, hurtling toward my only hope of safety, an elderly arthritic woman who at times could barely walk. But she had to have a phone, and maybe, just maybe . . .

My feet flew, my arms pumped. I ignored the burning in my lungs. I did nothing but run, and run, and run some more, arrowing toward sanctuary, aiming at the only chance I had. Behind me, hard footsteps grew closer. I could hear his panting breaths. There wasn't much time. I didn't have much time.

I pounded up wooden stairs onto Verity's deep front porch. The lights in her living room were flickering in a way that could only mean she was watching television. I banged on the door. "Help me! Please!" I glanced over my shoulder. Wished I hadn't. Turned around and pounded with both fists. "He killed Paige. He's trying to kill me! Please! Please help—"

The door flung open. Silhouetted in the doorway was an angular figure cradling a very long gun. "Stop right there," she snarled.

I held my hands up. This was how I was going to meet my end? By . . . mistake?

"You." She gestured at me with her chin. "Bookmobile cat lady. Inside. You," she said, narrowing her intent gaze behind me. "Stay right there."

I whirled. Will Wilcox was at the bottom of the porch steps, one foot on the bottom stair.

"Hey," he said, spreading his hands. "This is all a big mistake. The little lady and I were having an argument. Sure, it got out of hand, but we can settle this between ourselves. No reason for anyone else to get involved. Right, little lady?"

His broad smile terrified me. Who was Verity going to believe? A five-foot-nothing wide-eyed female who was currently incapable of saying a word, or a six-foot male oozing smooth words and confidence?

"Stop with the lies," Verity said. "I watched the whole thing. You were chasing her."

Wilcox smiled, shaking his head. "That's what you think you saw? No, that wasn't it. We were just playing a game, right, little lady? You can trust me, ma'am. Just a harmless game."

Verity eyed me and I shook my head.

"She says it's not a game," she told Wilcox. "And she's a librarian. If you can't trust a librarian, the world might as well end right now. You move a muscle and I'll shoot."

"On, come on." His smile became fixed. "None of us believe you'll actually shoot. How old is that thing anyway? Was it your husband's? Your dad's?"

Verity tipped her head in my direction and whispered, "Aiming high. Slug," as she snugged the butt of the gun firmly against her shoulder. And pulled the trigger.

Boom!

Crack!

A piece of the porch's decorative trim, shattered by the slug Verity had fired, spun around crazily and hit Wilcox square in the midsection.

"You shot me!" he screamed, tumbling to the ground and clutching his chest, which was decidedly not bleeding. "Call 911! Call an ambulance!"

"What are you waiting for?" Verity demanded. "Tie him up."

But I was already moving down the steps, pulling my cat-hair-laden scarf from around my neck. Wilcox was rocking back and forth, whimpering with fear and shock. Quick as I could, because it wouldn't be long before he realized he wasn't actually hurt, I grabbed his wrists one by one, pulled them behind his back, and tied some lovely tight knots.

I put a final oomph into the last one and stepped up and back, panting.

"Are you all right?"

I looked up to see Verity squinting down at me. She was cradling the shotgun in the crook of one arm and holding a cell phone in the other.

"Dispatch is asking," she said. "Police are on the way, but they want to know if you're okay."

I took in a deep breath, glancing at the sky, now clearing of clouds. Stars twinkled down at me, a sight that half an hour ago I wasn't sure I'd ever see again.

"Me?" I smiled. "Never been better."

Chapter 25

In the interview room, the wall clock's hour hand had rolled through the double digits and was making serious inroads on the singles.

Rafe, who hadn't left my side since we'd all arrived at the sheriff's office, yawned so wide I was concerned about jaw dislocation.

"Nice," I said. "Did Eddie teach you that?"

My husband pulled me so close that my cheek brushed up against his chin, now bristly with nearly a full day's growth of beard. "Maybe I taught it to him."

I did my best to snuggle in even tighter to the man whose side I didn't ever want to leave. "Nope. He was doing it long before you two met."

"Maybe we learned independently and simultaneously."

"Huh." I stifled my own yawn. "Seems unlikely."

"But not impossible."

"Alchemy," Ash said, coming into the room and plopping himself down across the battered table from us. He noted our blank expressions and sighed.

"The one thing that's impossible. Alchemy. You can't turn something into something else."

"Oh, I don't know." Rafe kissed the top of my head. "I've turned Ms. Minnie here into a married woman."

My throat, still raw from the shouting and the propane gas, closed up and my eyes stung with tears. Truly, I had the best husband in the world. How did I get so lucky? Sure, he was occasionally annoying and frustrating, but I'd never forget the look on his face when he'd shown up at Gainsborough.

I'd called him on Verity's phone as soon as I could, telling him I was fine and that everything was okay. He hadn't believed me, of course, and twenty minutes later, his truck had roared down the bluff into a sea of rotating lights. Fire trucks, EMT trucks, sheriff SUVs: a veritable smorgasbord of emergency vehicles had arrived to deal with Wilcox and the gas in the Duvall house. By the time Rafe reached the back of the ambulance where I'd been escorted, he was frantic. He'd flung open the truck's back door, seen me sitting up on the gurney, chatting with the paramedics, obviously hale and hearty, and his expression of relief was quickly followed by one of pure, simple, joyful love.

Ash, who'd arrived back in Chilson a bare ten minutes before Verity had called 911, tapped his pen on the table. "Are you crying? There's no crying in the sheriff's office."

"Disagree," a calm voice said, and the sheriff herself entered the room. Trim and straight-backed with a mind that worked faster than anyone's I'd ever met, Kit Richardson exuded competence and was someone else I wouldn't mind being when I grew up. "You'd know better," she said, taking her usual position of leaning against the wall and putting her hands in her pockets, "if you'd been in the room when I gave Hal his annual performance review."

The gray-haired Detective Hal Inwood, on the sheriff's heels, sat at the table and gave his boss a long-suffering look. Ash smirked, and I gave the sheriff a look that I hoped conveyed the gratitude I felt for the distraction she'd tossed in front of an unsuspecting Ash. She gave me a small wink in return, and I nodded, asking, "What's next?"

Hal extracted a small notebook from his shirt pocket. "At this point," he said, flipping pages, "most people plead to go home and vow that they'll return after they get some sleep. It is my belief, however, that Ms. Niswander will not want to do that, and will instead keep us all from our beds for another half hour while her curiosity is satisfied."

No matter how tired I might be, Hal Inwood could irritate me like no one else. "The curiosity that you're slandering," I said tartly, "found a murderer, so you're welcome."

The man didn't even look up from the notebook. "Yet at the end of the day, you called on law enforcement to extract you from a situation you created."

I pulled away from Rafe's embrace and sat up straight and as tall as possible. "No, the situation that Will Wilcox created. I wouldn't have been there if he hadn't killed Paige Ferrer in the first place."

"You wouldn't have been there if you'd left well enough—"

"Hal." The sheriff's single syllable was soft steel, cutting through our bickering and bringing it to a sharp halt.

"Yes, ma'am." He blew out a short breath. "Mr. Wilcox has requested that an attorney be provided for him. However, before that point, he was quite ... loquacious, and provided many details."

"Really?" I blinked. "That seems really dumb."

"It happens." The detective shrugged. "They think they're smarter than we are. That they can talk their way out of an arrest."

"Did Wilcox seriously think he could talk his way out of this?" I was dumbfounded. "He admitted that he killed Paige. And he tried to kill me!"

"Mr. Wilcox stated that, and I quote"—Hal paused to turn a page, turned another, then said—"'It was an accident. I needed copies of her case notes. All she had to do was hand them over. I'm no killer. It was an accident.'" Hal studied me over the top of the notebook.

"That makes no sense," I said flatly. "She was killed with a bow and arrow, for crying out loud. In the woods. At Gainsborough. What did he say he was doing? No, let me guess. He said he was hunting on private property without permission, property that just happened to be adjacent to a second home owned by the doctor he was suing for malpractice, and just happened to run into her?"

Hal nodded. "That sums it up nicely."

"What?" I exploded out of my chair. "Tell me you didn't believe him."

The detective smiled faintly. "Not a word."

"Oh. Well. Okay, then." I subsided. Rafe took my hand and squeezed it. I felt a bit ashamed of my outburst, but also figured I'd get over it quickly. "Did he say anything else?"

He glanced at the notepad. "Mr. Wilcox apparently felt compelled to explain why he wanted Dr. Ferrer's journals of case notes."

"Yeah, I didn't understand that at all."

"Mr. Wilcox's attorney and Dr. Ferrer's attorney had been in negotiations about the matter. The question was how many of the journals should be included. Dr. Ferrer's attorney wanted all of them as part of the court records, and if not all of them, enough of them to establish a pattern. Mr. Wilcox's attorney wanted to restrict it to the case notes regarding Rila Wilcox."

Light dawned. "They were all the same. From medical school on. Patient statistics, procedure, analysis of her work, notes to improve."

"Exactly." Hal nodded. "This would have established that the notes of things that could have been done better, the notes of how to improve, were not admissions of culpability, but were notes of a conscientious doctor."

I sat back. "Wilcox wanted to destroy them. The journals, I mean."

"Yes. They were scheduled to be provided at discovery the week Dr. Ferrer was killed."

"And that's why the case hadn't been scheduled in court." It was all making sense. "The attorneys were haggling over the case notes, so discovery wasn't final."

Hal flipped the notebook shut, tucked it back into his shirt pocket, folded his hands on the table, and waited.

"What?" I asked.

"There's a question I'm surprised you haven't asked yet."

"I have lots of questions," I said. "But as you

said, I'm keeping you from your bed, and I know you need your beauty rest."

Ash tried to stifle a snorting laugh. Failed.

Detective Hal Inwood ignored both of us and looked at Rafe. "Mr. Niswander?"

Rafe shrugged. "Well, I have been wondering one thing. Wilcox obviously knew about the hidden room. How?"

Hal sent Rafe a smile, something I couldn't ever remember him bestowing on me. "Exactly. Mr. Wilcox, while trying to reassure us that he'd meant no harm to Dr. Ferrer, said that as a teenager he'd been a summer guest in the house that was twin to Dr. Ferrer's, the Craymore house, I believe."

"Creighton," I corrected.

"No, that's not what he said."

"Don't care what he said," I retorted. "The name of the neighboring twin house is Creighton."

"That will have to be confirmed by—"

"And we're done." Sheriff Richardson gave us a quelling glance. "Hal. Ash." She tipped her head toward the hall. Chairs scraped, and the two men headed out.

Hal, however, paused in the doorway, not looking in my direction at all, and said, "Ms. Niswander, I do appreciate your assistance, your resourcefulness, and your ingenuity. I'm glad that you escaped uninjured."

My mouth dropped open. "Uh . . . I . . ."

But he was gone.

Sheriff Richardson smiled at me. "Still waters, yes?"

"He was tired," I said uncertainly. "I'm sure he didn't know what he was saying."

The sheriff did a sideways sort of nod, half yes, but also half no. "You'll come in tomorrow to sign your statement?" she asked, though it was more order than request.

"Yes, ma'am," I said, and closed my eyes. Exhaustion swamped through me, overtaking every part of my body, including my fingernails. Through the haze of sleep, I heard Sheriff Richardson murmur, "It's time to take your wife home."

"Yes, ma'am," Rafe said.

And he did.

The next morning, I half woke to a bed empty of husband, but full of Eddie. I gave him a long pet, snuggled up against his purr, and went back to sleep.

When I woke the second time, it was to the smell of coffee, bacon, and toast.

"If you sleep much longer," Rafe said, "this will be lunch, not breakfast."

I slid up to a sitting position, dislodging Eddie only slightly, rubbed my face with the palms of my hands, and looked at the tray of food my husband was putting across my lap.

"Flowers? I appreciate the sentiment, but it seems a bit over the top."

Rafe repositioned the small vase of pink carnations. "Your aunt brought them."

Aunt Frances. Right. There were a lot of people I'd need to fill in on the events of last night. I sighed. It was going to be a long day. "I suppose I need to call her," I said.

He sat on the end of the bed, facing me with his back against the footboard. "I already did. Told her enough to tide her over until tomorrow. Same with Kristen and your boss."

I blinked. "You did?"

"Well, yeah. That's my job. Taking care of you. I knew you'd be sleeping away the morning and that they'd all want to know what happened, so I headed them off at the pass."

I tried to swallow away the silly tears that were threatening to embarrass me. "What did I ever do to deserve such a wonderful husband?" I asked as I wrapped my hands around a steaming mug of coffee.

"Dunno," he said. "But I'm not calling your mom. Or your dad. Or your brother. That messing-with-the-messenger thing is real."

I snorted. "My family likes you better than they like me."

"And I don't want that to change." He grinned. "See how this works?"

"Puts you in danger of dropping off the Best Husband Ever list."

"Chance I'll have to take." He moved his foot, tapping my leg. "Food's getting cold. Eat."

After I ate and showered, we walked up slushy sidewalks and under shifting gray skies to the sheriff's office so I could read and sign my statement. Behind the glass window was the sheriff herself. When she saw us, she tipped her head at the interior door and buzzed us in.

"Morning, Minnie. Rafe," she said, waving us to the interview room. "It's days like this that make me think more seriously about retirement. And not the Hal Inwood kind of retirement. I'll have a deputy bring your paperwork. After that's settled, there's someone who wants to talk to you."

I stopped, halfway to my usual chair. "Oh? Who's that?"

But she was gone, and it wasn't until I'd finished reading, signing, and handing over that the deputy left and Rila Wilcox, hands in her coat pockets, was suddenly standing in the doorway.

Rafe eyed me. I shrugged, and gestured at the chair across the table.

She came in slowly and sat, looking at me with an expression I couldn't read. "I'm really sorry," she said softly.

Of all the possibilities that had run through my head in the last five seconds, an apology was not on the list. "Um . . ."

Rila put her hands flat on the table and studied them. "I get it if you don't want to talk to me, but I wanted to tell you that I never wanted that lawsuit against Dr. Ferrer in the first place. Will kept pushing and pushing and he wouldn't give up. It didn't matter to him how many times I said no, he just came back at me again. At some point"—she sighed, bending her head—"I just gave in."

It wasn't hard to imagine. He was a sales guy, after all. Probably had regular training in techniques of persuasion.

"Anyway," she said. "I should have been paying more attention. I'm so sorry. I should have stopped him. This is all my fault."

Wait, what? No, no, no. I could not allow this woman to walk through the rest of her life burdened with guilt for something she couldn't control.

I leaned forward, took her hands in mine, and spoke softly but very firmly. "It was Will and no one else. Do not take this on."

She smiled and met my gaze. Sort of. "Thanks. I won't."

But I was sure she would. At first, anyway. With time, though, and the help of friends, family, and professionals, she'd find her way. Besides, anyone who'd competed in a sport at an international level had to be full of drive and determination.

I gave her hands a squeeze and sat back against Rafe's arm. Once she made her mind up to come out of this whole, all she'd need was time.

"There's something else," Rila said. "At the cross-country meet, Bob Craw asked where I was when Dr. Ferrer was killed and I freaked out a little. Remember? She was killed at almost the exact same time I'd been talking to an attorney."

I frowned. "Um, not sure I'm following."

"A divorce attorney," she said. "Will didn't know. No one did. When Bob asked me that, I thought maybe he'd seen me go into the attorney's office or something, and he's not a guy to keep quiet. I was afraid he'd tell Will, and I wasn't ready for that yet."

Which was probably why Rila had been cleared of being a murder suspect so quickly.

"Not sure if Will being in jail waiting for a murder trial is going to make a divorce easier or more complicated," she said, "but I'll be finding out first thing Monday morning."

I almost smiled. Her drive and determination were already coming into play.

"And," she said, "I'll have to find another job. I was really lucky and got a partial signing bonus even though I never played pro ball, and put it all into the house. But even without a big mortgage, it costs a lot of money to live, you know?"

"How do you feel," I asked, now smiling broadly, "about working on the bookmobile?"

We spent the rest of Saturday at home, watching as much bad television as we could stand, cozy with a fire in the fireplace, eating pizza and popcorn like teenagers, with Rafe giving Eddie pets long enough to make his fur stand up from static electricity, once getting a spark that Eddie must have felt, because he immediately ran upstairs, where I later found him sprawled on Rafe's pillow, squashing it into an Eddie shape.

On Sunday, I girded up my mental loins and made the phone calls, starting at the top with my mom and dad, then my brother and his wife and family. Happily, the weather had cleared and a nice long walk outside in the crisp fall sunshine got the parental and sibling admonitions of "Really, Minnie, when are you going to start acting like an adult?" and "How do you manage to get yourself into so much trouble?" out of my head.

Then I called Verity Gauthier. We talked for a long time, and I learned that she had been one of the country's first female commercial pilots. I also learned that she was a big reader and that her usual source of library books was a friend who'd upped stakes and moved to Southern California to be closer to grandchildren. When I told her that the library's outreach program included bringing books to those who were homebound, she immediately signed up for when she had her surgery.

For lunch, Rafe and I went up the hill for an Aunt-Frances-and-Otto-prepared meal that contained hardly any scolding at all. We drove out to

Kristen and Scruffy's and were served the best cheesecake I'd ever had in my life. Any admonitions my best friend might have had in mind for me were upstaged by two infants in need of naps, and when Rafe and I were opening the front door, Kristen pulled me aside and gave me a huge hug.

"I'll yell at you later," she whispered, squeezing me so hard I squeaked. "And just so you know before anyone other than our parental units, the Scruff and I have decided that Chilson is where we want the twins to grow up. Not sure how it's going to work, careerwise, but we'll figure it out."

I beamed and squeezed her back. "That makes me very happy."

"Me too."

On the way home, I told Rafe about the Jurek/Gronkowski plans for the future.

"Huh," he said. "Does that mean we should get busy with our own plans for offspring? Don't want them to be too different in age."

Large parts of me clutched in abject fear. "Uh, sorry? What did you say?"

He laughed and reached out for my hand. "Never mind. It can wait."

I blew out a relieved sigh. "Most things can, right? Except our honeymoon location. We need to finalize that."

"This week," Rafe said, nodding. "This week or bust."

Off and on the rest of the day, we cast about for destinations, but every idea we came up with was either too expensive or already booked by people who planned their lives better than we did.

We headed to bed, hoping for a dream-inspired

solution, but when the Monday morning alarm went off, we were no closer to an answer. As I was toweling off my unruly hair, thinking that we might end up driving to Chicago after all, and thinking that we'd have fun even if it wasn't a super special destination, Rafe came upstairs.

"No milk," he said. "Forgot about it yesterday. What do you want to do for breakfast?"

Ten minutes later, we were at the Round Table, turning the white ceramic mugs over for Sabrina to fill with the hot steaming liquid that made living so much easier.

"Good morning, you two."

I looked up. Sophia Aguilar was just walking in, next to a fiftyish woman who looked familiar, but who I couldn't quite place.

"This is Whitney," Sophia said. "She's the county's equalization director and the person who talked me into signing up for the indoor pickleball league."

"Didn't know Chilson had one," Rafe said.

"Fastest-growing sport in the country," Whitney said, nodding. "Lots of fun. Come play a few games. I bet you'll love it."

Chasing small spherical objects was not my strong suit, but I was glad Sophia was finding a circle of friends. I looked at Rafe, hoping for backup, and saw that he was nodding. "It's not just for old folks," he said. "The kids at school are getting into the game."

"Well," I said, "I'm willing to try almost anything once, but maybe we should wait until after the holidays, when we get back from our honeymoon."

"You finally decided?" Sophia asked. "Where are you headed? Hawaii? The Caribbean?" Rafe and I shared a glance that must have said it all, because she started laughing. "Wait, still no destination? You two crack me up."

"London," Whitney said dreamily. "That's where my husband and I went."

Not once had we considered that as a destination. "London," I said slowly. "I've always wanted to go." So much history, so many things to do, so many things to see.

Rafe nodded. "Me, too."

"Then our work here is done." Sophia grinned and she and Whitney headed to a booth on the other side of the restaurant.

I looked at my husband. "London. I like it."

"Works for me."

And just like that, we had a honeymoon destination. We spent the rest of breakfast glued to our phones, looking at flights and hotels. "I can look more when I get to the library," I said as we forked up the last of our pancakes. "We'll finalize tonight."

"Ruthless efficiency," Rafe said, nodding. "I like it."

"About time, after those weeks of indecision and inactivity."

He grinned. "We were waiting for serendipity. And look, it worked out."

I wasn't sure that serendipity was something I wanted to rely on for major life decisions on a regular basis, but I smiled back. He was right. It was all working out.

I got home early—my coworkers and boss had shooed me out the door, saying that I needed to take care of myself after Friday night but more that I needed to get a move on with those flight reservations—and was welcomed by a cat who wouldn't stop winding himself around my ankles.

"What is wrong with you?" I picked him up, kissed the top of his fuzzy head, and then had to wipe the subsequent loose cat hair off my mouth. "And why are you shedding hair this time of year? It's almost winter. You should be keeping those to stay warm."

He squirmed out of my arms and jumped to the floor with a loud double thump.

"Then again," I said, "what do you need with a winter coat? The only time you're outside in the cold is the twenty feet between the house and the garage. And the ten feet between the car and the bookmobile."

"Mrr," he said.

I had no idea what he was trying to say. "Yeah, well, back at you. Do you want a treat?"

His little kitty sides heaved in a huge sigh.

Concerned, I crouched down and studied him. "You feeling okay?"

He stared straight ahead, at the closet under the stairs. "Mrr."

"Just a closet, pal. No hidden room." The inside of my skin crawled at the very idea. "Not now, probably not ever. Hope you're okay with that."

He slewed a cat glance at me, the one that so very obviously meant *Why are you so dumb that you don't understand what I'm trying to tell you*, and stalked off.

I trailed along. "Not following you," I said. "Just headed to the kitchen to get a . . . Hey! What are you doing?"

Just like he had the other day, Eddie was squir-reling himself over the top of my Nancy Drew books and pushing *The Hidden Staircase* onto the floor.

"Forgot to say," I said, scooping up the book and kneeling down. From behind the books, his yellow eyes peered out at me. "It was because of you mak-ing a mess of these books the other day that I re-membered seeing this on Paige's bookshelf." Yes, I was talking to a cat as if he understood every word I said. It was a good thing no one else was around.

"Mrr."

"You're going to make me say it out loud, aren't you?" I rolled my eyes. "Thank you. You basically saved my life."

"Mrr!"

"Okay, you did save my life."

He leapt out, scattering books left and right, and thumped his head against my leg so hard it almost knocked me over.

"For the sake of clarity," I said as I picked him up and snuggled him tight. "Is that cat for 'You're welcome'?"

There were times that I came close to thinking that not only did he understand what I was saying, but he also was trying to communicate things that I was apparently too stupid to understand. Ridicu-lous, of course, but still.

My furry forever friend looked up at me. Closed one eye in a slow wink.

And purred.

Ready to find
your next great read?

Let us help.

Visit prh.com/nextread